COUNTDOWN WW III: OPERATION CHOKE POINT

A novel by W. X. Davies with the Strategic Operations Group

D1414134

BERKLEY BOOKS, NEW YORK

This is the work of fiction. The characters, incidents, places and dialogues are products of the author's imagination and are not to be construed as real. The author's use of names of actual persons, living or dead, is incidental to the purposes of the plot and is not intended to change the entirely fictional character of the work.

COUNTDOWN WW III:
OPERATION CHOKE POINT

A Berkley Book / published by arrangement with
the author

PRINTING HISTORY
Berkley edition / September 1984

ISBN: 0-425-07135-9

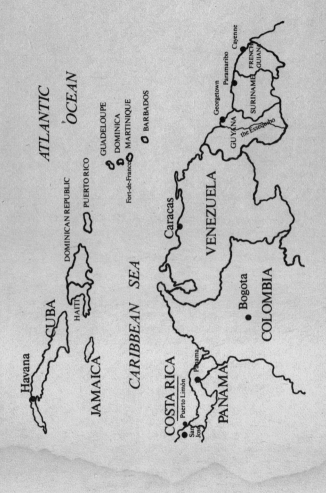

PROLOGUE

The mid-1980s have witnessed an unprecedented rivalry between the two superpowers that has reached crisis proportions. Guerrilla wars and insurrections which marked previous decades now threaten to give way to a vast global confrontation. The only question at the moment seems to be whether this confrontation will be limited to conventional weapons or nuclear ones.

In the spring of 1986 extremist elements, backed by the forces of Libyan dictator Muammar Qaddafi and bolstered by diplomatic and military support from the Kremlin, launched an attack against the most pro-Western states in North Africa: Morocco and Tunisia. The two-pronged assault, while a failure in Morocco, succeeded in Tunisia, with the ascension to power of a radical government. Suddenly NATO's dominion over the strategic Mediterranean basin was seriously jeopardized. The gauntlet had been thrown down.

Alert for any opportunity to capitalize on Western divisiveness, the Soviets in the autumn of that same year moved to back the Greeks when a longstanding political dispute with the Turks over air and sea rights in the Aegean Sea broke into open warfare. With two former

NATO allies clashing on the battlefield, it was no wonder that the Americans were unable to respond forcefully to the Red Army's invasion of Albania, the tiny, but strategically vital, communist satellite that for well over twenty years had managed to remain out of the Soviet orbit.

Six months have passed since then, and the Russians are about to turn their sights to yet another corner of the world, one much closer to American shores. While insurgencies have flared in Central America and the Caribbean for years, Washington is unprepared for the threat that is now about to confront it in the treacherous and uncharted jungles that separate Venezuela from the former British colony of Guyana on the northeast coast of South America.

Predictably, the Kremlin is relying on Cuba to advance its aims in this latest challenge to the West. But in an additional gamble, breathtaking in its audacity, the Soviets have dispatched to the shores of Guyana advisers from the Red Army. The way is open, for the first time since 1945 when U.S. and Soviet troops nearly collided in their rush to take over Nazi Germany, for a direct confrontation between armies of the most formidable powers the world has ever seen . . .

METRIC TOP SECRET OP   OP   OP
PRESIDENTIAL DIRECTIVE 1414
From: President
To: Secretary of State/Secretary of Defense/National Security Advisor 02118B   February 14, 1986

TOTALITY. All ack. personally.

1. In light of the aggravated tensions around the world, instigated and inflamed by the Soviet Union and its client states, the need for a new intelligence unit, answerable directly to the President of the United States, has become an urgent necessity.

2. This unit shall function as a small, close-knit group composed of individuals expert in political, economic, communications, and intelligence affairs.

3. Its purpose shall be to pinpoint those regions of the world where an international crisis is most likely to arise; to formulate contingency plans to prevent the crisis from occurring; and to arrest the crisis if it does occur.

4. In the event that direct intervention, requiring clandestine action on the part of the unit, is deemed necessary, the President shall have the power to mandate such intervention.

5. The name of this intelligence unit shall be the Global Crisis Task Force. In view of the three-pronged nature of the Global Crisis Task Force's mission, its code name shall be Triad.

Signed   *Creighton Turner,*
           President of the United States

COUNTDOWN WW III: OPERATION CHOKE POINT

1

All through the night until just before dawn, gunfire rang out in the desolate streets close to the City Hall and the great wooden cathedral of St. George. From time to time personnel carriers filled with soldiers of the People's Army—more formally known as the Guyana Defense Forces—rolled through the streets of the business district. Patrols continually pursued unknown gunmen from in front of the Stabroek Market, but for all their efforts, they failed to capture anyone.

Guests staying at the Pegasus Hotel, which had been turned into the headquarters of the National People's Congress, were awakened by repeated bursts of automatic fire and, impelled by curiosity, went to their windows. But there were no signs of life near the hotel. It was possible that the only people doing any shooting were members of the People's Army enforcing the curfew that would be in place until six the next morning. At seven o'clock the polling booths were scheduled to open for the first national election in four years.

But just after five a cold front moved in from the Caribbean, bringing a sudden downpour that sent even the guncrazed government soldiers scrambling for shelter.

Three bodies, apparently enemies of the government, would be discovered near the market when the rain subsided several hours later. Naturally there would be no mention of the shootings in the Guyana *Chronicle*. As a quasigovernmental organ, it would be expected not to publish any details that might prove embarrassing to the regime of Sydney Walling, who was commonly referred to by the citizens of Guyana as Comrade Leader.

Comrade Leader fully anticipated reelection, which was why the opposition paper, the *Mirror*, was not allowed to publish any article or editorial that could be considered an attack on his regime. Thus there were often huge blank spaces in the pages of the *Mirror*, mute testimony to the labors of the government censor.

Once daylight arrived, there was no question that the deluge was keeping early-morning voters from attending to their democratic duty. It descended unabated, hammering against the wooden rooftops of the faded white houses where the wealthier members of the community once lived, until the entire city seemed about to revert to the swamp and mud from which it had originally arisen.

Those guests at the Pegasus who had managed to sleep through the gunfire and the pummeling rain were finally brought to a rude awakening by a steel-drum band which got busy in the lobby shortly after eight in the morning in premature celebration of Sydney Walling's victory.

Among those seated in the Pegasus lobby at this soggy hour of the morning was a meticulously groomed man perhaps forty years of age. He sported a neatly trimmed beard and had chiseled, tanned features. The easy way he wore his elegant clothes suggested that he was used to having a great deal of money at his disposal. To anyone who asked, he replied that he was a Peruvian who was now a citizen of Mexico. His passport listed his occupation as "Journalist."

He was a great favorite among the younger women he met in his travels. They knew him simply as Hidalgo.

There were several foreign women at this hotel, the only establishment in all of Georgetown that the guidebooks designated as luxury class. While Georgetown, with its swampland, its rain, and its reckless politics, could hardly be considered a magnet for tourists, there was still important business to be conducted here. Deals were made involving the purchase of bauxite, sugar, and jute, and many of the men who came to Guyana brought their wives with them. After a few nights the wives grew bored, becoming used to the gunshots and the rare diversions. Certainly some of them found Hidalgo the most entertaining thing about the Pegasus.

While Hidalgo was known to be carrying on illicit affairs in Georgetown, no one would have suspected him of being an agent for Fidel Castro. His courtly manners and sartorial elegance were so at odds with the conventional image of a Cuban communist emissary, secret or otherwise, that they provided a more convincing cover than his false credentials.

Today, however, Hidalgo had no time to flirt with the foreign women. Today he was seated in the lobby of the Pegasus where, between blasts of steel-drum music, he was occupied in important conversation with a doleful-looking man who was attired like an out-of-work taxi driver. Though it was by now well into the morning, the latter appeared to have just awoken. His face seemed baggy with sleep. His jowls sagged, and his skin color resembled the greasy mud in the street outside the hotel. It could accurately be supposed that his heritage was racially mixed, which was the case with a great many of the 188,000 residents of the capital. He was part Asian Indian, part African, and part something else that went too far back to be properly identified.

The name of this haggard-looking man was Virgil Reade, and the post he occupied was that of deputy minister of defense. He was a trusted deputy of the Comrade Leader, and naturally he expected that the National People's Congress would have little difficulty securing another victory at the polls.

For long intervals he and the Cuban sat without speaking, vaguely attending to the medley of Broadway standards that the band was sending through the lobby.

The deputy minister was drinking rum punches. The earliness of the hour had failed to impede his drinking, but Hidalgo suspected that if he continued to imbibe his rum punches at the same rate, he would be comatose long before the election results were tallied that evening.

For the moment, at any rate, the deputy minister seemed able to hold his liquor, since his behavior didn't alter at all as the hours progressed toward noon. The only change that Hidalgo could detect was a fixity of expression on the other's face, an intensifying look of disgust and indisposition.

Eventually Hidalgo asked whether something was troubling him.

"Everything's gonna blow up in our faces," he said in his labored English. Though English was the Guyanese—and his—native language, Reade spoke it poorly.

"What are you saying? It is not going to blow up in our faces. Everything is arranged."

"Yes," the deputy minister agreed, "everything is arranged. But there's CIA. There's elements in this country who would subvert our government—bring it down."

"The CIA!" said Hidalgo with disdain. "You see how successful they were with us. Look how they tried to kill Patrice Lumumba!" He was referring to the Congolese leader who had led a rebellion against the U.S.-backed regime. "They saw in his photographs that Lumumba had very white teeth. Therefore they believed that he must brush them constantly. So they poisoned his toothpaste. It was absurd."

Reade gave him an incredulous look. "That isn't true —no!"

"I swear it is. It is published fact."

Reade considered this for a moment, then said, "But in the end they killed Lumumba anyway. Though with bullets, not toothpaste."

The rain had begun to let up and the sky began to lighten. The gunshots began again, loud enough to be heard over the steel band.

Hidalgo and Reade exchanged glances.

"Ah," Reade said with evident satisfaction, "the election seems to finally start."

By nightfall rum shops all over the city were crammed full of customers who were drinking either because they supported the National People's Congress and were consequently in the mood to celebrate or because they supported the opposition People's Progressive Party and wanted to dull the bitterness of defeat. No one doubted the outcome of the election for the simple reason that the government had stated some time before that it was going to steal it.

Ironically, the two opposing parties espoused the same policies; one was just slightly more to the left than the other. The rivalry between them lay more in race and the personalities of the party leadership than in political ideology. Blacks tended to favor the National People's Congress, and Guyanese of Asian background supported the People's Progressive Party. Since neither party exhibited much ability to govern the country it might have seemed irrelevant which side won. The contest should have had all the meaning of a soccer match that had been fixed in advance.

But the way the ruling party went about stealing the election created an enormous outcry. Though it was announced over state radio that the National People's Party had won by a wide margin even before the polls had officially closed, other stories were told by word of mouth: people who'd voted for the opposition had been harassed and beaten, ballot boxes had been stuffed, and thousands of ballots had been thrown away or voided illegally. In some cases soldiers of the People's Army, suspecting that the voting was going strongly against the government, had broken into polling stations and actually made off with the ballot boxes.

As a result of this gross chicanery, the announcement of a National People's Congress triumph caused hundreds of Guyanese to throng into the streets, where they hurled rocks and bottles at soldiers and called for the death of Walling and his ministers. The crowd then began to march toward the Pegasus where the victory party was proceeding on the veranda.

Improbably, even after consuming a full bottle of wine at dinner, Virgil Reade still remained upright, but his disposition was even more sour than it had been earlier in the day. Leaning over the wall of the veranda, he observed the crowds and shook his head gravely saying, "I knew this would happen. Now we'll have a riot on our hands."

Hidalgo, who had the same air of self-confidence he'd had at the beginning of the day, dismissed the protest. "It is their way of letting off steam," he said.

In the distance they could hear an uproar, then a sudden crack of gunfire, followed by a plume of smoke trailing up into the darkness. Unseen by those watching from the hotel, a bus had been overturned and set aflame, and glass continued to break in all quarters of the city, though by and large shopkeepers had learned from previous experience to shutter their windows.

A squadron of the People's Army had arrived and encircled the Pegasus, protecting it by training their guns outward on passersby. In the meantime, the victory party continued as though nothing untoward was occurring outside, although the disturbances were now taking place less than half a dozen blocks away. His supporters were excitedly waiting for the Comrade Leader to appear at any moment to accept their congratulations.

Other members of the People's Army could be seen from the veranda as they fanned out through the center of the town in an attempt to contain the demonstrators and keep them away from the City Hall and the Stabroek Market district. The staccato of gunfire grew more insistent as night moved in. Eventually an old, battered Centurian tank pulled into view around the side of the Pegasus, its gun sweeping from side to side, suggesting it either had a multitude of targets or none at all.

At one point the whole hotel seemed to shudder as the tank's gun opened up, firing in the direction of a raging, drunken crowd of opposition supporters coming from the flooded slums at the city's edge. The steel band played even louder, but it couldn't drown out the cries of the injured. Men and women began to flee back the way they'd come, anywhere to escape the attack. Another tank pulled in a side street at a right angle to the running mob and laid down a barrage that felled several more people.

Most of the celebrants were peering down at the dark, chaotic streets. The dimly seen carnage set them to talking excitedly while waiters circulated among them with trays full of rum punch.

"It is a messy business, to steal an election like this," Reade said almost with regret.

"Well, your government chose not to be subtle about it."

At that instant they were interrupted by loud cries inside the lobby. Turning, they observed the entrance of the Comrade Leader, Sydney Walling, onto the veranda and into the crowd of his supporters.

His arms held over his head in acknowledgment of the wild applause his presence had set off, Walling was an oddly unimposing figure. He had power and cunning and his face was dark and brooding, but he seemed too short for his important role. His chest seemed to have been stuffed with rags, making it bulge out prominently. Watching now, Hidalgo thought that he looked more like a greengrocer than a politician.

For the first time that day the steel band ceased playing, in order to allow Walling to speak. Triggered by the tug of a string, two large posters unrolled from the ceiling to reveal idealized portraits of Walling and Fidel Castro.

Walling stepped up to the ten microphones sprouting in front of the speaker's stand and called out, "Tonight, my friends, we have won a magnificent victory!" As he paused for the enthusiastic response, he studiously ignored the gunshots which cut through the applause. "As of this day, the National People's Congress begins its march down a new road, a road which will culminate in the triumph of socialism and the death of the capitalist-imperialist cabal."

At this point there was extended applause, with wild cheers and whistling.

"Let me continue. There are those elements of society who would see us take a different path. To these elements I would say, 'You are finished, you can no longer contaminate our society with your corruption and your greed.' "

"There are people who accuse us of betraying Guyana, of allowing outside interference. These people say poisonous things. They would have you believe that those very forces that are in the vanguard of fighting imperialism are seeking to meddle in our internal affairs."

Now he turned and raised his eyes almost reverentially toward the portrait of the Cuban dictator. "They mean, of course, the brave and peace-loving people of Cuba when they say such things. But I wish to make it absolutely clear that the Cubans are our friends, and we are lucky to have such friends."

Again there was a roar of approval from the assembled crowd.

"We Guyanese can take care of ourselves. We have no need to rely on others to help us. But let there be no mistaking the strength and solidarity of our two peoples as we go forward to our ultimate victory together!"

The few reporters from the international press who were covering Walling's reelection took the comment about Guyanese independence as a denial that Walling had any intention of inviting Cuban troops into his country. Rumors that this might soon happen had been circulating in the capital for weeks, and some political observers said that the Cuban troops would soon be helping to fight Venezuela, which had been asserting territorial claims against Guyana for decades. Others said it was more likely that Walling needed the Cuban presence simply to shore up his regime.

But the fact was, not only had the invitation been extended by Walling to Castro, but Cuban troops were already on their way.

2

It was four in the afternoon and John Zoccola was sitting in a café by the Hotel Bambou in the capital of the French protectorate of Martinique, waiting for a beautiful woman to arrive. He was suffering from certain misgivings about this woman, whose name was Adrienne Calenda. For one thing, she was somebody else's wife—the Indonesian foreign minister's, to be precise. For another, she was about to undertake an espionage mission for him—a small one, but dangerous nonetheless. Though he needed the information that she could obtain for him, he was extremely anxious that no harm befall her.

Adrienne was to come in by plane that evening. Because she had already been delayed forty-eight hours due to a strike at Orly Airport in Paris, Zoccola was becoming very impatient. He was not a man for whom vacations were a tonic; having time to kill only made him edgy.

He would rather get on with his business.

His business was to uncover information and to recruit agents for his employer, known officially as the Global Crisis Task Force and less formally to its four members as Triad. From time to time, his business with Triad also involved killing people.

To communicate with Triad, he carried at all times a microwave transmitter, miniature enough to be concealed in the palm of his hand, which could also encode and memorize the messages being relayed to and from Triad headquarters in Prince William County, Virginia.

John Zoccola had come to this café near the Bambou Hotel because it was frequented by agents acting on behalf of a variety of interests: the U.S., Russia, France, England, and especially Cuba. The man he wanted to see, the man he expected Adrienne to befriend, was a certain Cuban who went by the name of Hidalgo.

Of course all these agents, many of whom were veterans he knew by sight, had covers of one kind or another. Like them, Zoccola was acting a part. He was, if anyone should ask, a tourist, a businessman looking for a woman and a good time before he was obliged to return to an office suite on the thirty-second floor of a Manhattan skyscraper.

He looked the part too: he was lean and casually well-dressed and had the open manner of a typical American. He also had the looks to elicit the interest, if not always the admiration of women, with a full head of black hair and Mediterranean features. In him Latin and Arabic blood commingled to produce a man who was brilliant and cunning and who had the ironic sense that the world might be worth risking your life to save but it wasn't worth taking seriously.

He liked women as much as he did trouble, but the women he became involved with always ended up deciding they could love him only from a safe distance.

It was too soon to tell about Adrienne. She was alluring, to be sure, she had a knack for trouble herself or why else would she, an American anthropology student who had adventured around the world, marry a man like Adam Meureudu? Meureudu, after all, was as much a tyrant at home as he was in the political life of Indonesia.

Zoccola and she had first met in Morocco, in the ancient capital of Fez, where it was alleged a man could become lost in the labyrinth of its casbah. That meeting had occurred nearly a year before, but while the two had quickly realized an affinity for each other, there wasn't much they could do about exploring it, not with Adrienne's husband—and his bodyguards—hovering nearby, ready to pounce at any sign of infidelity.

Over the year they'd met only twice again, once in Istanbul and once in London, as each—the spy posing as a businessman and the lovely twenty-six-year-old American playing diplomatic spouse—made their way from one quarter of the world to another.

Adrienne detested her husband, but because she was afraid of him she wasn't ready to leave him. But she needed adventure, she needed excitement, just as Zoccola did, which was why she'd responded when he'd proposed that she help him gather information.

She still wasn't entirely clear about who Zoccola was working for, but she was sensible enough not to ask, knowing that she would only be rewarded with evasions, if not outright lies. She was in love with risk and, possibly, with Zoccola too.

"I don't often get interested in a man," she had told him in the dim hotel room in Istanbul. "But when I do, it can be dangerous. I want you to know that I've made wrong choices more often than not."

Her husband, he had recognized, was proof of that.

She wasn't finished, though. "It's possible that I am getting interested in you," she said matter-of-factly. "It doesn't happen so frequently that I can ignore it when it does. But you'd better watch out. This may be a bad choice for both of us."

The way Zoccola figured it, he *was* the wrong choice, but that didn't stop him from staying in contact with Adrienne by using much the same kind of coded messages he used to communicate with the operatives he ran for Triad. Earlier she'd informed him that she'd planned a vacation in Martinique alone, and he had sent a message to her, which finally reached her in Rome where her husband had gone to pay a courtesy call on the

Pope, that he would meet her on the Caribbean island.

She would be accompanied by her bodyguards, and so he wasn't able to go out to the airport and meet her in person.

As Zoccola sat in the café, he decided to call on the services of Edouard, a local character he had befriended the previous day. The overweight mulatto had a face grown soft from an abundance of rum and too many debauched evenings in the casinos. He sported shades and a frayed checkered cap and was forever bumming cigarettes from patrons in the cafés.

It was possible that when Edouard had first introduced himself to Zoccola he'd recognized the American as an agent of some sort. Or perhaps he had surmised that he was involved in an illegal business such as gun-running or drug peddling. Whatever his reason, he'd decided on his own that he could be of service to the well-heeled American.

Now, at five-thirty on the day Adrienne was to arrive, he appeared at the café just in time to give Zoccola an idea. But before he could think of how to explain it to the mulatto, the latter had joined him and begun to launch into a disquisition in French, a language Zoccola was fluent in, regarding Castro and Martinique.

"Castro has designs on Martinique," Edouard told him. "He thinks that with all that is happening in Central America no one will notice what he does here."

And there was indeed truth to Edouard's statement. At the time, Central America was in utter turmoil, with insurgencies going on in every nation in the area. Propagandists had a tendency to label one side right and the other left, but the actual situations were a great deal more complicated than that. In Nicaragua the left was in the ascent, but it faced an alliance of dissident leftists, oppressed Indians, and reactionary right-wing forces that had supported the ousted Somoza family years before. In Honduras the conservatives held sway but were engaged in armed conflict with Nicaragua, which was in turn supporting guerrillas in El Salvador, still under the rule of the right. Costa Rica, which had no army of its own, was falling under the influence of the left while its government continued to proclaim its neutrality. It was no wonder that, with all this going on, the U.S. administration might tend to overlook the tiny French protectorate of Martinique.

"I can identify all the spies and provocateurs who are working for Castro on the island," Edouard continued helpfully. "Why don't you buy me a drink?"

Zoccola ordered him a rum. "I don't want to hear about the Cubans," he said after the drink had arrived, still feeling it necessary to maintain his cover as a businessman.

Ignoring his comment, Edouard nodded in the direction of a man who'd just emerged from a Peugeot 604.

The man was impeccably dressed and had a trim beard. He bore the look of a very rich European who intended to squander a fortune in the few Martinique casinos with stakes high enough to suit him.

"There, that man," whispered Edouardo. "He is a Cuban emissary. He has just come here from Guyana. He calls himself Hidalgo."

So, Zoccola thought, this is Hidalgo. It was gratifying to have a good look at the man whose blurred, aging photograph he had recently seen in Triad files.

Hidalgo walked straight by them without giving them so much as a glance, exchanged a few words with the proprietor, and then vanished out into the street again.

"How do you know he was in Guyana?" Zoccola asked, deciding not to hide his interest any longer.

Edouard shrugged. "It is something I know. Didn't I tell you I am very well connected here?"

It was obvious that any attempt to pry an answer out of Edouard would be futile. His sources were of far less interest to Zoccola than the fact that Hidalgo was definitely on Martinique, just as earlier intelligence reaching Triad headquarters had indicated.

It was unfortunate, however, that Hidalgo was so handsome. Should Adrienne contrive to meet him, as he hoped, she might find herself forgetting that it was only information that she wanted from him.

Zoccola didn't entirely trust Edouard, but he was fairly certain he could rely on him to act as an intermediary for him. He only had to make Edouard think the clandestine affair with Adrienne involved sex, not espionage.

"I'd like you to do something for me, Edouard."

"Anything. *Just say the word*," he said, slipping into English. Zoccola guessed his use of the expression came from watching too much television or consorting with too many Americans.

"I'd like you to go to the airport and deliver a message for me."

"A secret message?" He looked at Zoccola with great hope.

"That's exactly it. A secret message."

There was nothing Edouard liked better.

3

MAY 25–26,
FORT-DE-FRANCE, MARTINIQUE

As soon as Adrienne Calenda stepped down from the Air France Airbus at 8:45 P.M., a ceremonial delegation on the tarmac, led by the short, elegantly dressed French prefect, and including several "paras" wearing camouflage suits and black and white uniforms, moved forward to greet her.

While Adrienne had been led to expect some sort of reception, she was surprised by the size of this one. Of course, she corrected herself, the honor was intended as much for her absent husband, Adam Meureudu, as for herself.

Photographers from the local press were right behind the French prefect's retinue. They scrambled for a better view of her, shouting to her to look in their direction. Her bodyguards, directly behind her, glowered at them, but made no effort to stop them.

As for Adrienne, enough paparazzi had photographed her since she had first made her appearance on the diplomatic scene that she was well accustomed to the attention by now. Yet it was evident that for all the pictures in *Paris Match*, *Quick*, *Stern*, and *Oggi*, the dignitaries of Martinique were unprepared for the impression she made.

She was a stunning woman who moved with calculated effect. Her hair, simply drawn back and pinned in place with a silver clasp, emphasized the graceful, aristocratic contours of her face that in certain lights was almost Nefertiti-like. Physically, she was just thin enough to effectively exhibit the latest fashions from New York and Paris, and this warm spring Martinique evening she was wearing a simple tropical white dress that showed her every movement.

The French perfect, a man of courtly manners, greeted her by bowing and placing a kiss on her extended hand.

He was startled to discover that she spoke French as well as she did. Though he listened for her American accent, he failed to detect a trace of it.

Once Adrienne would have been delighted, even overwhelmed, by such a lavish reception. Now the occasion simply made her feel she was only going through the motions. All the attention meant was that Indonesia was rich in oil. If it hadn't been, her arrival in Martinique would have gone virtually unnoticed. But since oil still played a pivotal role in the world economy, those countries amply endowed with it had to bear some of the responsibility for the soaring indebtedness of dozens of Third World nations, many of them in the Caribbean basin. So when these men looked upon her, they saw not just a beautiful woman but a vision of the rich black petroleum that made their economy function.

Adrienne and her party were guided through customs without inspection. Adrienne thought of the fine profit she could make by smuggling if she ever wanted to go into that line.

Almost before she realized it, a man with a white straw hat and checkered jacket had sidled up to her and taken hold of her hand. She had no time to react before he'd broken off the contact and slipped away. One of her bodyguards attempted to pursue the man but he had no difficulty vanishing into the crowd of arriving passengers.

Only after he had gone did she look at the message he

had deposited in her palm: "Staying at the Moulin. Call me there. Z."

The prefect, standing beside her, was mystified by the incident. "How did that man get by security?" he demanded of no one in particular.

"It's all right," Adrienne assured him. "No harm was done."

Outside the Lamentin Airport, a gray Mercedes, complete with flowers and champagne in back, was waiting to take the distinguished guest to her hotel, which was, naturally, one of the best on the island. The four-star PLM La Batelière, located a mile north of the capital on the seacoast, offered the discriminating visitor just about anything that he or she might want—a casino, a discotheque named "Club 21," six tennis courts, an open air terrace overlooking the pool, a beach, and a variety of water sports.

Early the following morning, Adrienne ventured out on the white beach, followed by two of her guards.

With her hair down and dressed only in a one-piece coral-blue bathing suit open at the sides, she seemed a different, more natural woman, and her stroll down the beach was watched with great interest by the few men up this early.

She elected to go out into the water on a pedal boat. The craft could accommodate only one person, and this was the principal reason she chose it. Her guards frowned at her choice but in the end relented, deciding that they could maintain their surveillance just as well by trailing her in a Sunfish.

A cloudless sky and a gentle southerly wind made for a day almost perfect for sailing. For nearly an hour Adrienne propelled her small craft in waters well within sight of her hotel, then she ventured farther out, advancing a half-mile up the coast, but each time she glanced back she saw the bright red and yellow sail of the Sunfish tracking her.

At one point, however, the wind dropped completely and the two bodyguards were forced to tack about to catch the slight breeze.

When they saw they had suddenly lost sight of her, one of them leaped into the water and began to swim, leaving his companion in charge of the boat.

A powerful swimmer, the guard was shortly in sight of the pedal boat again.

But Adrienne wasn't in it.

The boat was drifting in toward shore; he realized she had disappeared onto the beach.

Near shore the water was shallow enough for him to stand up, and he was soon walking onto the beach. She wasn't in sight. He climbed up the sloping beach, but could still see nothing from the small hill. But then, far to his left, he caught a glimpse of her running frantically in the direction of a gravel road that ran through the underbrush.

He was racing down the hill toward her when a taxi —a cumbersome black Mercedes—appeared down the road and, suddenly slowing, pulled up in front of Adrienne.

The rear door flew open and she vanished inside.

The bodyguard could only watch helplessly as the taxi sped away, leaving a cloud of dust hanging briefly in the air.

There was no question in the mind of the bodyguard that the rendezvous had been arranged in advance, and it took little imagination to surmise that it was a man she was meeting. Where she had gone with him was a mystery that the bodyguard, as he returned to his companion on the Sunfish, was confident of solving quite soon. While he didn't know what punishment might be meted out to Adrienne—that was for her husband to determine—he was quite certain what punishment the unknown lover would receive. In such matters the bodyguard and his colleague had absolute discretion.

While her bodyguards had returned to her hotel to begin the search, Adrienne had taken the prearranged cab to Zoccola's hotel in Fort-de-France. The Moulin was so close to the marketplace that the sounds of housewives haggling and the smells of bananas and fish drifted up to the windows of Zoccola's room.

During the half hour it had taken Adrienne to get there, Zoccola had done nothing but pace from one end of the large room to the other. He was barely aware of it when the cigarette he was clenching burned his fingers.

For all her effort, once Adrienne arrived she seemed no more tired than if she'd just returned from a leisurely walking tour of the capital.

Throwing her arms about Zoccola, she fought back the temptation to laugh; he looked so damn serious.

"Who," she asked, "was that strange creature who gave me your message?"

Zoccola explained about Edouard, then stepped back to observe her better. He was surprised by how different Adrienne appeared each time he was with her. It was as if each city—Fez, Istanbul, London, and now Fort-de-France—imbued her with a new quality or brought out some aspect of her that he hadn't noticed before.

Now she was radiant, flushed with excitement. She was obviously enjoying the intrigue. Her breasts rose and fell against the material of her swimsuit; a dark stain of perspiration had formed in the cleft.

When he went to kiss her, he tasted the salt of the Caribbean on her lips and in the tangle of her hair . . .

The last time, in London's May Fair, they had shared a room together for the better part of an hour. It had been clean and spacious, but by no means luxurious. His accommodations had been a part of his cover, which was that of an itinerant with far more time than money at his disposal. It was in the Mayfair room that they'd first made love. And it was there, too, that Zoccola had proposed that Adrienne collect information for him.

He'd realized that he might lose her, that she might think their long-distance love affair simply a pretext to recruit her. Even he hadn't been entirely sure he wasn't using her.

Yet, far from resisting the idea of being his agent, she'd embraced it. Her ardor for adventure was so great that over time Zoccola began to feel that she would do anything for him. Until the day came when she would leave him, repeating what every other woman in his life had done.

Now, in Martinique, he smiled. She liked his smile and touched his lips with her fingers as though to make sure it was genuine.

He said nothing. He simply took hold of her, pressing her buttocks, molding them, gathering her close to him.

Her breath was becoming shallow, her lips were drawn into a faraway smile, and her eyes were so slitted they were almost closed. He kissed her in the crook of her neck and heard her release a small stifled cry.

She gave a shudder as if an electric current had gone through her. With quick movements, she slipped the straps of her suit off her shoulders. Zoccola helped her, drawing the straps down until the top of the suit was lowered to her waist. In another moment the suit was entirely off and lay in a heap at her feet.

Zoccola guided her toward the bed, and suddenly they were there, tumbling back on it, her long legs flying into the air, her surprised laughter loud enough to be heard in the street below.

It was only later, when Adrienne realized she would have to get back to her hotel soon, that she recalled what she had to tell him. She'd been so happy to see Zoccola after so many months that she'd nearly forgotten it.

"That man you wanted me to see . . . Hidalgo?"

"You met him already?" Zoccola said, startled.

"Not exactly, but I met a man who says he knows him—a writer of leftist tracts and a contributor to one of the newspapers on the island. He was at a dinner the prefect gave for me last night and he assured me that Cuban troops being sent home from Angola were being diverted to Guyana."

This was new information. "Did he say how he knew this?" Zoccola asked.

"He told me he was a confidant of Hidalgo's. He said that every time Hidalgo came to Martinique, they'd get together for dinner. Of course I pretended not to have heard of him. 'But everyone on the island knows Hidalgo,' he told me. And apparently not for his politics. Evidently he's very popular with the local ladies.''

"I see. Did your writer friend happen to say when these Cubans were supposed to arrive in Guyana?"

"He implied it would be soon."

"Anything more?"

She thought for a moment. "No. That was really it. Of course I told this man I was interested in meeting Hidalgo sometime—given his reputation. He told me it could be arranged. So we'll just have to wait and see." Glancing at her watch she saw that it was almost four.

"I'll walk you downstairs," he said, noticing her concern.

She protested that it might be dangerous for him, but he insisted. "No farther than the entrance downstairs, then," she warned.

"Agreed," he replied, and they left the room hand in hand.

Adrienne's two protectors had experienced only slight difficulty discovering that she had gone into Fort-de-France. The sight of an attractive foreigner arriving in the fish market while clad only in a bathing suit and sandals was not something that locals could easily overlook.

Once in the market, however, there were so many contradictory reports about her that the bodyguards had no idea which way she had gone.

Along the Boulevard Allègre, a short distance from the fish market, they were accosted by a strange figure wearing a straw hat and a checkered jacket.

"Please, sirs," he addressed them with great ceremony, "I think I can be of service to you."

They would have ignored him and pushed him aside were it not for the fact that they remembered him from the airport.

"Who are you?" one of them demanded, taking his arm in an iron grip.

"That is of no consequence," he replied with dignity. "The important issue here is that I can conduct you to the hotel where the woman you want has gone." He suggested a generous sum for his services.

After the stronger one holding his arm agreed to the terms, Edouard led them through the narrow, crowded streets of the downtown area to Zoccola's hotel.

"There it is!" he declared proudly, pointing to the Moulin's crumbling stucco walls far down the narrow street. Flowers bloomed in the windows, but they were unable to disguise the hotel's air of poverty. The bodyguards frowned, disbelieving. How could Adrienne Calenda have gone to such a place?

They might have demanded back the money they'd given their guide when they suddenly spotted their quarry. She was at the front door of the hotel with a man, and as they watched from a distance, she gave him a lingering farewell kiss.

As she walked off, the man stood gazing after her. It was a grave mistake, for it allowed the two men to memorize the features of the man they eventually intended to kill.

4

Deep in the Virginia woods, protected by a series of defense perimeters that were sometimes conspicuous and sometimes not, stood the four-story headquarters of the Global Crisis Task Force, an imposing boxlike structure of granite that was designed to withstand anything less than a direct nuclear strike. A meandering road led several miles through the forest to the Task Force headquarters, and it was only at the very end of it that the traveler glimpsed any visible sign of security. Just before one reached the building there was a wooden bridge with a guardhouse on the far side. The security presence might seem minimal for a top-secret intelligence organization, but appearances in this case were deceptive, and meant to be so. At every point along the unmarked road the traveler was under electronic surveillance. Any unauthorized vehicle was tracked and, if necessary, interdicted by security personnel operating in the wooded terrain that stretched for miles on either side of the road.

The only indication to the unwary that they ought to remain on the highway was a simple handpainted sign at the turn-off reading: "NO TRESPASSING/PRIVATE ROAD."

Just before ten on the morning of May 27, three of the permanent members of the Task Force met in the fourth-floor conference room to discuss the message relayed to them by John Zoccola the previous evening from Fort-de-France.

These included William Drexell, the senior member of Triad, Jerry Hahn, the principal political analyst of the group, and James Lisker, who was an expert in communications, explosives, and assassination.

They were joined for this meeting by Drexell's aide, Marine Lieutenant Colonel Steven Cavanaugh, who handled the secretarial duties during these conferences.

There was no special urgency to Zoccola's message about Cubans heading for Guyana since the information was secondhand and had yet to be verified. On the other hand, if verification were obtained, it would suggest that a crisis of monumental proportions might be brewing in the Caribbean, with serious implications for American interests. The turmoil that already obtained throughout most of Central America was bad enough, but the prospect that Cuban communist troops might intervene directly on the South American continent—an event without precedent—was so alarming that Triad had been called together to work out emergency contingency plans.

Designed to help them in their planning, computerized maps of the Southern Hemisphere that could be magnified or broken down in response to commands typed into a Hewlett-Packard computer were projected onto three screens at the front of the room.

Before each place at the conference table, documents of varying degrees of confidentiality had been laid out. These the permanent members could study at their leisure after the briefing was completed.

Of the four men there, only one had no need to inspect the documents, and that was William Drexell. Most of the information they contained he knew by heart.

Drexell's personal history read like a history of the cold war. He was intimately involved on so many conflicts—underground as well as overt—that had defined the course of the cold war that it was difficult to see his life as a thing apart from it.

His face reflected some of this history. Now in his sixties, he had the look of a military man, hard and logical, with strong features that seemed unfinished, almost raw. One glance at him would tell you that he had had his share of bitter struggles, that he had lived much of his life in the open and had suffered as much from harsh environments as he had from the bullets and shrapnel that had left their mark on him and, in one instance, still lay inside him, a harmless but often painful souvenir of an Asian skirmish that was now only a footnote in the history books.

He was a commanding presence even when in the Oval Office, surrounded by cabinet members and advisers close to the President. But wherever he was he rarely asserted his real power; he chose to remain in the background, maintaining a self-effacing image that belied the importance of his usually covert responsibilities.

Drexell began today's emergency planning session by outlining the events of the last several months. "In one sense the world is a more peaceful place than it has been in some time," he said, his low, rough voice giving weight to his words. "Following the crisis in the Aegean area, which almost brought us into direct confrontation with the Soviets, we've seen a relaxation of tensions both in Europe and in Africa. The Turks and the Greeks still continue to hold to a cease-fire, and if they aren't seriously talking with each other at least they aren't shooting at each other. A significant achievement, to my way of thinking.

"In addition, we managed to convince Ankara to call off the blockade of the Bosporus after three days. That step, as you know, was necessary if NATO wasn't to end up in a war with the Soviets. That it cost us plenty you also know. But pouring a couple of billion dollars into Turkey and rescheduling their loans was a small price to pay to forestall open conflict between the super-powers.

"As you also know, the Kremlin announced that it understood the need for a peaceful gesture and suddenly withdrew several thousand troops from Albania and Afghanistan. Simultaneously a token division or two of the Red Army was moved out of Czechoslovakia and re-assigned to bases near the Urals. We have direct ground, as well as satellite confirmation that these withdrawals did in fact occur. Their real importance, of course, is something else again. Both Albania and Afghanistan are securely in the Soviet camp now; moving out several thousand troops was a minor luxury the Kremlin could afford. The President was correct to denounce the with-drawals as a propaganda ploy and demand that all Red Army troops leave both nations. First Secretary Kadiyev then declared that this would happen as soon as all im-perialist conspiracies had been put down. There was nothing really new in all this.

"While these withdrawals were obviously meaning-less, a significant development did occur beginning in April. I refer to SWAPO's abrupt change in its negoti-ating position, followed almost immediately by the an-nouncement out of Luanda in Angola that all Cuban troops would be departing for home in the immediate future."

SWAPO stood for the Southwest African People's Organization. SWAPO had fought against South Africa in the arid wastes and bush of its country—otherwise known as Namibia—as well as over the negotiating table at UN headquarters in New York. Long regarded as a United Nations-mandate territory, Southwest Africa had been held by South Africa for several years. The apartheid government in Pretoria had been reluctant to give up Southwest Africa so long as it thought that a government ill-disposed to its views might come to power there. Each time a treaty seemed in the offing, either Pretoria or SWAPO would back down. But on March 10, in New York, a spokesman for SWAPO had advanced a new negotiating position at a press conference at the Waldorf-Astoria. It proved to be the long-awaited breakthrough. Southwest Africa was to become fully independent on January 1 with a multiracial government (fashioned from a mind-bogglingly complicated formula) sitting in the capital of Windhoek.

"But if Zoccola's information is correct," Drexell continued, "it seems likely that all these movements of troops are, basically, diversionary tactics. The principal objective appears to be here in the Western Hemisphere where the Western alliance has been lulled into letting down its guard. Now let's get down to specifics."

It was Jerry Hahn who elected to speak next. While he'd spent the last several years working for the intelligence community, for both the CIA and the NSA, he had never quite lost the look of the academic he once was. One of the most enterprising and brilliant men to emerge from the Washington-Cambridge-Stanford think-tank axis, he had written two important books. One, titled *The World Crisis: A Structural Study*, was a scholarly exercise that was really an elaboration of his Columbia University doctoral thesis. The other, *Against the Odds: America's Search for Peace in the Twentieth Century*, was less bogged down with footnotes and appendices and was intended for a popular audience.

While he was thirty-six, his features still had a youthful, untested quality. He'd joined Triad expecting to be a consultant, but Drexell had thrust him into situations which took him far from his books and his computer screens. Drexell wasn't interested in a man who could merely analyze and consult; he needed someone with instinct and a penetrating intelligence who could divine the motives of kings and guerrilla leaders alike, someone who would not hesitate to hazard an opinion even in the midst of a crisis when thousands of lives might hinge on whether his opinion was the right one. It was a matter of looking—and leaping—at the same time.

Although the skills demanded of him by Drexell were not easily mastered, Hahn, in the year he'd served with Triad, had matured in many ways. If he was not the hustler Zoccola was or the war-scarred commando Lisker was, he could still hold his own under fire or in the back rooms of safe houses in enemy capitals.

It now fell to him to report to the group on the current situation in Venezuela and Guyana.

Relying on a series of diagrams to illustrate his briefing, he noted that Guyana, which in size was not much smaller than Great Britain, had a population of less than a million that could barely support itself on the bauxite, diamonds, and sugar produced by the country. Twenty percent of the work force was unemployed, the only industry worth mentioning was the country's sugar and rice factories, and the soil was so sandy and fallow that only .5 percent of Guyana's 83,000 square miles was under cultivation. Adding to these problems was Guyana's labor strife, which was marked by violence and strikes, and a severe shortage of foreign currency, which had impelled the leftist government in Georgetown to impose unpopular austerity measures on its people.

"There's no question that the Comrade Leader stole the election," Hahn went on. "Had it been an honest election he would have lost in spite of his charismatic personality because under him taxes have soared and the country still can't pay its bills.

"By contrast, Venezuela is amply endowed by geography. Without exhausting you with statistics, I'd like to point out one fact: the Jobo oil fields in the northeastern province of Monagas contain an estimated twelve billion barrels. And that, gentlemen, is a hell of a lot of oil."

On this point there was general agreement. Venezuela possessed enough oil to be a member of OPEC, but while it might charge the benchmark rate of forty dollars a barrel for the stuff, it still retained fairly close ties to the United States—closer by far than the Arab members of OPEC, who could not be depended upon by America even in the best of times.

Early in the decade Venezuela had made an unprecedented request for F-16's from the United States, and they had been delivered, though not without some controversy. Several congressmen wondered what in God's name Venezuela needed a squadron of F-16's for; it had no enemies poised on its borders.

Now there seemed to be an answer to this question.

"For a country as impoverished as Guyana it's ironic that anyone would want any of their territory," Hahn continued. "Even many Guyanese wouldn't care if someone took them over. But Venezuela does. Twenty-four years have passed since Venezuela first asserted territorial rights to what amounts to five-eighths of Guyana, basing its claim on old maps and deeds that existed before the border adjustments contrived by Great Britain, which ruled Guyana up until its independence. Naturally the Guyanese response to the Venezuelan claim has not exactly been favorable.

"During the last years the United Nations has attempted to mediate the issue to prevent the dispute from developing into an armed conflict. But nothing has come of the UN's efforts."

Lisker snorted, his gaunt features showing disgust. Intolerant by nature, he had never considered the UN a solution to anything. In his view, the world body was useful only for passing resolutions that said nothing in principle and meant less in practice. Lisker disagreed with the very idea of any sort of world government. He believed that diplomatic goals could be achieved without combat, but not without threat of force. At heart he was a military man who distrusted politicians, believing that they killed more people than generals ever had.

No one had an answer to the present world situation, of course. Whenever settlements were reached in international conflicts they were more the result of powerful third parties—like the United States in Lebanon—taking a role than anything the United Nations had done.

"What do you think's going to happen, Hahn?" Drexell demanded.

"The scenario I've worked out is that first we'll have a period of border incursions and skirmishes followed by more mediation efforts, perhaps by the UN but more likely by Great Britain and the United States, since both countries enjoy a certain influence in the region. But this scenario was devised before John's information came in. If Cuban troops are in fact on their way to Guyana I would expect one of two further things to happen. Either Venezuela will be intimidated by the prospect of confronting armed forces far better trained than the Guyanese army and refrain from taking any action, leading to its temporarily renouncing its territorial claims. Or else it might strike now, before Cuban troops arrive, to create a de facto situation where they will be in control of several thousand square miles of Guyanese territory. The Cubans would have a much tougher time rooting out Venezuelan units once they became entrenched."

"What's the border region like?" Lisker inquired. It was a practical question, since he had an inkling that he might be sent there and he wanted to know what to expect.

"It's someone's version of hell," Hahn replied. "Between the populated coastal area and the Venezuelan frontier there's little but jungle and mountains. Most of the area is unpopulated, with a scattering of itinerant diamond miners, Christian missionaries, and impoverished Amerindians who herd cattle. It's a very difficult place to move troops and matériel in."

"And a difficult place to monitor any such movements in," Lisker noted in a grave voice.

"The fact is," Drexell said, "we can't do anything until we're certain what's happening down there. Recon photos aren't much help in that jungle. We need a man on the ground." He looked from Lisker to Hahn and back again. "Any volunteers?"

Drexell posed the question more to see what responses he'd draw than to obtain an answer. He already knew whom he was about to choose.

5

James Lisker despised Georgetown. It was midafternoon, but with all the rain coming down, it felt like half-
past ten at night, and the whole city seemed to smell like
swamp rot.

Lisker especially didn't want to be sitting in a rum bar
down by the Demerara River, in a part of Georgetown
that, with enough rain, might one day sink underneath
ten feet of water and never be missed.

Lisker had arrived shortly after noon by way of a
cranky twin-engine jet from Trinidad. The jet engine
complained throughout the entire flight, making the
craft sound as if it would much prefer being down on
the ground than stuck in midair. Lisker, who was not
one to fear either heights or airplanes, had spent most of
the time staring out the oval window at the slate-gray
waters of the Caribbean, wondering what it would be
like to be floating around down there.

It was Drexell's idea that he pose as a journalist with
ties to a left-wing newspaper published out of Washington. The newspaper, *The Guardian Spirit*, had supported Comrade Leader Walling in his reelection bid,
though it was doubtful that even the most fanatically in-

clined of its readership cared a good goddamn who won in Guyana. Even those on the left seemed to care little about Guyana, and it took something like the Jonestown Massacre to get the world's attention.

James Lisker was now sitting at the rum bar waiting for his contact. Advised to steer clear of the U.S. Embassy and any of its personnel, including the few, unreliable, CIA assets posted to this desolate spot, he was told to rely on one of Triad's own people, a false missionary named Colin Harris. Apparently Harris had spent so long pretending to be a missionary that he'd begun to think like one.

"Don't be surprised if he talks a bit too much about God," Drexell had warned him before he left.

Lisker wasn't at all interested in hearing about God. He'd served in Nam and he'd served in other jungles as bad as the one flourishing between Venezuela and Guyana, and nowhere he'd gone had he ever witnessed anything that would indicate the existence of a deity. It was all madness and death. If Harris, assuming he eventually did appear, started in about God, he'd tell him to forget it. He wanted only facts—facts and a plan.

Lisker was here in Georgetown to find out if the Cubans were coming and if they were, how many of them could be expected to show up for the party.

Harris did materialize, fifteen minutes late. He was a man with a very red face, suggesting hypertension or alcoholism or both, and a shock of white hair that only served to make the redness that much more pronounced.

He was dressed in an open-collared white shirt and white slacks and was drenched with water and sweat.

Among the disconsolate-looking blacks, Lisker, in a light tan jacket and olive-green slacks, was readily identifiable to Harris.

Harris greeted the bartender and nodded to a few of the patrons. He was apparently known and seemed to feel moderately secure here.

Lisker found his handshake tentative while his eyes

flitted from one side of the room to the other, avoiding Lisker's steady gaze.

Lisker didn't think he was going to like this man of God, false or not.

A large cup of dark rum was set before Harris. After taking a mouthful, he gave a sigh of what may have been pleasure.

"I've heard a great deal about you, Mr. Lisker," he said with something of a stammer in his voice. He began by telling Lisker that he'd been traveling about the continent, ministering to the spiritually impoverished and ignorant for more years than he could remember, though later he said he had spent a quarter of a century among the heathen.

Gradually, after further consumption of the rum, he began to relax and admitted, still without looking directly at Lisker, that he enjoyed being a fraud. "You know, it's strange. I was a confirmed atheist, now I think that by trying to make others believe, I've turned myself into a believer. For the most part, though, I keep thinking that if I don't take myself too seriously, I'll be all right." He turned to Lisker, regarding him directly for the first time. "Mr. Lisker, you strike me as a man who does take himself too seriously."

What Harris said was true, but Lisker said nothing. An analysis of his personality was not what he'd come all the way to Georgetown for. "Tell me," Lisker said with deep sarcasm, "with all your missionary work here, have you heard anything about Cuban troops coming in?"

"Nothing," Harris responded. "But maybe it'll be easier for us to find them in the interior than in the capital. I'm still waiting for permission to go into the jungle, but I'm afraid that my credentials have yet to be approved. A deputy minister by the name of Virgil Reade has them now. All I can do is wait, but I'm not the only one. Even miners and other people with legitimate business can't get permission to go into the interior. Not that anyone tells you that it has anything to do with Venezuela. On the other hand, every ordinary person you talk to has seen troop transports going west.''

Lisker wasn't surprised by this; he had assumed that unofficial travel into the disputed region would run into impediments, either from nature or else from the government of Sydney Walling.

"What do you say to going into the interior without authorization?'' Lisker asked.

Harris contemplated this notion for a moment, then shook his head vigorously. "What would happen is you would go in there and never come out. You'd be arrested or shot on sight.''

Lisker could sense that Harris wasn't much for exposing himself to danger. He was close to sixty, from the looks of him, and he seemed to want to do nothing more than collect information and play missionary for the rest of his life. "What would you say to the idea of bribing your friend, the deputy minister?''

"Virgil Reade? Yes, quite possibly he could pull the necessary rabbits out of the proverbial hat. You have a substantial source of funds at your disposal, I assume.''

Lisker said that he did, either in American or Guyanese dollars.

"I should think he'd prefer American. Guyanese dollars don't travel very well, if you catch my gist. Just as soon as you come up with the money I will schedule an appointment. You know, it's possible Mr. Reade might actually enjoy seeing me again. My impression from the last time we met is that he is developing a definite hankering for religion.''

The telephone caught Lisker while he was dozing. He came awake in an instant and, glancing outside the window of his hotel room in the center of Georgetown, he saw that it had turned into night. The smell of rain still penetrated the room.

Harris was calling him, not to tell him of any results he had achieved with the deputy minister—an appointment had been made for ten the following morning

—but rather to inform him of a rumor that had just reached his ears.

"Something's happening out at the airport, something rather important. The People's Army has closed the road out to it and all regularly scheduled flights in or out have been canceled through tomorrow morning."

"What do you make of it?"

"I don't exactly know."

"I suggest then that we drive out there and see if we can't find out. Is there any other way of getting to the airport than the main road?"

"It might take us forever, but if we use the back roads we should at least be able to get close to it. Whether we can avoid the People's Army, I can't predict," Harris finished, apprehension showing in his voice.

Lisker said to meet him in an hour, at nine, in the nave of the Church of the Sacred Heart, one of the principal landmarks of the city. "You're a missionary, remember?" he told Harris sardonically. "It might be good for you to pray once in a while."

A four-wheel drive, closed in and suitable for driving through the overgrowth of Guyana's jungles, had been made available to Lisker through Triad. It was parked on a corner within sight of Georgetown's now darkened Stabroek Market—the central shopping district—just as the instructions to him had said it would be. The keys were under the seat.

After picking up Harris, he began to drive out in the direction of Timehri Airport. Having been in and around Georgetown long enough to know the alternate routes, Harris assumed the role of navigator and guide.

The part of the city that they started out in was one of the sorrier-looking sections Georgetown had to offer. Most of the houses were built of wood and appeared ready to collapse on the stilts that supported them above a sea of mud. Political slogans, an already fading legacy from the recent election, were painted on every available wall space: "Vote No to Walling!" "All Power to the PPP!" "Death to the NPC!" Blazing red hammers and sickles adorned many of these exhortations.

But the unrest and agitation suggested by the slogans were belied by the faces of the people who idled on the porches of the houses they passed. The natives exuded only an air of listlessness and resignation.

At intervals they would spot a military van or an olive-uniformed figure brandishing an automatic weapon. While their progress through the dark streets was watched with a certain ominous interest, no attempt was made to stop them.

However, as they traveled on the principal highway leading out to the airport, the military presence became far more pronounced. They soon passed a Soviet T-55 tank to the right of the highway, its guns trained on on-coming vehicles, and eventually they saw a self-pro-pelled 155mm howitzer illuminated a quarter of a mile up ahead.

Up to this point no one had attempted to force them to halt or to turn back. Nonetheless, Harris now pro-posed they turn off the main road.

They were soon riding on a pothole-filled asphalt road that evolved into an uneven, murky dirt track that could barely accommodate the width of their vehicle.

After a quarter of an hour, they drove into a village. In the headlights they could see that it was nothing more than a cluster of hovels set amid some withered palm trees. Fierce-looking but very emaciated dogs ran out in front of them, barking furiously. A few furtive figures appeared in lit doorways as they passed, but no more ac-tive human interest displayed itself.

"Indians," Harris remarked, drawing his arm inside the window before one of the wild dogs tried to snap it off. "If these people were supporters of Walling they'd live in the neat little brick houses you probably noticed in Georgetown. As they're not, they're simply ignored."

"Are you certain this is the way to the airport?" Lisker prodded.

"Well, let's say that it's in this general direction. We're traveling parallel to the main road."

As they passed out of the village, the jungle closed in on them again, and the illuminated vegetation was so thick, they had to slow to a crawl in order to keep with the dirt track.

In a few minutes Lisker sensed that they were approaching the coast; he thought he could smell the sea, though the jungle was as thick as ever.

Suddenly he put his foot to the brake, and doused the headlights. Harris pitched forward; only by propping his hands against the dashboard did he keep himself from falling. He regarded Lisker with puzzlement.

"Up ahead."

Perhaps two hundred yards distant, where the dirt road emerged from the jungle, an armored personnel carrier appeared dimly ahead of them. Lisker had sensed the rumbling of its engine even before it had come into sight.

"They've obviously decided to cover this route too," Harris noted dismally.

It wasn't clear if they'd been spotted yet, but they had to assume that they were. Since there was no possible way to get around the oncoming carrier the next best thing was to back up. And back up they did—right into the heart of the miserable Indian village they'd just come out of.

The sight of a four-wheel drive in reverse appearing out of the dark underbrush interested the few visible inhabitants of the village not at all. Only the dogs responded, once again barking and baring their teeth as they chased the receding front end of the vehicle.

Meanwhile, the armored personnel carrier was speeding after them, though it was hampered more than the four-wheel drive by the narrowness and roughness of the road. There was no question now that Lisker and Harris had been spotted and would soon be captured. Armed with light weapons—Lisker's was a Smith & Wesson M-13 .357 Magnum—they could not reasonably expect to fight it out with a squadron of the People's Army.

Instead of continuing to back up, Lisker chose to turn off the road, plunging into the heart of the village.

Seeing what Lisker was doing, Harris was appalled.

At the rate Lisker was going, he seemed liable to deci-
mate any villager who was still out. But while he scattered a few natives, he managed to avoid hitting anyone.

Shots whistled from behind them. Two plowed into
the vehicle's rear, but they seemed to cause no significant damage.

Ahead of them lay enough bush and palm trees to
have blotted out the sun in the daytime. Lisker raced the
vehicle directly toward the wall of vegetation less than
twenty yards away.

It was all Harris could do to hold on as the vehicle
proceeded headlong into the tangled underbrush. The
village could scarcely be seen when he looked back; nor
could he make out what had happened to the personnel
carrier. He was about to ask Lisker what in hell he
thought he was doing, but he couldn't succeed in getting
use of his voice, which seemed to have died in his throat.

But Lisker knew very well what he was doing. At the
last moment he suddenly slowed the four-wheel drive
and then, with a certain caution, took it into the brush
until it was completely out of sight of the village. Were
it daylight the sun would have been caught by the metal
surface of the vehicle and its reflection would have given
their presence away. But in the dark you would have
had to walk right up to the vehicle before you'd know it
was there.

Their getting out of the four-wheel drive was impeded
by the tangle of palms, breadfruit trees, and other
growth around them.

No sooner had they left the vehicle than they heard
the approaching rumble of the personnel carrier. It
seemed to be following the same route they had taken
into the jungle.

Then, abruptly, the carrier drew to a stop. It was apparent that the troops inside no longer had any idea
where their quarry had gone. Apparently the darkness
obscured the path the smaller vehicle had produced.
While Lisker and Harris watched from behind the safety
of the brush, half a dozen men descended from the carrier and began to fan out in search of them.

"I'm too old for this sort of thing," Harris murmured to himself, but Lisker ignored the comment.

The search continued for almost ten minutes without result. Then one of the men standing by the carrier called out to the others, directing them back. Three men were left behind to patrol the area. Obviously, the idea was that if Lisker and Harris could not be found, at least they could be kept from escaping.

But as soon as the personnel carrier pulled away, vanishing in the direction of the Indian village, Lisker gestured Harris back into the four-wheel drive.

"What are we going to do?" he whispered fearfully.

Lisker just shook his head as he brought the motor to life, instantly giving away their location to the People's Army patrol.

Putting the vehicle into reverse so that they were now heading toward the soldiers, Lisker pressed his foot hard on the accelerator. At the same time he yelled to his companion to keep his head down.

Automatic fire greeted them; there was a terrible racket as the bullets struck their rear and roof. One of the side windows disintegrated, sending shards of glass flying through the interior. When Lisker glanced down he saw that his arm was dripping blood, but he felt no pain and maintained the same steady grip on the wheel. Unable to put his head out his window to see where he was going, he was forced to rely on the rear-view mirror. But it was so dark that the mirror was of little help.

In spite of the jungle, the vehicle was gaining speed. All at once they heard a sickening thud followed by a ghost of a scream that died quickly away.

Someone had been dragged for a short distance under the wheels of the vehicle. Before the screaming stopped, Lisker realized he'd hit one of the members of the patrol.

Now a large section of windshield in front of Lisker came apart. As they'd continued in reverse, away from the militiamen, one of them had fired and hit the window squarely. The shower of glass made Lisker and Harris lower themselves still further. Lisker shot a sidelong glance at Harris and saw he was covered with blood. He knew he himself didn't look much different.

Through the newly created hole in the windshield Lisker had a brief glimpse of the fiery bursts from the soldier's weapon. As the four-wheel drive continued in reverse, their view of the man was soon blotted out by the thick jungle.

Shortly, Lisker put the vehicle into forward and drove on carefully for a few more minutes. Then, when they reached another dirt road that seemed to be leading to the airport, they stopped to inspect their wounds. In spite of all the blood, Lisker and Harris found that most of the cuts were superficial, and they dressed their injuries using the emergency medical kit that Lisker had brought along. Then they resumed their journey along the dirt road in the direction of the airport.

The four-wheel drive was still serviceable but there was no question that, in order to be inconspicuous, they would have to abandon it before they arrived at the airport and find another way back to Georgetown. It was especially important that they not be taken, for they were now responsible for killing a member of the People's Army.

Their most immediate priority, however, lay in getting to the airport.

Their luck held; although the roundabout way Harris chose cost them an additional hour they reached the outskirts of the airport without meeting any further opposition.

Fortunately, earlier attempts to clear away the underbrush and trees that bordered the field had been abandoned years before, and now the jungle grew dense and thick around it, concealing the perimeter fence from view.

Leaving the four-wheel drive carefully hidden in the underbrush, they proceeded on foot toward the wire fence that had been strung along the end of one of the runways.

"This fence is new," Harris observed. "It wasn't here when I last came out for a look."

As he said this they began to hear the distant throb of an airborne plane. It didn't take long for it to come within sight. As it approached, Lisker identified it as a large transport craft, bulbous and menacing in the night sky. It was an Antonov-12 and it went under the NATO code name Cub. Lisker knew it was capable of handling over 44,000 pounds of freight or 100 troops.

Signal beacons deployed across the airfield blinked repeatedly as the Antonov descended.

Lisker automatically noted the time: 10:08. Just a little over an hour had passed since they'd left the Church of the Sacred Heart.

Using the wire cutters from his kit bag, Lisker separated the strands of barbed wire. They made their way along the perimeter of the runway, careful not to let the lights expose them.

For Donald Singh, commander of the garrison at the airport, the arrival of the Antonov was an event of great importance. After months of practice drills to prepare them for Venezuelan bombing raids and direct attacks on the ground, his men were edgy with excitement. Now, with the arrival of the Antonov, they at least had an opportunity to show off their training.

As soon as the Antonov came to a stop, an honor guard would approach to greet the debarking passengers.

Meanwhile, a second unit had been mobilized to search the airfield for intruders one last time.

Ten men bearing automatic submachine guns spread out over the airfield while searchlights cut into the darkness.

In the meantime Singh, always a stickler for formality, briefed his honor guard on the etiquette that the situation demanded for them. "No laxity," he declared. "No sloppy postures. You shall stand erect and look straight ahead until I give the order to break rank."

The Antonov was in the process of taxiing up toward the terminal building when a burst of automatic fire rang out from the end of the runway.

"What on earth?" Singh shouted.

He fumbled with the switch on his walkie-talkie until he'd established contact with the leader of the surveillance force. He demanded to know what was happening.

"Cheddy says he saw someone," came the response.

"Who exactly did Cheddy see?"

"He can't be sure. We are looking now."

Singh was irritated at the delay. The Antonov was parked now and his permission was all that was needed for the door to be opened. Already the honor guard was lined up on the asphalt apron; the postures of the men were correct, at any rate.

Singh decided that he would wait for another few minutes; then, if no one was found, he would go ahead with the welcoming ceremony. Cheddy, he knew, was a rather stupid individual who would start shooting at the slightest provocation.

In order to have a better view of the Antonov, Lisker and Harris had crept along the perimeter of the airfield to within a hundred and fifty yards of the craft. Lisker managed to shoot half a dozen pictures with his miniature Olympus before Harris spotted a soldier approaching along the edge of the field.

He nudged Lisker, eliciting a look of mild annoyance from him before he realized what Harris was indicating.

A shot was fired and Harris instantly felt a burning sensation. His jacket suddenly gave off a stench of cordite. Apparently a bullet had just gone through it.

Lisker roughly pulled him back into the darkness at the edge of the field just as the rotating searchlight was about to reach them. They began running flat out away from the Antonov.

They heard a great deal of shouting in the brush behind them, but at least there was no longer any shooting.

Even so, they didn't stop running until they'd gotten behind a corrugated structure of indeterminate purpose. They were now caught in a position approximately sixty yards from the perimeter, halfway between the parked Antonov and the terminal building.

Lisker would have gone on, but Harris was completely out of breath. "I'm not cut out for this sort of thing," he muttered, but Lisker ignored the self-pitying statement.

They rested for a moment, cocking their ears for the sound of approaching troops. But when they hazarded a look outside the shed, they saw that the surveillance team had broken off its search.

At the same time they could see that a ramp was being lowered from the Antonov. Lisker raised his field glasses as the first men emerged from the craft.

They were wearing camouflage uniforms, and it looked as though they carried forty to sixty pounds of equipment in the packs on their backs. Kalashnikovs—AK-74's—were gripped in their hands.

"What are they, Cubans?" Harris asked.

Lisker waited before responding. He wasn't totally sure himself.

"Not Cubans," he said finally. "Russians."

6

"I think you are in grievous danger, sir," Edouard was saying, shaking his head gravely.

Zoccola was wondering whether it would ever be possible to get rid of this man. How Edouard had found him here at La Grand' Voile, a terraced restaurant directly above the Yacht Club—was anyone's guess. He may have followed Zoccola halfway across the city from his hotel. In comparison with the tumultuous market area where Edouard had first accosted Zoccola, La Grand' Voile provided for a tranquil and elegant setting. Nonetheless, Edouard seemed equally at home here as he did among the bins of bananas and crawfish. More and more Zoccola was convinced that the man was a spy, but he'd be damned if he could figure out who he was working for. Most likely himself.

"Very serious danger," Edouard repeated as he stood over Zoccola's table, regarding him with a look of gravity appropriate to his words.

Zoccola did not believe him for one moment. He continued eating his lunch in the hope that perhaps if he ignored him, he might vanish. He had too much on his mind to bother with Edouard this morning. When he wasn't thinking of Adrienne and how he was going to go about seeing her again, he was concerned with the fate of his colleagues in Triad.

Since giving Triad headquarters the information about suspected Cuban troop movements toward Guyana, Zoccola had accepted the fact that the semi-vacation he'd embarked upon had turned into something else entirely. Drexell had instructed him to remain where he was in view of the fact that Martinique seemed to be fertile ground for information as to what was happening in the Caribbean area, what with Cuban agents and leftist sympathizers roaming the streets of the capital and occasionally popping up at diplomatic receptions to which Adrienne had also been invited.

In particular, he was assigned to track Hidalgo's movements about the island. If he was as important a Cuban agent as Edouard and Adrienne had implied, then he might well provide a key to Castro's plans in the region. If Zoccola had been able to place more trust in Edouard—if he could have placed *any* trust in him—he would have asked him to assist him in this enterprise. But it was one thing to use him to arrange an assignation with a woman; it was quite another to put him onto the trail of a Cuban agent. To do so would immediately make it obvious that Zoccola couldn't possibly be a businessman.

So far as he knew, both Drexell and Hahn were waiting for further reports from Lisker and himself before they moved from their headquarters in Virginia. Until they had an idea as to what the Cubans were actually up to, it made no sense for them to head south too.

Turning now to Edouard, Zoccola asked him to explain himself.

"The men who are watching your lady friend are onto you."

"And how do you know this?"

"I know, I know," Edouard said, exasperated that he should for one moment be doubted. "They will kill you if you are not careful. I would advise you to stop seeing the lady."

Zoccola was growing angry. "That's none of your goddam business. I'd suggest you leave my table before I do something both of us will regret."

Edouard looked offended. "For a modest sum I can make sure that these men do not cause harm to you. And yet you reproach me! I admit I am insulted." He frowned and screwed up his face into an expression of petulance.

He rose from the table, saying as he did so, "I have gone out of my way to warn you because I am your friend. It is your choice to treat me shabbily, but you will regret it." With that final declaration he threaded his way among the tables and left the restaurant.

Zoccola sighed, hoping he had seen the last of him, but he knew better than to count on it. Yet when he scanned the tables around him he had the sinking sensation that Edouard, for all his deceit and avarice, might not have been mistaken abut the danger Zoccola was in.

Seated at a table close to the edge of the terrace were two men who appeared to be more interested in him than in the view of the Caribbean. Although the two didn't look remotely familiar to him, they held themselves like men who earned their livelihood in some branch of security; they could have been plainclothes police or spies—or bodyguards in the employ of Adrienne's husband. In any event, Zoccola had been working undercover long enough to recognize that they were agents of some kind.

Having no further appetite, he quickly paid the check and departed the restaurant. The pair who'd been observing him did the same, and this confirmed Zoccola's impression that they wanted him to be aware that he was being followed. He also knew that, in spite of the deliberately ominous air they affected, he should be most concerned not with these two but with those he couldn't see.

He ducked into a pay phone, for the moment losing his tails, and called the number Adrienne had given him. While she'd spent years training as an anthropologist, he'd discovered that she could also be as clever as any professional spy. At the moment, for example, he had no idea where the number he was calling was; he was only certain that it was not her hotel room.

She answered on the first ring. "I can't see you today," she said quickly. "I've accepted an invitation to go up to Rivière Salée with someone. But don't be angry. I think you'll approve of my decision when you hear who's invited me."

"Let's hear it," he said brusquely.

"Hidalgo," she replied.

"Where did you meet him?"

"At a big party last night given by one of the békés, a man named Roger Sansaire. I was introduced to him ten minutes after getting to the party and he wouldn't let go of me all night. He really is a very attractive man, though not my type."

"What about your guards?"

"I've told them about the expedition and they appear to have accepted the idea. They'll follow along in another car."

"He hasn't hinted at his true identity?"

"He's better than that, John. He's like you, he claims to be a journalist. And a Mexican citizen."

Zoccola asked what he intended to show her at Rivère Salée, which was southeast of the capital.

"Hidalgo says he has some friends on the island who own a vast banana plantation in the area. He tells me it's very beautiful and I simply must have a look at it."

"For a communist agent he seems to have a great preference for consorting with capitalists."

She laughed. "Look, I have to go now. I'll ring you sometime tonight and let you know what I've discovered."

Zoccola hoped that she would at least discover something important. The idea of sacrificing her for even a single day was abhorrent to him.

With nothing much to do, he found himself roving the streets of the capital, plunging ever deeper into the crowded, twisting streets of the downtown area, where people hung out of balconies and called down to friends passing by. The atmosphere was part French, part African, and part Caribbean and frenetic, though for all the motion and hustle not much seemed to be getting accomplished.

The men he'd seen in La Grand' Voile were no longer in evidence, but that didn't reassure him. He still had the feeling he was being watched; amid the tumult of downtown Fort-de-France it would not be a difficult thing to track somebody's movements without being spotted.

At a turn into the Rue de la Liberté, not far from the Departmental Museum, a man wearing a wide-brim hat tilted rakishly over his brow approached him. He was a mulatto with sienna-colored skin and a sparkling set of teeth. Stepping out into Zoccola's path and blocking the sidewalk, he addressed a question to him. It sounded like a question at any rate, but its substance was not at all comprehensible. His accent was so thick that Zoccola couldn't figure out whether he was speaking in French or English or Creole.

Shrugging to indicate his incomprehension, Zoccola attempted to go around him. The man, however, merely shifted position so that he was still in his way. The movement was enough to alert Zoccola that he had a problem.

Instinctively, he glanced behind him just in time to see two men coming up from behind him. One was black, with a torn undershirt and a smile made grotesque by several missing teeth. The other was white and bearded with a sour expression fixed on his face.

Both held machetes in their hands, the kind that were customarily employed on the sugar plantations.

While the street was crowded with people, no one seemed to notice the developing confrontation.

As soon as Zoccola redirected his attention to the man in the hat who'd stopped him, he saw that he, too, had a weapon in his hand, not a machete but a narrow knife blade that glinted in the midday sun.

All three moved in fast, evidently meaning to slash him quickly and vanish before passersby could summon the police. Zoccola leaped out of the way as they rushed him. Pressing his back to the wall directly behind him, he kicked out with his right leg, catching the mulatto in the solar plexus with such force that he let out a cry of pain before reeling away. The mulatto didn't go down, though, and he still retained hold of his knife.

The other two began to slash at him with quick broad strokes. He felt a stab of pain in his belly, but ignored it. He was armed but realized that too many seconds would be lost extricating his gun from the inside of his jacket.

Instead, he elected to use the hand-to-hand combat methods he'd been taught at Camp Perry, Virginia, more commonly known as "The Farm." Grabbing hold of the bearded assailant's right arm, he spun him completely around, wrenching his arm so hard in back of him that the machete dropped from his hand and clattered to the street. At the same time, he used him as a shield against his black companion, who seemed ready to send his machete straight into Zoccola's abdomen.

Then he pushed the bearded man stumbling forward, buying enough time to reach down and lay hold of his fallen machete.

By this time the third man—the mulatto—had recovered his wind and was approaching him, but more warily now, as if to acknowledge that Zoccola wasn't quite the vulnerable target he'd appeared to be at first. He was taking his time, performing a little dance, his smile widening on his face.

In the meantime an audience was gathering to see what all the excitement was about. It wasn't clear whether anyone would send for the police. They might prefer to see how this scrap ended before bringing the authorities into the picture.

Of his assailants, only the two who retained hold of their weapons decided to remain in the fray. The white man, disarmed, his right arm possibly broken, had scrambled away as soon as he had picked himself up off the street.

Meanwhile, one man feinted, trying to distract Zoccola's attention, while the other attacked. But Zoccola anticipated their strategy and jumped out of the way of the knife thrust. Then, before either man could respond, he sprang into the air, waving his machete about so furiously that both men backed off.

Now Zoccola wasn't even conscious of what he was doing; his only thought was to defeat his attackers, and the signals to which his body responded were originating from somewhere deep in his subconsciousness.

Sensing that the two combatants were hesitating, he lunged forward, raising the machete high above his head, then suddenly bringing it down in a sweeping motion that tore right into the mulatto's chest, describing a crimson trail from his shoulder virtually to his navel. He'd expected the man's reaction time to be swifter, the wound less catastrophic.

Blood descended from the entire length of the wound and spread until his whole chest was covered. The mulatto fell back with a howl of agony and clumsily made his way down Rue de la Liberté. From the rear he looked like a staggering drunk.

The last assailant, observing that the odds no longer favored him, disappeared into the crowd surging in the direction of the canal. Zoccola, happy to be alive, realized that there was nothing to be gained by trying to follow him.

Suddenly the adrenaline-charged fever that had mobilized him began to ebb while at the same time the pain from his belly wound started to burn. The pain and bleeding were much worse than they had seemed just moments before, and it was all he could do to remain upright. Buttoning his jacket to cover some of the blood, he concentrated all his energies into getting away from this street corner before the police arrived. He didn't want to be questioned by the authorities about either this confrontation or his presence in Martinique.

A great many people gaped at him as he moved off. Some even approached him and offered to help, but he waved them off. He felt as though he were hallucinating; everything seemed very far away, as if in a dream, and he could not be sure what people were saying to him. He maintained a constant smile on his face, however, in an effort to show them that there was no need to worry, that he could take care of himself just fine.

He quickly made his way into the throngs of shoppers circulating through the market district. Everywhere vendors importuned the crowd to purchase bizarre items such as octopus, iguanas, bats, goats, aphrodisiacs, and magical effigies.

The pain would ebb and then crest again, causing him to stop in his tracks. If he could only concentrate, he might have been able to figure out who his assailants were working for. Adrienne's bodyguards? Cuban agents who'd caught onto his purpose in Martinique? Local communists? He couldn't seem to focus on the answer.

Of primary concern was obtaining medical help. And that he could do best by returning to the hotel and calling Triad for aid. As he walked, he maintained as much pressure as he could on the wound, but the blood continued to seep down his shirt. He saw that he was drawing curious stares from the people around him, but it took him a while to understand that it was not his halting walk or the blood that was attracting their attention, but the gory machete he still gripped in his right hand.

Dropping it, he concentrated next on procuring a cab and getting himself back to his hotel. Once there, he slipped past the desk clerk and mounted the stairs to his room. There he used his microtransmitter to put in an emergency call to Triad. Equipped with encoding and memory functions in addition to its routine communication capability, the microtransmitter was, in last resort, the one thing he had to fall back on. Someone was always guaranteed to be at the other end to answer him.

What he needed was a physician who could be relied upon not to report him to the police. He reasoned that if such a man or woman existed, Triad would know of the person.

His assumption was correct. In twenty minutes—during which time he'd bound the wound as best he could with makeshift bandages—he received a reply in the form of the name and telephone number of a trusted American doctor whose specialty was helping out other Americans.

It took all of Zoccola's discipline to get himself downstairs and find another cab. Once he was in the back seat, he nearly blacked out, and it was necessary for the driver, a very solicitous and tactful fellow, to rouse him back to consciousness and establish his destination.

The doctor turned out to be an endlessly cheerful fellow with white hair and beard and an encouraging bedside manner. His office was in a bright pastel one-story structure that adjoined his house. The building overlooked the water of Fort-de-France Bay.

After giving Zoccola a shot to kill the pain, he examined the wound, which extended eight inches across his abdomen, and declared it serious but not desperate. "It will require surgery," he said. "Under ordinary circumstances I would prefer to perform it in a hospital, but as these are not ordinary circumstances, I will have to do it here. I have a very competent nurse to assist me so I wouldn't want you to think you won't have excellent care. It's just that our facilities are a bit limited here."

None of this mattered as much to Zoccola as the fact that he would be out for several hours. He resented the prospect of having to lose time recuperating while the world went to hell without him. It was now midafternoon, and for all he knew Adrienne was still touring the countryside with Hidalgo. She would try to call him tonight, but there would be no one there to take the message or to tell her what had happened to him.

Although the painkiller the doctor had given him was beginning to take effect, reducing the control he had over his mind, he managed to sit up and gesture for a pen and a piece of paper. Despite Triad's sanctioning this man, he wasn't certain he could trust him with the message he was about to write down. But he was in no position to do otherwise, so he scrawled the note and said, "Would you please get this to Adrienne Calenda at the PLM La Batelière. Make sure that it is delivered directly into her hands. Above all, make sure no one intercepts it.''

The drug was taking hold more rapidly and his words were slurring. Zoccola wondered whether he was making himself understood.

7

All morning James Lisker lounged about the veranda of the Pegasus Hotel, consuming one coffee after another as he read the day's Guyana *Chronicle* and then a slightly battered international edition of *Time* he'd found on sale in the lobby. Given the small but conspicuous cuts and contusions that were visible on his face and arms, one would have supposed him to have been in some kind of minor accident—something to do with a car perhaps or even a tumble down a set of stairs. Still, he felt better than he had any right to after last night's events. Perhaps, he considered, this feeling of well-being came most from the fact that he hadn't been woken out of his sleep last night by representatives of the People's Army and arrested for murdering one of their own.

It was true that he was probably being watched, but he wasn't especially unsettled by this. He naturally assumed that because he was a foreign journalist, and an American journalist at that, he would automatically create a certain suspicion, but he was sure no evidence existed to implicate him in the events of last night.

It had earlier begun to rain again, a light but steady

drizzle that showed no sign of abating. A small battalion of waiters loitered on the veranda of the Pegasus, waiting for somebody to serve, but with the exception of Lisker and a few bored Eastern Europeans who chatted among themselves in a Slavic tongue Lisker identified as Czech, there was no one to take orders from.

When it got close to noon, Lisker started to worry about Harris. As planned, Harris had gone to see Virgil Reade at ten to inquire after the permits allowing them into the interior. Lisker hoped that no harm had come to him; given the uncertain temperament of the country's rulers they could very well clap him in jail either because he'd proffered a bribe (even though it might have been accepted) or because the bribe simply wasn't big enough.

But at half-past twelve Harris, looking a bit bedraggled, appeared, a broad smile on his face.

"We've got them, we've got them, by God. I didn't have a chance to stay long in Mr. Reade's company—he gave me only five minutes of his time. But that was quite sufficient for the transaction to be consummated. Without saying a word, he signed the permits. From today until the fifteenth of next month we are authorized to visit the interior. The only exception is what's vaguely called the 'restricted military zone.' "

"What does that mean?"

Harris laughed. "Anything they want it to mean, I suppose. But you'll have to admit that it's better than nothing."

"No, you're right," Lisker conceded. "I'm very pleased."

"So when do you think we should be on our way?"

"Tomorrow, very early. We have to find ourselves a new four-wheel drive, for one thing, and load up on provisions. I'm also waiting for a response to last night's communication to Triad."

The communication he was alluding to related to his sighting of the Russian troop transport outside of Georgetown. From the rough count Lisker and Harris had put together, a minimum of sixty Soviet soldiers had debarked at Timehri Airport. In addition, rocket and grenade launchers, several howitzers and mortars, and a number of heavy machine guns had been off-loaded with the troops. Whether the Antonov they had observed was one of many, whether others had already landed or were scheduled to land, was something that neither witness could determine. It was Lisker's impression that what they'd seen did not constitute a full-scale introduction of Soviet forces and military equipment into the country. Both men agreed that this contingent represented something more like an advisory group. The weapons that accompanied them were sufficient only for defense purposes, and there was nothing to suggest these men would be used in any direct combat role.

That role, Lisker believed, was more likely intended for the Cubans. He was under the impression that several thousand troops, sent by Castro at Moscow's behest, might be expected to enter the country very shortly. An introduction of foreign troops on that massive a level could not go undetected for long no matter how diligently the People's Army sought to cover their presence.

Nonetheless, placing even a small unit of Red Army troops on South American soil was an ominous development, and one that was in contravention of the Monroe Doctrine. In light of the chaos enveloping Central America, where the Cubans were actively engaged in aiding leftist insurgencies, this event signaled a widening of the conflict to a point where the United States might be incapable of responding with any credibility.

It was possible that Triad might order him to remain in Georgetown to see if more Soviet troops would turn up. He had, however, advised Drexell that his position in Georgetown might soon become precarious. It was his inclination to get out of the city as quickly as possible.

As he and Harris continued to talk on the veranda, there was a burst of automatic fire somewhere in the distance. They looked up and glanced around but saw no evidence that the gunfire had disturbed either the waiters or the Czech trade delegation nearby.

Two minutes later, though, there was a tremendous roar from an explosion that no one inside the Pegasus could possibly ignore. An instant later there was another explosion, only slightly less violent than the first. Almost simultaneously a third explosion occurred in still another location.

Anxious to see what had happened, Lisker raced over to the banister to have a look. From what he could see, the explosions had occurred downtown, not far from the Stabroek Market. Harris stood behind him, gazing apprehensively about.

"Don't you think it wiser to go back in the lobby?" he asked.

Lisker shook his head. "This might be rather interesting. Care to come along?" he replied, indicating that he was about to leave the hotel.

Harris didn't care to come along at all. He wanted to stay right where he was. But when he saw that Lisker was serious about exploring, he sighed, lifted his eyes up toward heaven, and went out to join him.

Dark gray funnels of smoke trailed into the air and billowed out into cloudlike formations as sirens wailed from every quarter of the city. People began running in the streets, but they appeared confused as to the direction they should go; some were headed toward the center of the city, close to the Stabroek Market and the City Hall, while others could be seen going the opposite way. With the rain hammering down harder, the confusion was even more pronounced. Only Lisker seemed unconcerned as he proceeded toward the market, with Harris doing his best to keep up with him.

Jeeps and personnel carriers conveying units of the People's Army had to struggle through the throngs to get to the sites of the explosions. When repeated blasts of their horns failed to yield a path through the mobs, the vehicles could only inch forward and, from time to time, knock hapless pedestrians aside.

Police also moved into the intersections and with truncheons and tear gas grenades, maneuvered the surging mass of people back. The crowds turned ugly and hurled rocks and bottles, some of them Molotov cocktails, at the police.

Lisker and Harris did what they could to avoid the confrontations, turning into squalid alleyways or following the soggy embankments along the old Dutch canals in hope of eluding both a battering at the hands of the police and the noxious gas. Fortunately, Harris knew the central part of the city well enough so that he could guide Lisker toward the market and the City Hall without blundering into a cul-de-sac.

They continued down a passageway where, oblivious to the commotion elsewhere in the city, beggars were still sprawled, their drunken stupors uninterrupted. Refuse was everywhere while a stench of smoke and blood hung on the air.

At last they came out into a main street. On their right was a movie theater—the Metropole—with billboards advertising an old Bruce Lee epic. Directly across the street from it was the People's Progressive Party's headquarters. Or, rather, what was left of it.

It had been blow apart. Its walls were collapsed and its roof blown heavenward by the force of the explosion. In the ruins, fires burned uncontrollably. While uniformed men were in evidence, the fire department had yet to appear. Since this was the headquarters of the opposition party, Lisker thought it likely that the government was in no hurry to do anything about containing the damage. On the other hand, with all the other explosions that had rent the city within a few minutes of one another, the fire-fighting force might simply have been taxed beyond its means.

Guards, their uniforms sporting the insignia of the PPP, were running to and fro in an effort to douse the flames by tossing buckets of water on them. They'd have had as much luck if they'd sat back and waited for the rain, which had subsided for the moment, to do their work for them.

Other guards had evidently decided saving the building was hopeless and had turned their attention to the units of the People's Army which were taking up position around the site. Accusations were flung back and forth between party members and government troops as to who was responsible for the explosion.

In the street bodies were scattered about, their clothes soaked with blood. One man had been decapitated, and blood continued to ooze from the stump of his neck. A rather pretty young woman had been hurtled against the billboard of the Metropole by the force of the blast. Her dress was shredded, but there seemed to be surprisingly little blood on her. Moreover, though no one was tending to her, she was still alive.

Lisker, mindless of the suspicious stares he was drawing from the police, hurried over to her. Her eyes were glazed, her pulse weak. She was mumbling something, but he could not make out what she was saying. With a knife he sliced through the remains of her dress to see how badly she was injured. She was scraped and lacerated in several places, but there seemed to be no wound serious enough to account for her enfeebled condition.

He and Harris tried to move her to make her more comfortable. Suddenly the woman groaned, her head lolled back, and her eyes nearly burst from their sockets.

Then they saw why. The slight movement had allowed her back to open up, the skin and muscles drawing apart to release a torrent of blood. In another moment she was dead.

When the Americans looked over at the former headquarters, they observed that the arguments between the police and the PPP guards had grown more heated. One of the PPP guards was holding his rifle on his government counterpart, who reacted by screaming and leveling his own gun, at which point the PPP guard, who could have been no more than twenty years of age, fired.

This the policeman had not expected. He dropped his gun, clutched his side, and slumped over, remaining in a

kneeling posture for several seconds as though deliber-
ating on his next course of action. Then he fell over and
lay still.

No sooner had this happened than several of the
government police opened fire, turning the PPP man's
head into a red pulp. The lifeless body collapsed.

PPP guards, some of them retreating back into the
charred wreckage of their headquarters, responded with
a brief but heavy fusillade.

Neither they nor the police seemed particularly careful about where they were firing. Bullets flew all over
the street, several of them impacting in the aging facade
of the Metropole.

Lisker and Harris, like the others caught in the crossfire, sought cover in an adjoining street. They heard the
rattle of automatic fire coming from different directions, and the smoke became denser. It sounded as
though a revolution was in progress, but determining
what, in fact, was happening was impossible.

When they finally reached the Pegasus they discovered sullen People's Army men standing by the lobby
entrance, inspecting passports. Others were posted on
the veranda, training their rifles out on the street.
Despite the Pegasus' having been transformed into a
fortified bunker, the steel-drum band was playing up a
storm, presumably for the benefit of the bored tourists
and businessmen who were trapped there.

The passports Lisker and Harris presented to the
police were given only the most perfunctory appraisal.
If their names were on some wanted list, these men fortunately had not learned of it yet.

Once inside the hotel they found that practically no
one was paying attention to the steel-drum band.
Rather, they were gathered around the television set and
a shortwave radio. The sound was turned down on the
TV, which was no loss since the state broadcasting
network had decided that this was the perfect time to re-
broadcast a championship soccer match between Argen-
tina and Peru. The listeners left it going, hoping the

government might soon begin transmitting pictures of what was happening out on the streets.

The shortwave radio was hardly more helpful. On it, a government spokesman was assuring the country that there was no reason for panic and that the government of Sydney Walling was firmly in control. And if no organization had taken responsibility for the three explosions—one of which had destroyed a good section of the Stabroek Market and another of which had blown apart the Cuffy Ideological Institute, Guyana's socialist think tank—the Comrade Leader nonetheless had no difficulty in finding any number of parties to blame, among them the imperialist cabal, the People's Progressive Party (it allegedly blew up its own headquarters to gain sympathy for its cause), the CIA, and Venezuelan saboteurs.

Reports of casualties were sketchy and tended, from one hour to the next, to contradict one another. The one o'clock broadcast from Georgetown radio declared that 57 people had been killed and 130 injured in the three blasts. An hour later the count was up to 80 dead and well over 200 injured, though by four o'clock some of these figures had been revised downward.

There was no mention of the gun battles that had broken out in the aftermath of the explosions.

Late in the afternoon Lisker was alerted by his microtransmitter and in a moment had received word from Triad headquarters acknowledging receipt of his information about the landing of the Russian advisory force. Lisker was urged to telephone Drexell if circumstances allowed. Otherwise he should use his own judgment in determining his future course of action.

Lisker had a scrambler which he was prepared to employ upon dialing the international operator. But he was informed that it was impossible to get through to the United States; in fact, he was told, it was impossible to get a line anywhere out of the capital. He could expect to be no more successful reaching Queenstown up the coast than the suburbs of Washington, D.C.

Limited to his microwave-operated transmitter, Lisker sent a message back to Triad indicating that he planned to set out into the interior—toward the Venezuelan border—rather than remain in the capital any longer.

Throughout the chaotic afternoon, Lisker had felt ever more strongly that the explosions were not the work of imperialist or Venezuelan agents but were, instead, the responsibility of the government. It was not the National People's Congress party headquarters which had been reduced to rubble, but the opposition's, and there was no force better situated than the government to have so successfully orchestrated the bombings. Moreover the instantaneous response on the part of government troops would seem to indicate that they'd been primed beforehand to react to the chaos.

His suspicions were further borne out when at five o'clock the state radio announced that martial law was in effect and that, beginning in an hour's time, a curfew would be imposed on the capital and "other major centers of unrest" that would last until an hour before dawn. All civil rights, the state radio went on to declare, would be suspended indefinitely, adding almost in afterthought that the parliament had been dissolved by Comrade Leader Sydney Walling "until such time as national security can be restored." There was no hint in the broadcast as to when that might be.

In between bursts of martial music, a government spokesman periodically proclaimed that an undisclosed number of suspects, including several members of the People's Progressive Party, among them a former prime minister, had been taken into custody. He asserted that they would be tried before a martial-law tribunal and "called to account for their heinous crimes before all the world."

Given the impending clampdown, it was important for Lisker and Harris to leave as soon as possible. In spite of the permits they held, they had no guarantee that they would be allowed out of the city, and given the large numbers of people being rounded up, it was even conceivable that they would be detained simply because they were foreigners. In such a situation, even a journalist with impressive leftist credentials might be regarded with suspicion, if only because he was a journalist.

Their first problem occurred when they tried to leave the hotel. As soon as they reached the front steps, the guards posted at the entrance halted them.

"Curfew," an officer explained. "Can go noplace now."

Lisker pointed to his watch. "It's five-twenty. Curfew isn't until six."

The officer shook his head. He waved his pistol in Lisker's face, then gestured toward Harris right behind him, as if to say that he wouldn't mind shooting them both.

They retreated back into the lobby and sat, looking silently out at the back veranda, which was practically empty now. The swimming pool it overlooked was filled with debris, and the ocean beyond made for a sad gray spectacle in the intermittent rain. A lone guinea fowl made its way across the overgrown lawn and looked as though it were in desperate need of company. From time to time gunfire could be heard, but distantly, almost as if it were coming from a television set in the next room.

"Well, what do you propose we do?" Harris asked finally, fiddling with the cross that dangled from his neck.

"Do you have a gun on you?" Lisker asked abruptly.

Harris hesitated, not at all liking the sound of this.

"Well?"

"Yes, yes . . . I do. You don't propose to have me use it, do you?"

The undesired answer was suggested by Lisker's insistent silence.

Then Lisker outlined his plan.

"Absolutely not!" Harris protested upon hearing it.

Lisker waited to see if he'd come around.

"What you're asking me to do is suicide," Harris continued, as if Lisker could somehow be dissuaded.

"Not necessarily. There are two guards out front and I'll have my eye on them the whole time."

Harris began to waver under Lisker's determination. "Buy me a drink," he said at last, "and we'll see."

Lisker bought him a drink at the bar, 120-proof rum.

Harris downed the first drink, then the second, then placed a hand on his side where his gun created a slight bulge.

"I want you to know that I've never had to use this the whole time I have been in South America."

"And I see no reason for you to have to use it now, Harris. I'd be the last person to tell you to spoil your perfect record."

Harris was unconvinced. "I don't trust you."

"That doesn't surprise me," he said without elaborating.

"Well, then, let's get on with it. If I'm to be shot dead, better sooner than later," Harris decided with logic only alcohol was capable of inducing in him.

Holding himself erect, as if in preparation for the guillotine, he went to the front doors and, opening them swiftly, stepped out.

Both the guards whipped about, training their rifles on him.

"I am a man of God and I have an appointment at the Church of the Sacred Heart in fifteen minutes time," Harris declared, "and I do not wish to be late."

No sooner had he stated this in ringing tones than he began down the path leading to the street. The guards clearly didn't know what to make of this. It would not do to shoot on a foreigner outright, particularly one who proclaimed himself a man of God, but on the other hand, there was a curfew to enforce and they couldn't simply allow him to walk away from them.

"Halt!" one shouted, raising his M-16 and cocking it. The other did likewise.

At which point Lisker, with the quiet, stealthy step of a cat burglar, slipped up behind them. To the guard closest to him, he whispered, "Drop it!"

To underscore his seriousness he placed the tip of his

FN Browning against the back of the man's head.

Harris had now turned toward the second guard and, with his hands raised like a penitent, began appealing for his life. "Please. Please, don't fire!" he said.

He had the guard so distracted that it took him a few moments to realize that his colleague was being held at gunpoint.

When he turned to confront Lisker, Harris, with a steadiness of purpose that surprised Lisker, raced back the way he'd come with his gun drawn.

The second guard recognized that, if he chose to take Lisker's life, his own would be forfeit as well.

Concentrating hard to maintain a firm grip on the .32 he held with both hands, Harris stood at the foot of the stairs, aiming his weapon directly up at the guard's heart.

One M-16 clattered to the ground, followed a moment later by the other.

Lisker gathered them both up. By this time he'd drawn the attention of several of the hotel guests, who didn't dare come out and see what was happening for themselves. There was no telling where their sympathies lay—with the guards, who seemed terrified of losing their lives, or with the disheveled, red-faced man who called himself a missionary and the lean, hard-looking American with ice in his blue eyes.

Unloading the two rifles, Lisker tossed them as far as he could, then frisked the pair to make certain they had no other concealed sidearms.

That done, he nodded to Harris, signaling him to run.

Harris ran as fast as he'd ever run before. Lisker was right behind him and soon had come abreast of him. He was under no illusion that they wouldn't be pursued once the guards had recovered their wits sufficiently, but now they had the advantage.

Out in the street it was easy enough for them to lose themselves in the turbulent crowd. It seemed that in Georgetown, on this day, everyone wanted to get away from something.

An antiquated wooden bus, bearing the name King

George V, was pulling up at a stop three blocks beyond the Pegasus. It was already full to overflowing, which didn't stop additional passengers from attempting to clamber on. Among them, lost in the tidal wave of Guyanese, were Lisker and Harris.

When they stole a glance out the rear window of the bus, they saw the police helplessly scanning the crowd for their prey; their faces expressed their fury at having lost the Americans.

The bus was crammed with people, but an eerie silence prevailed. Both men and women behaved like criminals, avoiding any eye contact, as if hoping they would not be recognized and hauled off into the oblivion of prison or worse. Their sense of unease communicated itself even to the few children on the bus who also held themselves stiffly, their lips pursed, their eyes downcast.

Harris now allowed himself the privilege of fear. His whole body began to tremble and his face became as pale as the rainy skies over the city. "They'll trace us through the register and they'll soon know our identities," he whispered. "Then our permits won't do us any good. As soon as we present them they'll arrest us. If we're *lucky* they'll arrest us, not shoot us right away."

Lisker nodded that this was a possibility, but he said that with so much chaos reigning in the capital, and presumably in the surrounding countryside, the police and paramilitary forces would have more on their minds than the apprehension of a missionary and a leftist journalist on their way into the jungle. "I wouldn't worry too much yet. Let's just concentrate on getting out of Georgetown."

"That reminds me, do you have any idea where this bus is going?"

"None at all," Lisker said. "Except that it's taking us away."

VENEZUELA DENIES MASSACRE

CARACAS, May 30 (Reuters)—A spokesman for the government of Guillame Lopez Canares denied categorically that Venezuela was responsible for a massacre that allegedly occurred in the border region separating Guyana from Venezuela. Last week the Guyanese government of Prime Minister Sydney Walling accused elements of the Venezuelan armed forces of violating Guyanese territory and murdering close to 250 Amerindians dwelling in a village close to the western end of the Mazaruni River. "No such intervention or massacre occurred," the spokesman said. "Either it is a complete fabrication cooked up by Guyanese propagandists or else it is the Guyanese themselves who are responsible for the deaths of the Indians. We would like to suggest that the Red Cross or the United Nations or any other neutral outside observer inspect the village where this carnage was said to have happened. We are firmly convinced that Venezuela will be vindicated." There has been no comment about this suggestion from Georgetown. A source close to the government in Caracas said that because the border region is nearly impenetrable independent verification of the incident might never be possible.

8

MAY 31,
CAMP DAVID, MARYLAND

The Bell Huey Cobra, carrying William Drexell and his
aide Steven Cavanaugh, hovered for a moment above
the warren of lodges and security stations that made up
the Presidential retreat of Camp David, then began its
descent. The blue ridge of the Cotoctin Mountains was
soon obscured by a wall of pines and evergreens.

A platoon of Secret Servicemen materialized from the
woods to greet the new arrivals.

Drexell had been to Camp David twice before, once
to brief the President on the North African situation in
the aftermath of the Soviet-backed Libyan assault on
Tunisia and Morocco and once to discuss the Balkan
crisis, which had erupted when Greece went to war with
Turkey. In both instances he'd found the President
more relaxed, more susceptible to new ideas that he
might have rejected out of hand if they'd been holding
their meeting in the Oval Office.

As soon as the helicopter put down, Drexell and
Cavanaugh were immediately escorted to the Dogwood
Lodge, where they would be temporarily quartered.
Only after lunch had been served—it included poached
salmon, rice, and string beans—did an aide appear to

say that the President was ready to see them in the Holly Lodge.

With the President were the only other men in the administration who were aware of Triad and its secretly authorized mission: Jeffrey Schelling, Secretary of State, Martin Rhiel, Secretary of Defense, and Morse Peckum, the President's chief of staff and, quite possibly, one of the most important men in Washington, given the power he exercised in the President's name.

Drexell regretted that these men were also present at the meeting. With the President alone he had a chance to get his views fully aired and understood. But the addition of the other three men, each with his own turf to protect, put him in a much more vulnerable position. The others resented Drexell's power and influence, but above all they resented the fact that he could operate completely out of the public eye; his agency did not have to be called to account either by Congress or the press, since neither Congress nor the press knew of its existence.

Ironically, these three men each possessed more forceful personalities than the President himself. Schelling might be ineffectual, but he cut a handsome figure in society, and with the self-assured air that he projected he had attracted a following among the public far in excess of the power he actually enjoyed in the administration. Rhiel, who like his predecessors believed that there was no such thing as too much money for the Pentagon, had the weight of world events on his side; every time the Soviets provoked another crisis—or every time the facts could be manipulated so that it looked as though the Soviets were responsible—he would appear before Defense Appropriations Committee on the Hill, demand additional billions for a new submarine or a new Stealth bomber, and come away happy.

It was Morse Peckum, however, who wielded more real power than either of these men. He was a dull, brooding man who disdained the press and tended to upbraid congressional leaders for not falling in line with Presidential policy, and there was no one, Drexell included, who could quite figure out why the President heeded his advice to the extent that he did. Peckum had begun as a poll-taker and political adviser to the President, and it was this background that Peckum used to make judgments.

Acutely aware of the impact of any Presidential action on the public, he cared little about the details of foreign policy as long as that policy had the support of a plurality of the American people.

In meetings such as the one that was about to get under way, Peckum might say very little, but as Drexell knew, he often preferred to act behind the scenes. He'd let everyone have his say, knowing that, once they'd all gone home, he would still have the President's ear. And it was widely thought that the last one to have the President's ear was the individual whose opinion prevailed.

As far as anyone knew, the President's wife, who under ordinary circumstances might be expected to have this influential role in her husband's life, seldom had an opinion to express.

The main room of the Holly Lodge was newly decorated and, with its dark paneling and commodious leather chairs, was designed to convey an aura of masculine strength. It was a wonder that no one had thought to mount a trophy or two over the fireplace. On entering, Drexell could just as well have imagined that they were here, not to discuss Guyana and Venezuela, but to lay out that day's deer hunt.

It was the President who began the meeting, which was accompanied by cider and cake served by an unobtrusive waiter. "I've read over copies of those reports you sent over here, Bill. The ones about Guyana's Russian advisory group, or whatever the hell it is. What puzzles me is that we've had no concurring reports from any other source. I've spoken with everyone at Langley who would be in a position to substantiate this, and all I've gotten are blanks."

Drexell was tempted to say that his sources were superior to the CIA's but refrained.

"The man I have on the ground in Guyana is one of

the best operatives in the country," Drexell said evenly. "If he says that a Soviet force numbering about sixty men has landed in Georgetown, then I believe him."

The President looked over in the direction of his Defense Secretary.

Rhiel picked up on the cue. "If any transport jets were used to convey the Soviets, the only way they could have gotten to Guyana without our knowing about it would be from a staging area in the Caribbean or Central America. We've got Cuba pretty well covered; we're tracking the air and sea traffic coming in and out of the island on a continual twenty-four-hour basis. I am not making a judgment as to whether this report about the Russians is correct or not. All I am saying is that if they didn't come via Cuba, where the hell would they be coming from?"

"Bill?"

"I can't give you an answer on that. We're still trying to determine the embarkation site. But how they got to Georgetown is I think less important—at this point anyway—than the fact that they have established a definite military presence there, one we are going to have to recognize and come to grips with."

"I can't imagine Kadiyev doing something like this," the President said. "The use of Cuban troops—at least in small numbers—is nothing new. But how can he have the effrontery to introduce Soviet armed forces into this hemisphere? He must know that we'll have no choice but to respond forcefully to a provocation like that."

Drexell was tempted to say that it was because of the President's hesitancy in the past that the Soviets might have been disposed to undertake such a step. He said, "Don't you think it possible, Mr. President, that this could be a diversion? In the last year we've seen two strategic moves against our positions—in the Balkans and in North Africa. Up to now the conflict has centered about the Mediterranean basin. We've bolstered our forces there and upgraded the Sixth Fleet, using shows of force in Egypt, Somalia, and in the Persian Gulf, to make it clear that the Soviets have gone just as far as we'll let them in that area. It makes some kind of sense that they'd change the rules of the game and challenge us in our own backyard. All they need is a few advisers to cause us to react. Our major problem is that we're overextended already.''

"There's some truth to that," Rhiel agreed. "What you're saying is that they're hoping we'll pull some of our men out of the Mediterranean and redeploy them in our bases in Central America."

"Exactly," said Drexell. "But I don't think we ought to fall for that gambit."

The President looked at his Secretary of State to solicit his assessment.

"I think we ought to hold off on any kind of policy decision until we have further information," Schelling said. If anything, he was more cautious than the President. "To act prematurely might put us in the same mess Carter got into when he went public saying that there was an unauthorized Russian battalion stationed on Cuba. For all his saber-rattling all the Cubans and the Russians did was laugh. The Russians never went away and we lacked the capacity to back up our threat. I wouldn't want to see us get into the same sort of situation—particularly without some substantive evidence." Looking at Drexell, he added, "I don't doubt that your man in Guyana is an excellent agent, but his report simply doesn't provide enough basis to change national policy right now."

"Frankly, I think, Mr. Secretary, you're missing the point," Drexell said, doing his best to maintain his equanimity. "I am not proposing that we take immediate action now. What I'm saying is that we should accept—tentatively—that Soviet troops, however small their number, have entered Guyana. We also have information that suggests that several thousand Cuban troops are on their way to Guyana as well. Putting two and two together, I believe we can safely say that the introduction of these troops is a prelude to some significant military adventure in the area."

"What kind of military adventure?" Rhiel said.

"If you've been following the situation down there, you'll recall that Venezuela has for years been claiming a big chunk of Guyana. In recent weeks the dispute has approached a boiling point. Caracas and Georgetown have both started to trade accusations and atrocity stories again."

"So you're saying that the Cubans and the Soviets have been invited into the country to defend it against a Venezuelan attack," the President said. "Don't you think that kind of thing is pretty unlikely?"

"The Argentines went into the Falklands, and certainly Great Britain wasn't prepared for it," Drexell reminded him. "It took the British several weeks to assemble their fleet and get it to the South Atlantic. But, no, I don't believe that Venezuela is about to launch any sort of military campaign into Guyana. What I do believe is the reverse."

"You mean the Cubans will cross the border into Venezuela?" the President said in horror.

"Yes, Mr. President."

"Preposterous!" Morse Peckum exploded in his first contribution to the meeting. "The Cubans and Venezuelans might not be the best of friends, but they're getting along. Venezuela's not Bolivia or some backwater banana republic. There's poverty there, but not so much that a million revolutionaries are going to come scrambling out of their mud shacks to welcome the Fidelistas with open arms."

"First of all," Drexell replied coldly, "this has very little to do with Castro. The decision about Guyana isn't being made in Havana, it's being made in Moscow. So what the state of relations is between Venezuela and Cuba is really beside the point. With its procommunist government, Guyana is fertile ground to become a Soviet satellite every bit as compliant as Cuba has turned out to be."

"But what the hell does Moscow need with another impoverished satellite?" the President insisted. "It has enough problems just subsidizing Cuba. And Guyana, gentlemen, has nothing much to speak of except some bauxite and a scattering of sugar and rice factories."

"Venezuela has oil," Schelling said, anticipating him.

"I don't go for it," said Peckum before anyone else could reply. "I think it's fantasy from beginning to end. What do you want us to do, go in and bomb the shit out of Cuba?"

"No, of course I'm not advising that. First of all, it wouldn't do us much good. The Cuban troops are coming from Africa, not Cuba. I'd be willing to bet you that they're never going to touch Cuban soil. They'll be using another staging area—possibly the same one the Soviet transport plane took off from—elsewhere in the region, most likely somewhere in Central America, maybe Nicaragua, maybe El Salvador."

Peckum still wasn't having any of it. "We haven't any independent confirmation that there's a single Cuban or Soviet soldier on Guyanese territory. All we've got is your word for it. Nothing from the National Security Agency, nothing from State, nothing from CIA."

"That's true, Bill," the President said. "We're dealing with a very precarious situation here and I don't want to go off half-cocked."

"The American public won't accept any military involvement in South America," Peckum declared flatly. For him, that was the plain bottom line.

"The problem comes down to securing more data," the President stated. Turning to Rhiel, he asked him the status of information coming in from their surveillance and reconnaissance satellites.

Of the two types of satellites, the former conducted monitoring activities on a more or less continual basis, while the latter was used in specific instances. A surveillance satellite over the Soviet Union might pick up a sudden fluctuation in troop movements or the installation of a new missile silo. A recon satellite, on the other hand, would be put into orbit over a site where an adversary might have become suddenly active.

The recon satellites were generally orbited as low as

possible for the purpose of obtaining the best sensor resolution possible.

"We already have Big Bird II, launched less than a year ago, in sunsynchronous orbit, covering the Central American area, and a second series of scout satellites designed for rapid launch which we are in the process of putting in orbit over specific trouble spots in the area." Rhiel spoke with great authority although it wasn't always certain that he had anything of particular relevance to say. "These trouble spots include regions in Honduras, Guatemala, and El Salvador, places where insurgent activity and unrest are taking place. One difficulty we're encountering is that dummy staging areas and military bases may have been set up to fool us. We have several suspected locations—even the sort of possible staging areas that Bill spoke of earlier—but at this point we're uncertain as to which are genuine and which have been constructed for the sole purpose of deceiving our recon satellites. I can only tell you that we're still analyzing the data."

This assessment didn't make the President any happier. "Well, how do we go about determining where this staging area is, if it in fact exists?"

"I think we are just going to have to go with the old-fashioned way and rely on our operatives on the ground," said Rhiel. "You can talk to your boys at Langley, maybe they'll come up with something."

The President responded by saying that he had been in touch with the CIA Director that very morning, but so far the results had not been impressive. "He tells me that several of his best people in the region have either been shopped or eliminated or else gone underground."

His eyes met Drexell's. "What about your people?"

"My sources are still intact, Mr. President. If there is a staging area, we'll find it."

9

JUNE 1-2,
SAN JOSÉ, COSTA RICA

Jerry Hahn was sitting in his room at the Ambassador, boning up on his Spanish with the help of the morning's edition of *La Republica*, when he heard an eruption of gunfire. He ran to his window, looked out, but all he could see were other equally curious faces in other windows. There was no indication as to where the gunfire had originated although the sound of it seemed to be coming from the central business district. The gunfire had lasted no more than a minute and had ended just as suddenly as it began. An eerie silence obtained for a moment before the normal nighttime sounds of traffic in San José began again.

Jerry Hahn was in the capital of Costa Rica because that, as far as was known, was where the enigmatic Cuban agent Hidalgo had temporarily taken up residence. Before John Zoccola had left Martinique—headed for Walter Reed Army Medical Center in Washington to recuperate from his knife wound—he'd managed to speak briefly with Adrienne Calenda, and it was from her that he'd learned of Hidalgo's destination.

Drexell had voiced his doubts about this information. Greeting Zoccola at Dulles International, he'd asked him whether Hidalgo might not have simply misled her about his plans. While Zoccola's enfeebled condition did not allow him to discuss the matter at length, he did point out that as Hidalgo had no reason to think Adrienne suspected him of being an agent, there was consequently no compelling reason to deceive her. In fact, he had even invited her to accompany him to San José, an invitation Adrienne had politely declined, telling him that, as the wife of the Indonesian foreign minister, she could not very well travel alone with a man who was virtually a stranger to her. The looming presence of her bodyguards gave added weight to her words, and Hidalgo didn't press the matter.

While Triad did not yet understand how significant an agent Hidalgo was, his movements in the last month underscored the fact that he was well worth paying attention to. On the eighth of May he was reportedly still in Havana, but by the tenth, he had turned up in Moscow. Sometime between the fourteenth and nineteenth he visited Sofia, Bucharest, and Prague. A day later he was sighted on the Unter den Linden in East Berlin. Until he surfaced in Georgetown, Guyana, on the twenty-third, it was assumed that he'd been in Fort-de-France on Martinique. From Georgetown he'd returned to Martinique. Now he was presumably somewhere in San José.

While informants at the customs control at Juan Santamaria Airport had confirmed that Hidalgo had entered the country thirty-six hours prior to Hahn's arrival, they had no idea what had happened to him after he procured transportation into the capital. Hahn had assigned the two operatives Triad made use of in San José to the task of checking out all the hotels and pensions in the area to see if a purported Mexican national by the name of Hidalgo had registered in any of them. As of ten P.M. the reports were all negative.

Hahn suspected that either the Cuban had registered at a hotel with a passport other than the one he had presented at customs or he was being put up at a private residence. Two other possibilities suggested themselves

to him: one was that Hidalgo would let himself be found
so as to lead the Americans on what amounted to a wild-
goose chase and the other was that he had yet to realize
that his cover was blown and would, sooner or later,
lead Hahn to the location of the true Soviet-Cuban staging area. Naturally, Hahn hoped that it was the latter;
he was in no mood to go chasing around Central America on a futile mission.

At least he had some photographs to aid him in his
search. During the one-day outing Adrienne had spent
with the Cuban on Martinique, she'd succeeded in getting him to pose for her. A male photographer might
have found him strangely shy of such a request, but he
had proven susceptible to a beautiful woman's wishes.

The photographs disclosed a man who looked less like
a spy than a jaded roué who was accustomed to spending his life in nightclubs and in the beds of other men's
wives. It was unfortunate that Adrienne had not been
able to come with him to Costa Rica, Hahn thought, for
she could have rendered an important service to Triad
by keeping him constantly in sight. Instead, she had
gone on to Caracas, on behalf of her husband. Indonesia and Venezuela were members of OPEC; and as the
two were both oil-rich non-Arab states, they had more
in common than their geographical disparity would
have suggested.

Knowing what he did about Hidalgo, Hahn expected
that should he ever succeed in locating the mysterious
agent he would have to rely on another woman to en-
snare him. This should not present a formidable problem; there were a great many beautiful, and cunning,
women in the world, and quite a few of them were in
Costa Rica, if what Hahn had seen so far was any indication.

At half-past ten there was more gunfire in the streets.
This time when Hahn peered from the window, he saw
sporadic flashes of light coming from the west, beyond
the old Sabana airport and the national sports stadium.
Sirens erupted all over the city, and as he watched police
vans tore down Avenue Central.

Unsure of what was happening, Hahn went down to the lobby to get information. Gathered in the lobby were three khaki-uniformed Civil Guards. They were Costa Rica's only armed forces, the army itself having been abolished in 1949. They scrutinized those entering the hotel, occasionally checking their luggage and hand-bags for bombs and concealed weapons, but otherwise doing nothing to hamper their passage. Nor did they stop anyone who wished to leave.

The somber-faced manager, who presided from behind the registry desk, however, was advising his guests that it was best not to venture out onto the streets unless one had no other choice.

"*Terroristas,*" he told Hahn, making an unhappy face.

While the conditions in the capital had not deteriorated to the extent that they had in Georgetown or elsewhere in Central America, and while there was neither martial law nor any all-night curfew, life had nonetheless changed considerably in San José in the last year.

Up until the early 1980s, Costa Rica had been the wealthiest country in the region, but when prices for its main export—coffee—had fallen on the world market, unemployment rose markedly and the government began to go into hock to bolster its sagging economy with loans from international banks.

Once practically quarantined from the conflagration that was devouring its neighbors, Costa Rica, too, was becoming a theater for battles between the right and the left. Rightist guerrillas began to use its northern territory for bases against the leftists in control of Nicaragua, while leftist guerrillas began to do the same in the south against the rightists in control of Panama. There were now unconfirmed reports that units of the Nicaraguan security forces had moved across the border, and as to the insurgency in the swampland between Panama and Costa Rica, no one was quite sure what was happening there. At the moment anyhow, the regime in Panama City was firmly entrenched, and given the stra-

tegic significance the United States attached to free
movement through the canal, it would probably remain
so for the foreseeable future.

Costa Rica, its security threatened from within and
without, had sent a succession of emissaries to Washington, appealing first for millions of dollars in economic
aid, in the form of low interest loans or outright grants,
then for military aid. By this time El Salvador, Guatemala, and Honduras had all had their share of American advisers. And while they were under orders not to
participate in military activities, it was common knowledge that they frequently had violated, if not the letter,
then certainly the spirit of their instructions.

As Hahn well knew, the problem with dispatching advisers to Costa Rica was the President himself. His
predecessors in office had authorized the introduction
of lightly armed technical and military advisers in Central America, but all Turner was doing in the cases of
Guatemala, El Salvador, and Honduras was maintaining the status quo.

But sending substantial numbers of advisers to Costa
Rica was a decision he was reluctant to make, especially
since he had campaigned for office by declaring in the
strongest terms possible that he would not involve the
United States in war in the Western Hemisphere unless
there was a flagrant violation of the Monroe Doctrine.

From Triad's present assessment of the situation in
Guyana—which was also linked to the situation in
Central America and Costa Rica—the Monroe Doctrine
had been flagrantly violated. Yet the President was
loath to acknowledge the fact, if yesterday's meeting at
Camp David was an accurate reflection of his attitude.
So Costa Rica teetered on the brink of outright collapse,
waiting for its fate to be decided upon by forces beyond
its borders.

The only word from the State Department was that
"Costa Rica's political and military requests are under
study." There was no assurance, Drexell felt, that once
this study was completed anything in the way of defini-
tive action would take place.

• • •

Hahn found a taxi idling right outside the hotel, and he directed the driver to take him through the mostly dark streets to the Kuang Chaow restaurant on Calle 11.

One of the few Chinese restaurants in the city, the Kuang Chaow was practically deserted when he arrived. It wasn't the lateness of the hour that accounted for the absence of customers, but the violence that had begun to take hold of the streets of San José. One could pay a call on the El Barraquo Disco, the Discotheque Infinito, or any of the dance casinos on Avenue 2, and find only a few couples sitting at tables while the voices of Stevie Wonder and Donna Summer thundered over vacant dance floors. Even the popular Le Club was bereft of customers these days.

A man was waiting for Hahn in the back of the restaurant. Sitting disconsolately at a small table, the thin, bearded mestizo was spooning hot-and-sour soup into his mouth. This man had come to San José after working on a banana plantation for United Fruit, but though he had contacts with the communist and left-wing insurgents, he was not a communist himself. Rather, he considered himself a Costa Rican patriot who was anxious not to see his country suffer the same ravages that the countries around it had. It was for this reason that he had expressed a willingness to assist the Americans. Not the CIA; he did not trust the CIA or consider it efficient. Triad, however, he thought was different.

Hahn had never met this man, had spoken to him just once, on the phone earlier in the day, and knew him only as Jorge.

"I hope you do not mind that I started eating," he said quietly in Spanish, a language Hahn was familiar with. "I was hungry and the waiters and cooks are getting impatient to close."

Hahn, who'd eaten earlier, said that he had no objection. He asked if Jorge had discovered any information of value in regard to Hidalgo's whereabouts.

Without raising his eyes from his food, Jorge replied that he had both good news and bad. "The good news is that I have found Hidalgo.''

"And the bad news?''

"The bad news is that he is no longer here in San José. He was reported to have left this morning on the eleven o'clock train to Limón. He arrived late in the afternoon and booked a room at the Puerto Hotel, but I very much doubt he will remain for very long there.''

"Why do you say that?''

"His ultimate destination would not be Limón if he is on his way to the staging area you are seeking. I will, for argument's sake, assume that there is such a staging area even though it is still a matter of speculation here in San José. Some of my friends say that it is all a fabrication of your CIA. Others believe that such a place exists.''

Now he drew a pen and paper out of his pocket, pushed aside his food, and proceeded to outline a rough map of Costa Rica, with Nicaragua to the north and Panama to the south.

"If this staging area for the Cubans and perhaps the Russians is present in our country then there are two places to look for it. One is here.'' He indicated a stretch of terrain that ran the length of Costa Rica's southern border with Panama. "But it is very swampy, very bad for planes. The only advantage is that it is very inaccessible. The second possibility is up in the north, along the coast, which is not very inhabited. There are already Sandinista troops from Nicaragua in this part of the country. They might provide protection for such a staging area.''

"What about an airfield?''

"Yes, this is possible too.''

"It's your impression then that Hidalgo would be heading north from Limón?''

"I suspect this is so.''

"Is there any way of getting to Limón tonight?''

"Tonight?'' Jorge looked shocked. "Señor, it is impossible tonight. How would you go?''

"I don't know, I'm asking you.''

Jorge continued shaking his head as if Hahn had taken leave of his senses. "There are no planes anymore. The Civil Guard has appropriated them all for military use. And the train does not leave from here until tomorrow at eleven."

"What about a car?"

"To travel tonight in a car is madness. You would be ambushed—*phht*." He made a cutting gesture across the base of his neck with his hand. "Even the Civil Guard are killed when they try to patrol the road between the capital and Limón. To tell you the truth, it is not wise to go by car during the daylight either. The guerrillas make raids. Sometimes they rob you, sometimes they kill. No, I advise you to go tomorrow to the train station—it is just in back of the Parque Nacional —and at eleven o'clock you will find a train to Limón."

"Isn't the train dangerous?"

"Of course. Everything now in Costa Rica is dangerous. But of all the choices, the train is the least dangerous. The Civil Guard tries to keep the rail line secure. Sometimes they fail and the passengers are left to do as they can. For your sake, señor, I hope this is not a mistake."

Hahn looked at the man glumly.

Even at 10:45 A.M., the platform was sparsely populated. In better times, Hahn was given to understand, there might be hundreds of people waiting to board the daily train to Puerto Limón, the country's second largest city and major Atlantic port. But with the heightened tensions and the prospect of robbery or, worse, confronting passengers, most travel plans had apparently been put aside until tranquility returned to the country.

If anything, there were as many Civil Guardsmen present on the platform as civilians. A voice over the loudspeaker urged people to report pieces of abandoned luggage to the nearest authorities. Such innocent-looking items were frequently known to contain saboteurs' bombs.

It was, however, a gorgeous day, with a cloudless blue sky and just enough of a breeze in the air to make the heat tolerable. Hahn found it difficult to reconcile himself to the idea that the country was being rent by civil insurrection. Apart from the conspicuous military presence on the platform, there was little hint that there might be a war on.

First-class was so reasonably priced—just shy of four dollars—that Hahn felt no reason to stint even though he was under instructions to economize whenever possible. (Because Triad's budget came out of secret, but limited, Presidential contingency funds, it was under financial constraints that the CIA was not. The CIA Director could appear before a Senate subcommittee and explain why he needed additional funds. William Drexell, however, could not.)

He carried with him two suitcases, one of which he needed for personal use; the other was to justify his cover. This second suitcase contained books about the Indians who had settled in the region prior to the coming of the Spaniards to Costa Rica in 1502. There were, in addition, pages of notes which were to support the declaration in his passport that he was an anthropology professor from the University of Pennsylvania.

To emphasize the physical aspect of his cover, Hahn sported a pair of horn-rimmed glasses and wore the sort of olive-green jacket that looked as if it had come from an Army surplus store. He presented a decidedly incongruous sight; even without the academic trappings, he would have looked as though he'd been plucked from a decent, hardworking American community and set down in the middle of a foreign revolution without having the slightest inkling of how he got there. His skin was too pale, his expression too inquisitive, his hands too soft. He seemed the odd man out, too reflective for his own good, and as was happening now on the railroad platform, people had the tendency to either underestimate him or ignore him completely. However, as someone who practiced espionage for a living, Hahn could only feel protected by these appearances.

The first-class car he selected was sparsely occupied, as he'd suspected it would be. There was one married couple loaded down with luggage, but otherwise the passengers seemed to be businessmen and low-level politicians, in short, anyone who lacked sufficient political clout to get a lift to Limón by air.

The journey, if it went without a hitch, was to last no more than nine hours. But there was no one, the conductor included, who was willing to give assurances to Hahn that no such hitches would develop along the way.

Nonetheless, for the first few hours Hahn had reason to be hopeful. The landscape sped by so quickly that he began to think that perhaps the Americans, with their deteriorating rail system, might take a lesson from the Costa Rican railway authorities. Moreover, the scenery was magnificent, from the continental divide at Cartago, through the narrow wooded Reventazón valley, past Siquirres. As a veteran traveler, Hahn felt it was truly one of the most beautiful rail trips in the world.

Unwilling to believe that they would avoid trouble indefinitely, he removed from his pocket a slip of paper Jorge had given him the night before. It specified the person he was to contact on Limón—a woman named Maria who could be found at the Café Faisan. According to Jorge, she would know where to find Hidalgo if he was in Limón. He glanced at the paper once more to make sure he had memorized the information correctly and ripped it carefully into shreds.

It was just beyond Siquirres that there was an inkling of trouble. The train abruptly slowed, reducing its pace to a crawl. For the first time one of the Civil Guardsmen appeared in the car, an M-16 gripped carelessly in his hands. While responding to none of the questioning gazes he was eliciting from the passengers on either side of the aisle, he kept peering out the weather-stained windows, intimating that he anticipated trouble. All that was now visible was a row of banana trees, behind which could be seen as profligate a display of tropical vegetation as Hahn had ever laid eyes on. There was no telling what, or who, was out there in the brush, but the grave expression fixed on the Civil Guard's face was enough to raise everyone's apprehensions.

The man sitting with his wife stopped the Civil Guard and asked him what the matter was. The somber way he said it suggested that he already knew.

"We are taking precautions," the Civil Guard responded, and moved on.

Hahn felt fortunate that his Spanish was as dependable as it was; in this situation, not to comprehend what was being said around him would have only increased his sense of helplessness.

If any attack on the train did materialize, it was not at all clear how they could adequately defend themselves. Hahn imagined there were no more than a dozen Civil Guardsmen on board, and even that might have been an overestimation. While he carried a .32 with him, he had no intention of using it except in the most exigent circumstances. Certainly he was in no position to fend off a raiding party of guerrillas, if they were in fact lurking in ambush among the trees.

Still the train continued on, though with such painstaking slowness that the landscape seemed scarcely to move by. No conductor appeared to explain what was responsible for the slowdown.

Then, just as the engine began to pick up speed again, an explosion tore up several ties in its path, hurtling them up in the air with enough smoke to momentarily cast a pall over the sky. Almost instantaneously the engineer applied the brakes, causing an enormous jolt that threw the passengers back and sent many of them falling into the aisles. Trays full of light refreshments tumbled noisily to the floor. Hahn, picking himself up and getting back into his seat, noticed that the car's one woman passenger had sustained a forehead gash that was bleeding copiously. Her husband seemed too dazed to immediately react.

With a shrieking protest of wheels and journals, the train ground to a halt. The Civil Guard who'd passed through the car earlier reappeared. He called out to the passengers to stay down, then proceeded to roll down a window and thrust his M-16 out of it.

For several moments all anyone could hear was the occasional cawing of birds in the forest that flanked the rail line. The absence of any other sound was unnerving to the passengers.

Even the Civil Guardsman looked frustrated as he scanned the terrain, shifting his weapon from one direction to another. Then he seemed to spot someone moving and discharged his gun. All he succeeded in doing, though, was to excite his comrades, who opened up an instant later. Hahn listened for return fire, but heard none. When the Civil Guardsmen realized this themselves, they stopped shooting. Now even the birds were silent.

"How long must we endure this?" one man demanded.

There was no reply.

"We could be here forever," he went on.

Fifteen minutes had gone by since the explosion had occurred. Against the Civil Guardsman's instructions, many of the passengers began to raise themselves up, adjusting the window shades in order to steal glimpses for themselves. But aside from the banana trees there was nothing to see.

After some minutes had passed, four guardsmen emerged from the train, keeping low, their rifles trained on the brush. Evidently they'd decided to inspect the damage done to the tracks to see if it might be possible to repair them. They hoped the bombs had been detonated by radio; the guerrillas needn't be nearby at all.

Ten men and one woman, brandishing Kalashnikovs, watched the soldiers' progress from the cover of the brush and palms. The woman was short, almost petite, and slender, but after three years of fighting in the jungle, she'd been toughened and there was no one among the guerrilla force who would dare question her strength. But even in fatigues, with a beret pulled down on her brow, she was still an attractive woman.

With full calculation, she selected the man who would be killed first and trained him in the sight of her gun as he paced back and forth in front of the train. As she studied him in the sight, her mind played with him, imagining him as lover and husband. Then she pulled the trigger.

He staggered and began to fall. Instantaneously, an entire volley caught him, tearing into him. In a moment, he was dead.

On the train the conductor, a wiry man with a mustache that would not have looked out of place in a comic opera, was in the midst of reassuring the passengers that the authorities in San Jose had been informed by radio of the sabotage and that assistance would soon be forthcoming.

The first burst of gunfire made him stop speaking. He held out his hands in a vague gesture of appeal.

"Calm, everybody be calm," he stammered, and ran quickly to the next car.

Hahn saw a Civil Guardsman rushing headlong to the open door to peer out.

A second fusillade came a second later, and the passengers heard the guardsman cry out. When they next looked, he was lurching back in their direction, his face contorted in pain, his uniform darkening with blood. His M-16 slipped from his grasp, and he collapsed in the aisle.

Outside the train, Hahn could hear the guardsmen—though he couldn't see them—as they sought cover from the hail of bullets directed at them.

A man to the rear of Hahn screamed. The others around him regarded the prostrate figure of the guardsman with bewildered shock, as if they couldn't make out exactly what he was doing, bleeding like that.

Outside, the insurgents moved up, revealing themselves. The five surviving guardsmen had managed to withdraw and had taken up positions inside the train four cars down from the one Hahn occupied.

Led by the woman, whose code name was Tania, the

insurgents advanced a few paces toward the tracks, then dropped to the ground and fired, blowing out the glass from the windows. A great deal of shrieking came from the cars.

Tania then scrambled to her feet, simultaneously heaving a grenade at the car from which most of the opposition fire was originating.

The grenade was well targeted, its trajectory taking it through one of the blown-in windows. An instant later an explosion rocked the car and blew a hole through its roof. A cascade of smoke belched through the hole, then a part of the side wall disintegrated as well, leaving a gap through which the attackers could see charred bodies half-obscured by smoke.

Firing continued from a few places in the train, but it was sporadic and the insurgents had no difficulty in silencing it.

The passengers in Hahn's car cowered in their seats, some of them holding their hands above their heads in a gesture of surrender.

Hahn, however, decided to stay below seat level for the moment.

Many of his fellow passengers could not refrain from screaming or sobbing to themselves. There was no question that most expected to be killed.

One particularly well-fed man quickly got to his feet and made a run for it.

He reached the passageway at the far end of the car just as the guerrillas appeared in the doorway. For a moment he stood face-to-face with Tania. She extended her automatic, tickling his chin with the end of it. Little by little he shambled backwards; his raised arms were visibly shaking.

Once he'd slumped into his seat, Tania launched into a fervent speech in which she denounced both the central government and the imperialists. "I am calling upon all of you to contribute to the cause of the people and socialism!" she announced, making it clear that everyone was to contribute.

Throughout her impassioned remarks, she continued

to ignore the body of the Civil Guardsman who lay bleeding at her feet.

It was with some relief that Hahn realized that her speech implied the guerrillas did not mean to execute them or take them prisoner, but merely to rob them of their money and valuables. The woman, however, did hint at a more dire fate for those who turned out to be "exploiters of the people." Naturally, she and her comrades would be the ones to decide who fit into this category.

Hahn composed himself as much as possible. While it was unlikely that his true purpose in the country was known, he could not entirely rule out the possibility. His was a world of subterfuge and the unexpected where, at any instant, someone might find himself shopped by the opposition. What guarantee did he have that somebody like Jorge might not have sent word to Limón that he was an American agent in search of Hidalgo? No matter that the man's credentials had been checked and cleared by Triad; there could be no final guarantee of his loyalty.

One by one the guerrillas inspected their passports every bit as thoroughly as customs officials. They then proceeded to confiscate wallets, rings, necklaces, bracelets, and whatever else they considered of interest, including transistor radios. The married couple proved of particular concern to Tania. She scrutinized the husband again and again as she leafed through his passport. At last she ordered him out of the train. Just him, not his wife.

His wife protested vehemently, but the guerrilla silenced her by bringing up her rifle as if he meant to butt her in the face. Meanwhile her husband, his head bowed penitently, complied by carefully stepping over the fallen Civil Guardsman and starting toward the end of the car.

"What will you do to him?" the wife asked tearfully.

She received no response.

Tania suddenly stepped up to Hahn.

"American?" she said upon opening his passport.

Hahn replied in Spanish.

"You speak our language quite well," she said suspiciously. Noting the entry date on his papers, she asked him if he'd been in Costa Rica before.

"You can see for yourself," he said politely, indicating the many stamps which showed he'd been in and out of the country half a dozen times in the past year. They were all false—this was his first visit—but it would hardly do to have an anthropologist and supposed expert on the history of Costa Rica lacking in experience in the field.

"Ah, yes," she said, narrowing her eyes. Then, "May I look at your bags?"

"You will no matter what I say, so go ahead," he replied casually.

She ordered him to open them. The bag full of books and notes especially intrigued her. Examining one of the Spanish volumes, she nodded with satisfaction. "I read this in the university. If you are able to understand our history perhaps then you can also begin to understand our struggle. When you return to your country, tell your people that we are not murderers and perpetrators of atrocities, in spite of what your government and your newspapers and television say."

Hahn said that he would be happy to communicate whatever message she wished.

She regarded him dubiously. "I will not even ask you for a contribution, although one would be appreciated."

Deciding that it would be wiser to volunteer, Hahn offered her twenty dollars.

She snatched it away from him and stuffed the bills in her pocket. "Next time the cost will be much greater. Consider yourself fortunate, American."

As Tania disappeared from the car, Hahn began to hear the distant rumble of helicopters. He assumed that the assistance requested from San José by the engineer was approaching. The guerrillas appeared to believe this as well, for they departed the train in seconds, taking with them four men who they'd apparently found to be exploiters of the people. What would happen to them wasn't clear, but it was Hahn's guess that they would be tried by a people's court in some rebel encampment and either lined up against a wall or else held, pending an exchange of prisoners with the government at a later date.

The woman whose husband had been seized was weeping uncontrollably now as she pressed her face up to the window for a last glimpse before he vanished with the guerrillas into the wall of grass and underbrush.

A minute after they'd disappeared from sight a pair of government Huey helicopters hove into view, their brown bodies catching the westering sun as they came in low over the jungle. Somewhat higher up in the sky an OV-10 counterinsurgency aircraft could be seen. Dispatching an OV-10 to this site underscored how seriously the government regarded the ambush; each one of these aircraft cost $10 million.

At the moment, however, the OV-10 appeared to be providing only backup support as the Hueys banked and suddenly started spraying the jungle with 30mm chain guns. Whether they were accomplishing anything by this barrage was impossible for Hahn to tell.

Of course, the four captives were equally imperiled by the air strike as the guerrillas were, a fact not lost on the woman whose husband had just been kidnapped. Hammering her fists against the window, she screamed hysterically until two nearby passengers succeeded in restraining her.

The uppermost branches of the trees disintegrated as the bullets came streaking down toward the guerrillas, who were herding their hostages before them.

Two of Tania's men were brought down in the first attack. The others managed to escape by taking refuge under the generous cover of palm fronds.

But then the OV-10 appeared overhead, banked, and dived in to drop a succession of cluster bombs. One landed only a short distance away from where the guerrillas lay concealed, forcing them to move again.

It was then that the Hueys returned. One came dangerously low and spat out a withering burst of fire that caught the first five men in the column, including three of the hostages. Tania was about to direct her men back when her chest opened up and she fell to her knees. She could not abide the thought that she was going to die, not here at any rate. Groaning, she lifted herself up, clutching at the tatters of her uniform as though she meant to stem the flow of blood spilling from her. The pain was so intense that Tania could barely cling to consciousness. Her eyes burned, her vision was darkening. The smell of the bullets and the bombs was terrible. There were screams all around her, some, she realized in a haze of pain, were her own.

She could hardly see. Squinting, she looked down at the blood on the ground under her. She stopped clutching her uniform and something fell out of her. Then something else, larger, began slipping out. She realized distantly that her intestines were uncoiling and soaking through the grass. She couldn't understand why she wasn't dead. Then she vomited and fell into a distant blackness.

Those remaining on the train were luckier. Half an hour after the aircraft appeared, armored personnel carriers arrived on the Puerto Limón highway, which adjoined the rail line, to convey the passengers to their destination.

The country's only deep-water port on the Caribbean, Puerto Limón was set amid a landscape so rocky that there wasn't a half-decent beach anywhere within the city limits. Until the insurgency had spread to Costa Rica, there were only 30,000 people living here, but their numbers had swollen with refugees from neighboring villages and towns that had come under attack.

Hahn asked the guardsmen to drop him off near the center of the city, which seemed to consist largely of cantinas blasting jukebox tunes from the United States and second-rate movie theaters showing Mexican sex films.

Hahn had only to make a few inquiries to learn where the Café Faisan was. When he entered, he was instantly greeted by a lonely proprietor apparently eager for customers. Without asking, he brought Hahn an *agua sapo*, in English, frog water. Hahn discovered that he heartily disliked the mixture of lemonade, brown sugar, and ginger, but he drank it to be polite, then inquired after Maria.

The proprietor gave him a huge smile and nodded agreeably, but said nothing.

Presently, though, a woman appeared from the back of the cafe and Hahn knew immediately that this was the right woman.

She was between thirty and forty years old. Somewhat on the heavy side, she still retained a certain delicate beauty that suggested an ancient Indian heritage uncontaminated by any Spanish influence.

After introducing herself, she told Hahn that she knew where Hidalgo was. Hahn was relieved that the Cuban had not yet departed Limón for the north. On the contrary, Maria said, at that very moment he was taking a stroll on the city's famous palm promenade. As of fifteen minutes ago, she added, he was alone.

She was so sure of her information because the informants she relied upon were shoeshine boys and beggars who affected blindness and vendors of lottery tickets—her own people, who were far more observant of the comings and goings of pedestrians than even professional spies.

"He has gone to Vargas Park," Maria told Hahn. "We will find out where."

As if on cue, a youngster of no more than eight materialized from out of the gloom. Like almost everyone else that Hahn had seen in his first hour in the port city, the youngster was black.

Maria instructed him to race on ahead and discover precisely where Hidalgo had gone. When he'd sighted him, he was to come back and tell them.

While they waited, he and Maria spoke little. Hahn sensed that this was not a woman who would appreciate chatter about the weather. She was someone used to danger, probably thriving on it, and who went about her work with quiet efficiency.

Even though Maria reported that the insurgents were bivouacked in jungle camps less than fifteen miles away, the atmosphere in Limón did not seem anywhere as tense as it had in the capital. Still, Hahn felt that all was not as it should be. Outside the café, traffic was sparse, confined mostly to taxis and the occasional military vehicle, and the streetlights were dim, as though a brownout had been instituted. Those people who were still about at this hour walked quickly, nervously.

At last the youngster reappeared and beckoned to Maria. "Come," she said to Hahn. "You can leave your luggage here. It will be safe."

The three of them soon found themselves in Vargas Park. Whenever Hahn glanced up at the tree branches he saw eyes peering down on him. He didn't know what to make of this until he realized that the indigenous sloths were undoubtedly disturbed by their presence.

As they approached a clearing, in which there was a wide, flat circle of grass rimmed by tropical flowers, the boy pointed to a lone figure standing about fifty feet away and silhouetted in the hazy light of a lamp. It was Hidalgo.

Maria dismissed the boy, who instantly disappeared into the darkness, and then turned to Hahn.

"We wait," was all she said, then motioned him back so that they were behind a bush, out of the Cuban's sight.

After perhaps five minutes another man came into view from the opposite direction. From his vantage point, Hahn could see the second man clearly. He was heavyset and balding, and as he stepped forward to greet Hidalgo, his face was caught by the light of the lamp.

Hahn was so taken aback that his mouth actually

dropped open. Maria gave him a questioning look.

"Do you know who he is?"

"Yes," Hahn replied tightly.

In Triad headquarters this man was known as Mr. Clean, a code name derived from the complete lack of hair on his head. And while he was now dressed in civilian clothes, in what looked to be a rather ill-fitting and uncomfortably warm suit, Hahn knew he cut a far more imposing figure in a military uniform.

The last Hahn had heard, he was posted to the Soviet embassy in Athens as a military attaché. Puerto Limón was a long ways from Athens, and the question now was what exactly was Maxim Kolnikov, a colonel in Red Army intelligence, doing here?

10

JUNE 2,
THE GUYANA INTERIOR

"We've managed to get to the middle of nowhere," observed Colin Harris. There was no indication, however, that being in the middle of nowhere especially troubled him.

Lisker looked through a side window of their turbo-prop plane and regarded the terrain far below with only casual interest. He, too, was used to vast stretches of impenetrable territory. The 58,000 square miles of unexplored forest and savanna below was the sort of thing he'd often contended with, always successfully.

Lisker and Harris had obtained their passage into the wild western region of Guyana while they were in a remote town called Barika, which they'd reached after leaving Georgetown. Once they'd eluded the police near the Pegasus Hotel, they'd gone directly to a prearranged site in the city where another four-wheel drive had been left for them, courtesy of the same mysterious Triad asset who'd provided the first one.

The six other passengers on board this flight were prospectors whose interest in the interior was less political than monetary.

There was oil in this region, and uranium and gold

and hardwoods like the famous Guyanese greenheart, but most of it was a bitch to get at. There were allegations that it was for these unexploited resources, and not for any nationalistic reason having to do with a mistakenly drawn border on a map in 1899, that Venezuela claimed this territory. Officials in Caracas hotly disputed this, blaming the British for having appropriated to Guyana, when they had owned the country, land that was rightfully part of Venezuela.

As far as the prospectors in the plane were concerned, Venezuela had all the oil it needed, and they hoped it would leave them alone in their explorations of the disputed border area. They seemed to regard the government in Georgetown with no more enthusiasm. But it was becoming clear, with rising tensions in the area, that they were in increasing danger from both sides.

Finally, two days before, the Comrade Leader decided to nationalize the few remaining private industries of Guyana. As they talked now, the prospectors could not comprehend how the regime could hope to operate the companies that they worked for. The chief motivation for foreign companies to come into the area had been in hopes of making a high risk pay off big sometime down the road. It was with this hope that they had put their money, their manpower, and their technology to work in the forbidding jungle. There was little question that, with the government moving to take them over, the companies would now pull up stakes. Significantly, the first companies to receive notice of the nationalization measures were American and Canadian, underscoring the regime's antipathy toward its powerful northern neighbors.

On first boarding, Lisker had given the other men the impression that he was an employee of one of these firms and that he had happened to fall into the company of a man of the cloth traveling in the same direction. He pretended almost total ignorance of the political situation so that his questions wouldn't arouse any unnecessary suspicion.

"Was it true?" he asked, "that there's been fighting

between Venezuelan and Guyanese troops?"

All the prospectors—who called themselves pork knockers—agreed that they'd heard of such combat, but all they could do was repeat secondhand stories. One of the men said he'd been told that there'd been a massacre of Indians near the Mazaruni River, but he couldn't say for sure whether it was the Guyanese or the Venezuelans who'd committed it.

After nearly an hour the plane came down in a clearing that could be considered an airstrip only by the most generous definition of the word. Even Lisker found himself holding his breath as the pilot landed in the confined jungle area.

Upon debarking, they were greeted by a representative of the Holland Mineral and Mining Consortium, a man whose face had the texture of reworked leather. His name was Charlie Grove, and he had a small, rusted van with which he was to convey Lisker and Harris, together with the prospectors, back to the dredging site three miles away.

As part of their contact, some of the prospectors would remain with the Holland operation. Others would continue farther into the jungle to search for their fortune independently.

According to earlier information received by Lisker via transmitter in Barika, Charlie Grove could be relied on to provide them both with transportation and with photography equipment. He was, however, the last contact that they'd have in this part of the world; once they left the dredging site, they'd be on their own.

Grove gave no hint that he was aware that the two Americans had arrived in the middle of the jungle for any purpose other than what they avowed. Lisker was treated as a new employee, Harris as an idealistic missionary on his way into the brush to convert the heathen.

"You boys are probably going to be the last ones to be sent out here for a while," Grove said. "There isn't any telling how much longer *any* of us will be here."

Grove, it turned out, had been in this part of Guyana

for fifteen years. He'd had a home in Wisconsin, but he'd left it, his wife and six children. He told them that there wasn't a day in his life when he ever regretted his decision.

To Harris he said, "You think the Indians are going to listen to you? What do they care about Christ? They won't understand what you're saying anyway. They don't know English, they don't know Spanish, they don't even know Creole."

Harris was undaunted. "I've made more headway with the Indians than you can imagine."

Lisker said, "He can't help himself. Converting's like an itch with him."

Harris shot him an irritated look.

Twenty minutes after leaving the airstrip they arrived at the site of the dredging operation. A collection of structures, some of aluminum, some jerry-built out of dried mud and hardwood, overlooked a turgid river where the dredging was going on. The machinery created so much racket that the treetops had been emptied of the local bird population. Prospectors in hard hats and boots up to their knees plodded about in the thick, viscous mud that bordered the bank of the river.

Above the clatter of the dredging another sound made itself heard. Glancing up, the new arrivals were confronted with the sight of a squadron of helicopters proceeding in the direction of the Venezuelan border, which was still fifty miles away to the southwest.

Lisker, affecting to be no more interested in the spectacle than the others, raised his field glasses to his eyes.

He had no trouble establishing what type of helicopters these were. More than half of them were Soviet Haze choppers, introduced in the early 1970's; the others were Hip E's, one of the most heavily armed helicopters in operation, capable of transporting nearly 200 57mm air-to-surface rockets and deploying antitank missiles and bombs. He guessed that these craft would be ferrying troops as well as weapons into the border area.

Speaking quietly to Harris, Lisker said, "I'm sure

either Cubans or Russians are manning those. The Guyanese army doesn't have any transport choppers.''

Charlie Grove hadn't heard what Lisker said. ''We see them all the time,'' he explained. ''Back and forth, back and forth, every day. But nobody tells us what's happening.''

After the prospectors had gone back to their business, Lisker asked Charlie what he knew of the troop movements into the interior, but like the prospectors on the plane, he'd heard stories of battles and massacres, but nothing solid. ''Obviously there's a big military build-up going on upriver,'' Charlie concluded, ''but whether it's for show or preparation for a major battle, I haven't the foggiest.''

''How soon can you get us the equipment and transportation we need?'' Lisker asked with some urgency.

''Anytime you want.''

''Aren't we going to stay here a day to rest up?'' Harris asked uneasily.

''Why don't you?'' Charlie Grove suggested. ''Have some food, get a good night's sleep. Tomorrow you can see about going on.''

Lisker shook his head. ''We'll trouble you for a bite to eat, then we'll be on our way.''

He was already chafing over the full day they'd had to wait for the plane in Barika. He didn't want to delay any longer.

Harris argued, ''I agreed to come in order to help you get information. I did *not* come with you to get myself killed in a crossfire between Venezuela and Guyana. I'm simply not as combat ready as you.''

Lisker shrugged. ''Stay here if you want, then.''

Harris cursed him in a manner which belied his missionary persona. Then, as Lisker had foreseen he would, he consented to go too. ''But I intend to teach you a few prayers first,'' he added resentfully, ''so you can say the appropriate words over my bullet-riddled body!''

An hour later, after consuming some biscuits and tea

in the workers' mess shack, Lisker and Harris were
presented with a jeep by Charlie Grove.

"It's got a full tank of gas," he said, adding,
"There's no need to return it. Holland Consortium will
just write it off their taxes."

In back of the jeep there was a small suitcase in which
were neatly cached the photographic equipment Lisker
had requested from Triad. It included a fascinating array of devices capable of shooting at high speeds and at
night or in the worst kinds of weather the interior could
provide.

The road Lisker and Harris followed in the jeep had
been paved once upon a time, but it had long since
become overgrown with grass, and was now pitted and
broken apart by erosion. For a ways the road ran by the
side of the river, past small rice-growing islands. Once
they spotted an Indian paddling a canoe, but he was the
only sign of human life visible on the water. Brilliantly
colored birds occasionally swooped down to perch on
the tips of trees that were just out of sight. Clusters of
brown rocks, covered with extravagantly beautiful
flowers, jutted out of the water near the banks.

The weather began to change around four in the
afternoon. A mist began to form, shrouding the river
just ahead of them. The brush, filled with ferns and
creepers, seemed to move in the haze, but there was no
way to determine what caused the effect. For several
minutes as they drove along, the thrum of the jeep's
engine was all they could hear; it was as if the gathering
mist was not only blotting out sight but sound as well.

It occurred to Lisker that they might be getting close
to the landing area that the Soviet craft had put down
in. "I think we ought to go the rest of the way on foot,"
he announced suddenly to Harris.

He explained that he didn't want to alert several hundred armed men by their approach in the jeep.

Concealing the vehicle amid a cluster of palms, he
and Harris continued on. After walking along the road
for a mile, they began to make out the sound of voices,
which were clearly speaking Spanish. Motor engines

rumbled through the mist from their right.

Just as Lisker was deciding whether or not to proceed any farther, they became aware of footsteps coming in their direction. An instant later a Cuban soldier materialized out of the brush directly in front of them.

If they were surprised, the Cuban was no less so. He stared at them uncomprehendingly, unable to determine who they were or what they were doing here.

While Harris hesitated, Lisker lunged forward. In one deft, graceful motion, he seized hold of the Cuban's gun hand, yanked it back and up at such an angle that Harris heard the bone break. The Kalashnikov fell from his grasp, and he let out a savage howl of pain that was immediately cut off by Lisker's knife slicing into his throat. It was a stainless steel bush knife, handcrafted and worth well over $200, and it did its job very proficiently. Blood spurted from the ruptured jugular and his head lolled to one side.

Lisker dragged the Cuban into the shelter of the forest and set him down among the creepers, ferns, and grass, hiding him from anyone traveling along the road. A great deal of blood, bright red against the lush green vegetation, had been spilled, but there was nothing to be done about that.

Harris hadn't moved. He looked as if he were in shock.

"Did you really have to do that?" he demanded anxiously.

"Unavoidable," Lisker said, suddenly grabbing hold of Harris and pulling him into the same brush where he'd just deposited the body.

A minute later, a jeep carrying three of the Cuban's comrades appeared, proceeding with painstaking slowness down the road. It came to a halt about twenty feet away and the three men leaped out, their automatic weapons ready to fire. They were undoubtedly in search of the missing soldier.

Harris gave Lisker a reproachful look, as though this was all his fault. Seldom used to being around dead bodies, Harris was trying not to breathe too deeply; the odor of the Cuban seemed so powerful to him that he imagined the three soldiers surely must be able to smell the blood too.

But the Cubans gave no sign that they had any idea where to look. One began to call out the name Carlos, which Lisker assumed belonged to their fallen comrade.

Meanwhile, although the last thing he wanted to do was start shooting at anyone, Harris had gotten his own gun out and was holding it unsteadily in his hands.

The Cubans cautiously approached the brush where they were hidden, yet there was still little about their behavior to suggest that they had any idea anyone was hiding from them. Several tense minutes went by during which the patrol continued to reconnoiter a narrow strip of forest flanking either side of the road, but at no time did they dare venture into the forest itself. For one thing, the mist reduced visibility and none of them wanted to risk becoming lost. For another, they were understandably reluctant to commit themselves to a course of action that might lead to their deaths.

At last they decided to give up and return to their vehicle. Half a minute later they were speeding down the road, leaving Harris and Lisker in peace.

Lisker recommended remaining where they were until the mist lifted enough for them to orient themselves. There was no sense in blundering into still more Cubans. All around them they could hear the sound of military movements: the whirring rotors of helicopters, the squeal of tires against mud-softened ground, the voices of enlisted men being mobilized into formation, and the sporadic bursts of sound from walkie-talkies and field radios. But the sounds seemed to frequently shift direction, coming now from the west, now from the northeast, now from the south. Lisker thought the mist was probably responsible for the confusing acoustical effect.

Forty-five minutes after the patrolling jeep had gone on its way, the mist began to dissipate, and a bit of the late-afternoon sun could be seen. Lisker decided that now was the time to move.

Just as they had picked themselves up, they caught a glimpse of an oncoming half-track along the road. Simultaneously from the opposite direction, two jeeps appeared, each with a machine gun mounted on the hood.

Lisker immediately understood what had happened; their jeep had been discovered and an alert had gone out to conduct a thorough search for its owners. Now they faced a score of adversaries who, unlike the earlier ones, could not be counted on to abandon their efforts so quickly.

The only advantage that they held was that they still had not been sighted. Wasting no time, they plunged deeper into the brush, ignoring the barbed underbrush that clung to them.

Their luck couldn't be expected to last for much longer—and it didn't. An advance party of Cubans somewhere to their right became aware of them because of the racket they were making as they fled. They still had not actually been sighted because when the Cubans fired, their bullets went wide, impacting against the palm trees above and landing harmlessly in the soggy earth.

They continued to draw relatively harmless fire as they ran; the thing that Lisker feared most was dashing headlong into a second patrol and becoming trapped.

But instead of finding themselves confronted with a second patrol, Lisker and Harris emerged from the forest to discover that they were now on the periphery of a military encampment.

Unable to go either back or ahead, they dropped down in the high grass bordering the camp in order to make themselves as inconspicuous as possible. While they were certain that the patrol was still somewhere to the rear of them, it appeared to have completely lost their trail; as attentively as they listened, they heard no sound of the pursuers.

At any rate, spread before them in the hour just before twilight, was the spectacle they'd come all the way into the interior to capture on film and tape. Even though Charlie Grove had indicated that the military build-up in the area had been proceeding steadily, it still seemed something of a miracle to Lisker that the Cubans had succeeded in hacking out of the jungle an encampment of this size in just a few weeks. Now, while several men were busy stringing barbed wire about the perimeter of the temporary installation, others were erecting corrugated shelters and watchtowers, all with components that had been dropped in on landings made during the previous few days. Most of the helicopters and both of the British-made transport planes were gone, but three Mi-8 transport helicopters were still parked on the airstrip.

In the middle of the encampment, set off by a wire fence, were several half-ton GAZ Russian field cars, one amphibious wheeled Russian APC carrier with heavy 14.5mm KPV machineguns; a pair of Soviet BMP APC tanks with Sagger missile launchers and a 73mm cannon; and an array of self-propelled howitzers and mortars, some of Soviet make, some of Czech and even British and Belgian manufacture. Strobe lights were also in view in the fenced-off area although most of them had yet to be hooked up.

Lisker and Harris also observed soldiers closer to where they lay concealed, undertaking the more pedestrian aspects of establishing a camp: pitching tents, installing sanitary facilities, and setting up a kitchen. At the moment huge black kettles filled with black bean soup were being heated by a series of coal-fueled fires.

"Well, let's get to it," Lisker whispered sharply.

Harris immediately dug out the photographic and recording equipment buried in their gear, and together the two of them set to work.

They had to work quickly, operating against two obstacles—the falling light and the risk of discovery. While Lisker possessed the technical know-how to get the most from any equipment he might be asked to use, Harris fumbled as he made the proper adjustments and seemed to snap away almost indiscriminately. Not that skill was a necessity; these cameras and recorders were so sophisticated that they could usually produce good results even in the hands of utter incompetents.

However, the weather refused to hold, and minutes after the appearance of some dark, evil-looking clouds overhead, the heavens opened up, releasing a torrential shower against which the palm trees above were scant protection. But the downpour made most of the soldiers abandon their work and scramble for shelter. Only a few remained outside to struggle with erecting the tents as they cursed their fate and the dismal meteorological conditions.

To Lisker the rain, uncomfortable as it was, lent him and Harris an unforeseen advantage. Under cover of the rain, he decided to hazard a further exploration of the camp.

Predictably, Harris objected. "Haven't we gotten enough?" he complained.

"I'd like to get in closer to the airstrip," Lisker said in a quiet, commanding voice.

Harris had no wish to stay where he was, alone and wet, and he reluctantly followed Lisker as he began to make his way around the edge of the camp in the direction of the airstrip, which in the rain was barely visible. All that could be seen of it was a spit of muddy land on which three Soviet helicopters sat, ominous and ghost-like.

Barbed wire extended only halfway about this part of the perimeter, the Cubans having forsaken the task of putting up fencing until the rain let up. Spools of unused wire lay upended in the thick grass.

Periodically Lisker would stop and use one of his cameras, usually the 35mm but sometimes the Tesar with the infrared attachment, to shoot something that caught his interest. It astonished Harris to see how oblivious the other man was to the rain or to the possibility that a Cuban might emerge from his shelter and spot him.

Once they'd come abreast of the helicopters, Lisker became even more involved with what he was doing, sparing no effort to film the trio of Mi-8 helicopters.

• • •

Pablo Guzman and Gabriel Mendez had been assigned to watch the helicopters at the far end of the encampment, a dismal task that neither of them welcomed, especially with this downpour. Having spent a year in the jungles of Angola, in rain and humidity every bit as bad as the rain and humidity of Guyana, they'd been looking forward to being reunited with their families. That they had not been told how long they would have to remain here only demoralized them further.

Because the encampment had not been fully established, there was no shelter for them and so they had been obliged to improvise one, setting up four bamboo poles and stretching a sheet of canvas over them. There were several leaks as they stood about, miserably observing the rain turn the ground to thick mud and moving now and again to avoid the water seeping in.

"Where in the name of God are the Venezuelans?" Guzman inquired, peering into the soggy undergrowth. "Where in the name of God are we anyway? Venezuela or Guyana?"

"We're somewhere," Mendez replied. "We are near one border or another; what difference does it make?"

"It makes a big difference, you son of a whore. When I run I want to know where the enemy is so I can go in the opposite direction."

"And betray the revolution?" Mendez said only half seriously.

"I've done what I can for the revolution and I will do more," Guzman replied. "But first let me see my wife." He smacked his lips at her memory. "I have a picture of her."

He got out a photograph that was so worn that the image had almost completely faded.

Mendez had a difficult time trying to puzzle out what she looked like, but he declared diplomatically that she was beautiful indeed and that it was understandable why a man would be anxious to get back to her.

"And you?"

"I have a girl," Mendez admitted, "but in all this time who knows whether she'll still be there. They all like to fuck around, just between you and me."

"Not my Mercedes," said Guzman angrily. "She is faithful to the core."

Mendez snorted derisively. "Such a thing is possible only in a mother."

"Mercedes *is* a mother. I have three children. I will show you their pictures—"

Mendez interrupted him. "Wait. Quiet! I hear something."

"You hear the rain," Guzman said, rummaging through his pack to find the photographs.

"No, no, I'm sure. Listen carefully."

Mendez trained his Kalashnikov toward the underbrush and aimed the beam of his flashlight in the same direction.

"Nothing is there," Guzman said too loudly.

Mendez prodded him violently with his elbow, causing him to look between the first helicopter and the second.

Guzman just caught sight of a man scrambling behind the fuselage of the middle chopper. He carefully raised his gun. His hands were trembling; he was surprised by how fearful he was.

Mendez told him to stay where he was and ran to the fence where a klaxon had been installed. As soon as he triggered the shrill blasting alarm, he hastened back to his companion under the shelter.

Although Guzman hardly thought it necessary, Mendez now ventured out in search of the intruders. With the blasting noise from the klaxon, Guzman assumed that they would already be running away.

No more than a dozen paces from the helicopters, Mendez suddenly fired. With the blinding rain, Guzman couldn't tell who or what his friend was firing at. Nonetheless, he followed right behind Mendez and discharged his gun in the same direction he'd just seen Mendez do.

There was a crackle of gunfire in response. "They're

heading toward the brush!'' Mendez cried.

As Guzman attempted to follow him, he slipped in the mud and fell, almost losing hold of his Kalashnikov.

When he succeeded in drawing himself upright, he looked about but failed to see any sign of Mendez. He glanced in back but couldn't see anything at all in the rain, though he expected reinforcements to arrive at any moment.

Then he heard a furious exchange of fire and rushed toward it.

Just as he regained sight of Mendez, several shots came from the brush. At least two struck Mendez and he let out a scream and catapulted backward.

Panicked, Guzman released a steady barrage into the brush with his AK-74. Without waiting to see whether he'd hit anyone, he went to Mendez's aid. When he got to him, the other man was still alive, groaning in the mud.

With no further gunfire from the brush, Guzman surmised that he'd either eliminated the intruders or driven them away. He bent down next to Mendez, but he was so mud-spattered that it was impossible to determine how badly he was wounded.

"Gabriel, Gabriel, talk to me, I'm here, Gabriel," he said, but elicited no response.

Mendez's eyes rolled back in his head and his body began thrashing, wildly.

Guzman then placed his hands underneath his shoulders and attempted to lift him up.

At that moment he detected movement ahead of him in the brush. Before he had a chance to react, there was a muffled pop and a bullet tore into his brain, entering just above the ridge of his nose. The wound from the front was small, a hole the size of a dime; in back, though, the hole exploded with pieces of brain and skull fragments.

Guzman's hands released Mendez and he fell back without a sound.

Mendez seemed to become vaguely aware of what was happening. He struggled to sit upright, but another bullet impacted in his throat and he sank, dead, back into the mud.

Satisfied that he had put an end to the immediate threat, Lisker beckoned Harris away from the airstrip. In spite of the elements and the uncertain terrain, they managed to make fair progress in their flight from the encampment, and the sound of the klaxon eventually diminished to nothing.

An hour later, when Lisker decided they were far enough out of danger to stop, he extracted the disks of film he'd taken of the base and handed them to Harris. "Do you think you can make it back to the prospectors' camp alone?" he asked gravely.

Without the use of the jeep, Harris was dubious, but the prospectors' camp was the safest place he could think of under the circumstances, and he allowed that, going by way of the road, he probably could.

"Well, see if you can't get there by the time that plane comes in tomorrow morning. It's imperative that you deliver these to Triad—in person—as soon as possible."

"What about you?"

"I'm staying here in the interior."

Harris narrowed his eyes. He wasn't sure he believed what he was hearing. "You're staying here? For God's sake, why? What more can you hope to accomplish?"

"Things are only beginning here. I want to see what else happens."

"I don't mind telling you that I think you're mad," Harris said, not unkindly.

Walking away from the other man, he was almost sure he heard the sound of Lisker's laughter. But when he turned to look, the laughter had stopped and Lisker was gone.

11

"The one thing I'm concerned about here is the possibility of a leak."

It was obvious to Drexell that the President was only echoing his chief of staff when he made this remark. Although Morse Peckum was unable to attend this confidential meeting in the Oval Office, his presence could be felt, hovering over the proceedings like a ghost.

Besides the President and Drexell, both Secretary of State Schelling and Secretary of Defense Rhiel had been summoned to the White House. It was nearly midnight, less than two hours after the photographs had arrived from Guyana.

They were in the form of disks, one of the latest advances in photography, and because they were compatible with video equipment and could be watched like slides on a television screen, they were immediately ready for viewing by the President and the other men at the meeting.

It had taken half an hour for the four men to examine the results of Lisker and Harris' clandestine photography. During that time, the President asked repeatedly to have another look at one or another of the pictures that had just flashed by. It was as though he kept hoping that he hadn't seen what was there.

But the photographs were too numerous and too clear to be wished away. The evidence that the President had demanded of Drexell at Camp David was here in abundance. While there was still no solid substantiation to back up Lisker's claim that Soviet advisers had been deployed in Guyana, there could be no question whatsoever that Cuban troops were active in the country and that they had taken up positions along the border with Venezuela.

"How many troops did Castro have stationed in Angola?" the President asked wearily.

"Approximately fifteen thousand, Mr. President," Rhiel replied.

"And of that number how many have returned to Cuba?"

"We can't say for certain," Rhiel replied, "but our naval and satellite intelligence indicate that of the ten transport ships that set out from Mocamedes, only two of them are known to have reached Cuba. Four are still in the mid-Atlantic. Our theory is that they've been given orders to reduce speed to a minimum pending a decision as to the final disposition of the troops."

"That's six out of ten. Where are the other four?"

Although Rhiel had expected the question, he was hesitant to answer.

"We aren't sure."

The President shot a glance at Drexell as though he might have the answer, but Drexell remained, wisely, silent.

"What do you mean, we aren't sure? We have millions of dollars worth of satellites in orbit and millions of dollars worth of radars in planes and balloons, and you say we aren't sure?"

"I'm afraid that's the case. Two of the ships were definitely sighted in the Caribbean, heading toward the

Honduran coastline, but we aren't certain of their ultimate destination. The other two we cannot account for at all." He then began to stammer out an explanation for this negligence that entailed technical details about sunsynchronous orbits.

From the expression on the President's face it was clear he had little comprehension of, or interest in, what the Defense Secretary was talking about.

"I suppose we should assume that these ships are landing troops somewhere in Central America," Turner said resignedly. "Has the Task Force succeeded in pinning down the location of this secret staging area?"

Drexell was heartened to see that the President had now accepted the fact that such a staging area did exist and wasn't just a product of Triad's overheated imagination.

Thinking of Jerry Hahn, who at last report was still in Puerto Limón, he said that while the precise location had yet to be ascertained it was very likely in the north of Costa Rica. "I have a man working on it right now and I expect that we should have an answer within a day or two."

"What do you think about all this?" The President turned now to the Secretary of State, who had maintained a scrupulous silence up until this point.

"I suppose we have to recognize that the Soviets are involved, and deal with them accordingly," Schelling said matter-of-factly. Having so long counseled holding off until all the facts were in, he now seemed to understand that some kind of decisive action was called for. "While we still aren't absolutely certain they have troops or advisers in either Costa Rica or Guyana there can be no question that the Kremlin is pulling the strings on this one. Castro would hardly dare dispatch his troops to Guyana and place them in a position where they might end up in combat against Venezuela unless the Russians gave him the orders and backing to do so. I think we ought to talk to Marchenko directly—the hell with Rudnitsky. Marchenko's in New York for the UN

disarmament conference. I can meet him there privately
tomorrow morning and see what he has to say for himself."

Valeri Marchenko was the Soviet Foreign Minister,
who'd only recently replaced the venerable Andrei
Gromyko in this capacity. As a member of the Politburo and longtime friend of First Secretary Kadiyev, he
was, at the comparatively young age of fifty-seven,
regarded by U.S. intelligence as one of the most influential figures in the Kremlin. As Soviet Ambassador to the
U.S., Rudnitsky held a rank of much less importance.

"Of course he'll stonewall it," the President said
flatly.

"Not necessarily," Schelling countered. "Not if we
confront Marchenko with the evidence and tell him
we'll present it to the United Nations."

"Suppose he says that he's not responsible for what
the Cubans choose to do. If pressed to the wall, you
know what'll happen? The Guyanese government will
admit that they're there and say that it's only a temporary measure for protection against Venezuelan aggression."

"I wouldn't doubt for a moment that's what they'll
do," Drexell interjected. "But I think that with the evidence we have, we'll score a few propaganda points
and, at least diplomatically, back the Soviets into a corner."

"That makes some sense," the President agreed.
"That's about all the UN's good for anyhow, isn't it—
scoring a few propaganda points? What do you think
the next step should be?"

The question was addressed to everyone in the room,
but it was Drexell who responded.

"I think there's no harm in speaking to Marchenko,"
Drexell said. "Feel him out, try to determine what Moscow's intentions might be in all this. Hint that we know
there are Soviets in Guyana as well as Cubans. That
might throw them. It's something they definitely don't
want to come to light. I wouldn't show him any evi-

dence, though; it might jeopardize Triad's intelligence sources.''

Schelling had no comment but it was apparent that he would have preferred to do without Drexell's opinion, even if it happened to coincide with his own at this point.

''But it's not enough,'' the President went on. ''We have to impress upon him that we're ready to back our words with forceful action. The problem is, how the hell do we do that? The latest CBS/New York Times poll— it'll be out in tomorrow morning's edition—shows that sixty-six percent of the population are opposed to committing ground forces to action outside the U.S. for any purpose but to defend American soil. Twenty-two percent support a limited war anywhere in the world where our interests might be threatened. The rest were, naturally, undecided. But, you see, with that kind of margin we're not about to find the people in Congress who'll back us in the event that introducing American forces in the Southern Hemisphere becomes necessary.''

''You're worried about the War Powers Act?'' Rhiel asked.

''Exactly. There's no chance anyone on the Hill is going to vote for something that will result in our boys fighting Cubans and Russians. Not unless we play it like Reagan in Grenada and show that there's some immediate threat to convince them. That's why I'm worried about leaks on this. As soon as the public gets wind of a new flashpoint, the opposition will only get worse. We'll be lucky to have even twenty-two percent on our side then. After what's gone down in the last several months people are jittery. The antinuke rally in New York last weekend drew how many people?''

''Half a million,'' Rhiel said.

''Some say it was more like three-quarters,'' Schelling put in.

''They're scared and I can't blame them. I'm scared too. But the point is we have to do something in this Guyana situation,'' the President said.

He directed his gaze at Drexell.

"Why not put together a clandestine force?" Drexell suggested. "There are enough exiles from Cuba, El Salvador, Nicaragua, and Guatemala who are already in training in the South for the kind of operation I have in mind."

Rhiel was openly scornful of such a proposal: "You want to get us involved in another Bay of Pigs. This isn't 1961 and this administration isn't Camelot."

"You haven't let me finish, Marty," Drexell continued, his gravelly voice as calm as before. "I'm not suggesting going into either Venezuela or Guyana. We don't know what'll develop there and until we do it would be damn foolish to become involved. What I'm proposing is that we sabotage the supply lines. Once we know precisely where this staging area is—and I'm assuming that it'll turn up in Costa Rica somewhere—then we destroy the air base, wreck the landing facilities, maybe blow up the aircraft and ships that are being used to transport troops and supplies to Guyana.

"At the same time I'd recommend we do what we can to bolster Venezuela's defense. It'll be a hell of a lot easier for Congress to approve the sale of a dozen F-18's to Caracas than to send the Marines."

Silence greeted Drexell's words. Then the President spoke.

"About how many men do you think you could collect for an operation like this?"

"Three hundred would be all that I'd need. The object is to get in, wreak as much devastation as possible, and get out as quickly as possible. I'm speaking of a very limited type of mission here, not a full-scale invasion or an attempt to topple a government. And remember too that neither the Cubans nor the Soviets want to acknowledge the fact that they've built up military installations on Costa Rican territory against the express wishes of its government. If they sustain a severe loss they're more likely to crawl away and lick their wounds than bitch to the UN. They do that, somebody might ask them what they were doing there in the first place.''

"I see what you're saying," Rhiel said. He might not
have agreed, but at least he had a glimmer of understanding.

"Of course, no matter what happens," the President
warned, "we can't have anyone tie this expeditionary
force to us. I don't want the controversy Reagan had
with the Coatras in Nicaraqua.''

"That won't be a problem," Drexell said.

"How long do you think it'll take to put the plan into
operation?" the President demanded.

"Once we've identified the staging area—or areas, as
the case may be—I'll be in a better position to judge."

The buzzer on the President's phone interrupted their
exchange. It was his personal secretary reminding him
that the Speaker of the House was waiting to see him.
It was about an important $10 billion appropriations
measure the President was pushing for, and without the
Speaker's clout behind him, there was no way he was
going to see it passed.

"You'll have to excuse me now, gentlemen," he said.
"I have to get in some late-night lobbying."

As the others filed out, he signaled Drexell to stay.
"From this point on," he shot at Drexell when the
others had left, "I don't want to know what you do,
you understand? But by next week, I expect those supply lines to be cut."

"I understand completely, sir." The two shook
hands.

While it was well after midnight, Drexell still had one
more obligatory visit to make before he could go home.

His car was waiting for him outside on Pennsylvania
Avenue.

"Where to now, sir?" the driver, a bodyguard bor-
rowed from Secret Service, asked.

"Walter Reed."

In spite of his debilitated condition Zoccola had
begun to disregard his physician's orders and stayed

awake each night reading and watching television until two or three in the morning. This night, Drexell knew that visiting hours were long since over and that his presence in the wards was against the rules. But he was in the habit of breaking rules, and those that happened to prevail at Walter Reed daunted him no more than those ordained by Congress.

Zoccola looked forward to his chief's nocturnal visits, and he understood that the press of business was such that Drexell could not get away earlier in the day.

Drexell had no difficulty getting to his room. The security staff on duty recognized him, and while they didn't know exactly what his position in government was, they had been informed that his rank was extremely high, and they always let him pass.

But this time when he arrived in Zoccola's private room, there was no one there. He immediately summoned one of the on-duty nurses, who peered into the room in confusion. "He was here an hour ago," she said. "Let me check with the resident."

While she went to find the doctor, Drexell inspected the room. Not only was its occupant gone, so were all his clothes. However, the books, the video cassettes, the flowers (sent by female admirers whose names were inscribed on cards piled on his bedside table), and the prescription medicine had all been left behind.

When he appeared, the resident looked no less astonished than the nurse before him. "I don't know what happened," he said. "I've looked in the men's room, I've searched the corridors. There's no sign of him."

Drexell turned to him and very quietly asked whether Zoccola had somehow slipped out of the hospital, either on his own, or with somebody's help.

"That's the only possibility," the doctor admitted.

Silently Drexell cursed Zoccola. It was bad enough that they had to find a way to counter a Soviet presence in the Western Hemisphere; now he had to find a missing operative. He didn't know which would be harder.

MEETING REPORTED BETWEEN SCHELLING AND MARCHENKO

Special to the New York Times

NEW YORK, June 4—Secretary of State Jeffrey Schelling and Soviet Foreign Minister Valeri Marchenko were reported to have held a forty-five minute meeting at the Hotel Pierre this afternoon. There was no immediate indication from either man as to what the apparently impromptu session was about. A State Department spokesman, Warren Held, said that he had not heard of any such meeting and would have no comment.

Marchenko is in New York to attend a special United Nations disarmament conference that will get under way tomorrow. He is expected to make a major foreign policy address, spelling out Soviet proposals to create a nuclear-free zone in central Europe.

SOUTH AMERICAN CRISIS FIGURES IN TALKS

NEW YORK, June 4 (Reuters)—A source close to the Secretary of State, Jeffrey Schelling, said here today that an hour-long meeting between him and Soviet Foreign Minister Valeri Marchenko involved discussions about the situation in South and Central America. According to his source, who refused to be identified, the urgent meeting, which took place at New York's Hotel Pierre, was called by the Secretary of State. Concern was reportedly expressed by Mr. Schelling over a build-up of Cuban forces in the border region separating Guyana and Venezuela.

The two states have been squabbling over territorial claims in the area for several years. According to the source, Mr. Schelling asserted that the

United States was in possession of "solid evidence" of this build-up and would take all measures necessary to achieve the removal of any Cuban armed forces from the disputed area. Mr. Marchenko was said to have denied the charges, calling them "baseless, provocative, and malicious." Neither man had any comment regarding the meeting.

CASTRO DENIES TROOP ALLEGATIONS

HAVANA, June 4—Fidel Castro, Cuba's communist leader, stated categorically that there were no Cuban forces currently based in Guyana, according to ATS, the Swiss news agency. While he expressed "sympathy and solidarity" with the government of Guyana, headed by Sydney Walling, he said that the people of Guyana were fully capable of looking after their own interests.

12

One of the things that Adrienne Calenda most wanted
to see while she was in Venezuela as official guest of the
government was the Angel Falls, situated in the heart of
the Grand Sabana. The highest cataract in the world,
Angel Falls was twenty times higher than Niagara Falls.
Discovered by an intrepid World War I aviator whose
name, appropriately enough, was Jimmy Angel, it was
surrounded by voluptuous green, savannas and flat-
topped buttes.

In ordinary times tens of thousands of tourists would
be ferried into the area by Avensa airlines. But these
were no ordinary times. By order of the interior ministry, all package tours, all tours of any kind, were suspended until further notice. Although no explanation
accompanied the order the local press speculated that it
was because of the growing tensions between Venezuela
and Guyana; beyond Venezuela's Grand Sabana lay the
disputed border with Guyana.

But because Adrienne was a VIP, and because she
was able to employ her looks to advance her aims whenever necessary, her request for a special visit to Angel

Falls was not summarily dismissed. She was told by the Interior Ministry that her request would be studied and she would be informed of the ministry's decision in a few days' time.

But four days had passed and she'd heard nothing. Never one to take no for an answer, she'd tried phoning the relevant officials only to be informed that she would have to be patient, that she would have to understand that the situation in the area was "abnormal."

In Caracas, however, there was no evidence that the situation was in any way abnormal; the city was as fervently alive as ever. The nightclubs were packed and there were still long lines waiting to get into the City Hall discotheque. The population was accustomed to the vitriolic exchanges between their government and Sydney Walling's and it had long since ceased to pay much attention to them. Since the Port of Spain Treaty had expired in June 1982, though—the treaty held the dispute in check for the twelve previous years—the quarrel had continued to get worse. Still, it was Adrienne's sense that nobody actually expected that the war of words would become a war of guns. This general attitude had not changed in spite of a breakdown of the bilateral talks that had been going on since '82 and the more recent collapse of a UN mediation effort.

On the night of June 5 Adrienne was invited to a dinner party at the Caracas home of Julio Arbanez in the wealthy residential district of Altamira. Although most of the other guests were unknown to her, she had no difficulty in making friends with many of them. To the consternation of some of the wives, the men gravitated easily to her side, each trying to outdo the other in displaying the extent of the power he wielded in Venezuela and abroad.

Besides the businessmen, there was also a scattering of politicians present, who daily commuted between the Palacio Miraflores and the Palacio Blanco on the Avenue Urdaneta.

When she mentioned her problem getting permission

to see the famous Angel Falls, no less than three men assured her that they would personally see to it that the situation was speedily rectified. "It is a matter of cutting through the red tape," a man introduced to her as Señor Obarez said.

Asked about the abnormal situation in the border region, Obarez conceded, "It is true. There are some difficulties and, realistically, I would expect these difficulties to increase in the next few weeks."

This man was older than the others, a balding figure who exuded so much confidence that Adrienne judged him to be either extremely powerful or extremely rich, or both. He told her he was an adviser to President Lopez. "Tomorrow I will call you. All the arrangements necessary for your expedition will be completed then. How many will be in your party?"

Adrienne hesitated to say that she planned to go by herself. There were her bodyguards, of course. Since Martinique they'd been unusually scrupulous about keeping her within sight. Even here, at this dinner party, one was stationed in the parlor while his colleague waited restlessly in the car outside. She had no doubt that this man might well be able to elude her guards, but then she would have to contend with him. She didn't think that she would appreciate his company or the complications his company might produce.

"It will be a party of four," she said. "My security staff and a friend."

"A friend?"

"An old and dear friend," she offered, though in truth she had no one in mind for this role.

"Very well. My secretary will give you a call in the morning. And then perhaps when you return from Angel Falls you will do me the honor of having dinner with me and letting me know how the trip went?"

As he said this his eyes traveled down from her face to the rather generous cleavage revealed by the cut of her chiffon dress.

"I would be delighted," she said, whereupon Obarez

gathered up her hand and planted a dry kiss on it.

In a short time, a gray Cadillac limousine, with one bodyguard at the wheel and the other idly smoking a Gauloise in the back seat, was punctually waiting for her in front of the house. In half an hour she was delivered back to her hotel—the Tamanaco—universally regarded as the capital's best. Only those with influence or luck were able to secure accommodations here, since its reputation had spread far beyond the borders of the country.

Adrienne's bodyguards occupied the suite next to hers. She suspected that they had bugged her suite, for how else would they know when she stepped out into the hallway? She had only to open the door and one of them would be there, smiling politely, asking if there was anything he could do for her.

As if that were not enough, her husband found the time to call her from Indonesia practically every night, often ringing at two or three in the morning, then apologizing profusely for awakening her. "I didn't realize what time it was in Caracas," he'd say. The excuse wouldn't wash. She knew that he was very much aware of the time difference; his only concern was to discover whether she was in her hotel room at night. As for whether she was alone in her hotel room, that was a task he had to leave to his security. She wouldn't have been surprised to learn that her husband called them as well to be briefed as to what she had done during the day and whom she had seen.

She assumed that he knew about both Zoccola and Hidalgo, although there was never any hint of his suspicions in his conversation with her on the phone. Nor did he have occasion to repeat his threat, made in the privacy of their home in Jakarta and in hotel rooms around the world, that should she ever leave him or even sleep with another man, he would kill her.

She supposed that he felt he'd so impressed upon her the gravity of any possible unfaithfulness that he needn't do it again now.

She was sure he would be able to make her death look like an accident, and she sometimes pictured him at her funeral, tears flowing from his eyes even as he congratulated himself on the success of his revenge against her.

As she unlocked the door to her hotel room, her guards stood watching her for a moment. Even with her back turned, she felt their eyes boring into her. She had no doubt that if they had not feared her husband's vengeance, they would long ago have tried to rape her.

"Good night," she said sharply.

"Good night, Mrs. Meureudu," they responded in unison, emphasizing the *Mrs.*

Shutting the door behind her, she closed her eyes and breathed deeply before snapping on the lights.

It was then that she saw her visitor.

"My God, what are you doing here?" she exclaimed in a loud whisper.

John Zoccola, seated comfortably on her double bed, gave her a faint smile. "Thought I'd pay you a visit. We never did get a chance to say good-bye in Martinique." She had received communications from him about what had happened to him since they had last met, and now she found herself more concerned about danger to him than herself.

His normally handsome dark features looked wan and drawn and his eyes were sunken. The strain of what he'd been through in the time that had passed since she'd last seen him showed itself even when he smiled. It was a smile that could easily be mistaken for a grimace.

Suddenly recalling that the suite might be bugged, she put a finger to her lips and gestured toward the walls. Zoccola understood immediately, and withdrew into the bathroom.

She followed him. There they continued their conversation while water surged from the taps and the shower nozzle; the white noise produced as a result could not be completely counted on to blot out the sound of their voices, but it was the best that Zoccola could think of under the circumstances. More than likely, her watch-dogs in the next room would assume she was taking a shower and not listen too carefully.

"You're not supposed to be here," she said, almost chiding him. "How did you get in?"

"Wasn't hard," he said. "I persuaded one of the maids to open the door. A little charm, a little money. No problem."

"But you should be in the hospital," she insisted. "Look at you!" She turned him around so that he faced the mirror, which was fast becoming clouded with steam.

"I don't need to be reminded of what I look like," he said, turning back toward her. "I'd much rather look at you."

"Would I be wrong if I thought that you left the hospital without permission?"

"Let's just say I didn't say good-bye to them."

"And what about your friends in the cloak-and-dagger business?"

"No good-bye there either."

"But why? Why would you jeopardize your career and your health?"

"To see you," he said with a ghost of his old charming smile.

She shook her head in wonder. "I knew you were impulsive—"

The steam had begun to fill the bathroom. Zoccola threaded his arms about her waist and pulled her close to him. He kissed her long and hard.

"Well!" she said, drawing away for a moment. "You don't seem to have lost all your strength."

He undid the small pearl buttons that lined the back of her dress. "I've waited a long time for this," he said.

"We should turn off the taps," she suggested.

He didn't give a damn about the taps. The steam continued to build.

He slid the dress off her shoulders and lowered it so it hung from her waist. Her nipples were visible through the black lace of her bra. He gently squeezed the nipple of her right breast between his fingers until it became erect.

A sigh went through her, an airy sound from deep within. He drew off the feather-weight bra, and let it fall lightly to the tile floor.

He sank to his knees and began to cover her breasts and the smooth flat surface of her stomach with kisses. She braced herself against him, leaning back with her eyes closed. When she looked again, she could barely see the dark top of his head through the whorls of steam.

In a moment they were in bed, and as she mounted him, pressing herself against him, he cried out so loudly from the painful wound that she was afraid the bodyguards next door would hear.

They lay still, holding their breath. Seconds later there was a loud rapping at the door.

"Yes, what is it?" Adrienne shouted. Rising from the bed and gathering a nightgown about her, she went to the door and opened it a crack.

It was one of the bodyguards. "I heard a cry," he demanded. "Are you all right?"

She smiled anxiously. "I was just having a bad dream."

He gave her a skeptical look but was evidently satisfied enough that he could return to his own room.

Back in the bed, she discovered that her earlier buoyant mood had disappeared, replaced by anxiety and a feeling that her husband and his henchmen would never stop hounding her.

"I shouldn't have come," Zoccola said in a whisper.

Getting up and seating herself on the edge of the bed she leaned down and said directly into his ear, "It's all right. I'm happy you did."

But after they had later expended their passion for each other, she lay awake for the remainder of the night, her eyes fixed on the door as though expecting the bodyguard to force his way in at any moment. It never happened, though, and eventually, just before dawn, sleep came to her.

In a few hours, Adrienne was jolted awake by the telephone ringing.

As she reached for it, she assumed that it must be Adam. Who else would be calling her this early? Glancing at the sleeping form of Zoccola next to her, she was overcome by a momentary panic. Maybe she was crediting her husband with telepathic powers, but she almost felt as if he already knew of her infidelity, even from far-off Jakarta.

Her fears were groundless. It wasn't her husband calling her; rather, it was a woman who said that she was secretary for Señor Obarez.

At first Adrienne was confused, thinking that the woman had gotten hold of the wrong party. Then she recalled that Señor Obarez was the man she'd met at the dinner the night before. "Oh yes. This is Miss Calenda," she said.

"All the necessary arrangements for your journey to Angel Falls have been made," the secretary told her. "You are scheduled to leave at ten this morning from Maiquetia Airport. Please be at Gate 2 of the Avensa terminal half an hour beforehand."

"Won't I need papers?"

"None are required. If there should be any difficulties you can telephone me and I will see to it that they are straightened out." She then gave her her number.

When Adrienne replaced the receiver, she saw that Zoccola was awake. He still looked pale, but not quite so exhausted.

"I seem to have committed myself to a tour of Angel Falls," she told him after turning up the bedside radio full blast. "I should be back in Caracas in a couple of days," she said apologetically. After spending just one unexpected night with Zoccola, she was reluctant to run out on him again. On the other hand, she couldn't see how he could stay with her undetected even if she should remain on in Caracas.

"I'll go with you," Zoccola said simply.

"You *can't*. It's impossible."

Having survived three machete-wielding assailants in Martinique and slipped out unobserved from Walter Reed in Washington, Zoccola was fairly confident that he could deal with any further difficulties.

"Let me be the judge of that," he assured her.

"What about my watchdogs?"

"I think that they can be made to disappear." Anticipating her reaction, he added, "And in a way that your husband can't hold you responsible for."

She regarded him dubiously.

"I'm going to kidnap you," he explained, smiling broadly.

"For ransom?"

"No. For love."

It had never occurred to him to admit his feelings before, and he suddenly wasn't certain that he should have. He wasn't sure it was what either of them wanted right now.

To all appearances, there was nothing unusual about the manner in which Adrienne conducted herself when she emerged from her room at eight o'clock that morning.

Inevitably, her two bodyguards were waiting for her by the door, and greeted her with curt nods, but they displayed no more reserve than normal toward her. However, because they were so practiced at their occupation it was impossible to determine whether they were on to her or not.

She informed them that they would depart for the airport shortly before nine. In the meantime they would have breakfast in one of the hotel's restaurants. In silence they went down in the elevator together.

When breakfast was concluded, Adrienne asked one of the guards to return to her suite and bring down the few bags she was taking on the trip.

Several minutes passed in silence while she and the other guard waited for him to come back.

"I don't know what's taking him so long," Adrienne said fretfully. She looked at her watch impatiently. "If we don't get going soon we'll never make it to the airport on time."

At her insistence, the second guard rose from the table and announced that he would go upstairs to look for his partner. He refused, however, to allow her to remain by herself, leaving her no other choice but to accompany him.

Noting that the door to her suite was ajar, he extracted a PPK Walther from the holster concealed under his jacket and motioned Adrienne back.

He then kicked the door open, revealing the second guard on the floor, his hands trussed behind him. The man looked like he might be dead but he wasn't. He was unconscious, and his breathing was shallow and when his eyelids were pried open by the other man, his eyes failed to react to the intrusion of light.

Adrienne remained out in the hall as the guard scanned the room warily. He went into the bathroom, but found no one there. As he opened the closets in the main room, he held his weapon as if prepared to fire, but again he found nothing.

"Is he all right?" Adrienne asked from the threshold of the suite, gesturing toward the prostrate figure.

"We should call a doctor," the guard replied in a tense voice as he approached the phone.

At that moment a man bearing an umbrella appeared in the hallway and peered in. "Is something the matter here?" he said quizzically.

If the guard recognized him he gave no sign of it. And the way Zoccola had hiked up the collar of his jacket and tilted his wide-brim hat, it was unlikely that he would have identified him even if his memory did reach back to the day he'd spotted him in Fort-de-France.

The guard stepped away from the phone and ordered

Zoccola to move. "This is none of your business," he warned.

Zoccola made as though he hadn't heard him. Coming in and kneeling by the side of the guard he'd brought down only minutes previously, he pretended to be taking his pulse.

"You have to go now," the guard said sternly, seizing Zoccola's arm.

Adrienne watched this spectacle as though it were imaginary. She fervently hoped that Zoccola knew what he was doing. The sight of the PPK Walther in the guard's hands terrified her, but it was obvious that he regarded Zoccola only as an annoyance, not a threat, and there was no indication that he meant to use the weapon.

As he pulled Zoccola upright, the latter spiked his ankle with the tip of his umbrella. The guard winced and then relaxed his hold enough for Zoccola to free himself.

Still maintaining his pose as an innocent guest who'd just happened by, he quickly apologized in a stilted, formal voice: "I'm sorry. It was an accident, I assure you."

The guard's face expressed great disdain as he growled, "Get out. *Now.*"

Zoccola allowed him to grip his shoulders and steer him in the direction of the door. As he went by Adrienne, he shot her a mischievous look that the guard didn't catch.

No sooner had the guard gotten Zoccola to the door than his grip loosened, and, like a man gone suddenly punch drunk, he wobbled on the balls of his feet.

Adrienne could tell the guard's eyes were losing their focus, for he kept squinting as though having immense difficulty fixing Zoccola in his sight.

The toxin had taken him by such surprise, and with such speed, that he had yet to make the connection between the small wound created by Zoccola's umbrella and what was happening to him now.

Just before he collapsed to the floor, he realized that Zoccola was in some way responsible for his condition, and tried to bring his gun up.

Zoccola sprang to the right just as the collapsing man fired. With its silencer attachment the Walther made very little noise, but a chunk of the wall in the outside corridor exploded into fragments.

Slamming the side of his hand against the guard's arm, Zoccola succeeded in dislodging the gun from his grip. By then the man was too far gone to offer any resistance. He fell back into the room and lay still.

Adrienne had come into the room during the struggle, and now Zoccola closed the door and bound the unconscious guard with the same type of wire he had used on his companion.

"What did you do to them?" Adrienne asked, astonished by the efficiency with which Zoccola had disabled the pair.

"Gave them something that'll keep them out for the next twenty-four hours. When they regain consciousness they'll feel like they've had a dozen martinis each—a terrible hangover and a very hazy memory of how they managed to acquire it."

He and Adrienne dragged the two men into the closet. "I wouldn't want the maids to discover them right away," he said, shutting the closet doors. Now there was nothing in the room to hint at the presence of the two comatose men.

"And what am I going to say when they do regain consciousness and call Adam?" she asked.

"Tomorrow, when they wake up, they'll discover a note demanding a large sum of money for your return. They'll probably want to have a little talk with your friend, Señor Obarez. Naturally he won't be able to tell them anything more than that you went to Angel Falls. When you do come back, you can simply tell them that you escaped your captors.

"They won't believe you, of course. On the other hand, they'll be so relieved that you did come back they

probably won't do anything. I imagine they won't even
report you missing to your husband unless they get
really desperate. And you're not going to be gone that
long.''

Adrienne couldn't dispute his logic, but that didn't
mean she was any the less troubled by the plan.

From Canaima airfield, Adrienne and Zoccola were
conveyed to the park's tourist camp by a tractor-driven
charabanc. From there they would board another plane
the following morning for the final stretch of the journey to Angel Falls.

The camp was situated near the Carrao River, which
led upstream into the jungles of Guyana. Looming over
it was Auyán Tepuy Mountain, whose slopes ran with
water cascading down from the summit.

To their surprise, they discovered that the camp had
been vacated by tourists and was now occupied only by
Venezuelan troops and frontier police.

A lieutenant who couldn't have been much older than
twenty approached them, introducing himself as Luis
Zummullo.

"I was told to expect you," he said, and though his
words welcomed both of them, his eyes were riveted on
Adrienne.

In her olive-green blouse and matching skirt, she provided him with a sight far more intriguing than even the
beauty of Auyán Tepuy Mountain could offer.

"What happened to the tourists?" Adrienne inquired.

Lieutenant Zummullo pulled on his mustache and
shrugged. "All gone. Any day now we expect the fighting to come here." He said this so matter-of-factly that
he might have been reflecting on an unfortunate but in-
evitable change in the weather. "It is only because you
are a friend of Señor Obarez that you are being per-
mitted here."

They were escorted to the only one of the fifty-eight
cabins in the tourist camp that had been left vacant for

VIPs. All the others had been converted into barracks.

They accepted the lieutenant's invitation to dine with him that evening, and all through the meal he feasted as much on Adrienne as on the beefsteak and rice. To Zoccola's questions regarding the proximity of Guyanese and Cuban troops, he seemed to have no answers, only eloquent shrugs.

"Who is to know? I am a soldier, not an intelligence officer," he said time and again.

Lieutenant Zummullo proposed that his guests remain after the meal and share a drink with him—he'd procured a bottle of bogus scotch that he was convinced was the real thing—but his guests, claiming weariness, declined.

No sooner had they reached their cabin, though, than they heard the hollow whine of a shell in the distance, followed an instant later by a deafening roar. They rushed back outside and gazed toward Auyán Tepuy Mountain.

Its slopes were lit by a faint reddish glow.

"Fires," Zoccola said. "They've been set by the explosions. We couldn't hear them before because they're too far away." He surmised that Guyanese and Cuban batteries were in the process of shelling front-line Venezuelan positions, softening them up in anticipation of an all-out assault. He estimated that the tourist camp they were staying in was now forty and fifty miles away from the front.

More shells were descending now. They were coming nearer, landing on this side of the mountain.

At least, Zoccola thought, he no longer had to rely on Lieutenant Zummullo to discover how close the fighting was.

"What are you doing?" Adrienne asked as he got out his microtransmitter. He figured it was time he let Drexell know where he was. He assumed that Drexell would be interested to learn that, in pursuing a woman, he'd managed to find himself a war.

GUYANA AND VENEZUELA IN BORDER CLASH

GEORGETOWN, Guyana, June 7 (Reuters)—Reports reaching here say that units of the Guyanese army—the so-called People's Army—have clashed with forward units of the Venezuelan army in the disputed border region between the two countries. The government of Sydney Walling issued a statement this morning blaming the Venezuelan government for violating Guyanese territorial borders and asserting that "the invaders have been repelled and pushed back." There was no word on how many casualties resulted from the engagement.

VENEZUELA ACCUSES GUYANA IN BORDER INCIDENT

CARACAS, Venezuela, June 7 (Agence France Presse)—A spokesman for the Venezuelan government said that an exchange of artillery fire had occurred in the border region separating Venezuela and Guyana. While reaffirming Venezuela's historical right to five-eighths of Guyanese territory, the spokesman denied that Venezuela had penetrated beyond the international border and said that the government held Guyana responsible for the incident. Skirmishes involving close to 100 troops were said to have taken place throughout last night. Venezuela claimed that four of its men were killed and another 14 wounded in the clash. According to the spokesman, more than twice this number of casualties were inflicted on Guyanese forces. No independent confirmation of this claim could be established.

UN SECRETARY GENERAL CALLS FOR CALM

NEW YORK, June 7 (UPI)—Raoul Hueller, Secretary-General of the United Nations, issued a statement here today calling on both Guyana and Venezuela to refrain from further military activity. Responding to reports that the armed forces of the two countries had engaged in combat, he appealed for a cessation of hostilities and said that he would redouble his efforts to work for a peaceful solution to the border dispute that has been simmering between the countries for decades.

STATE DEPARTMENT HAS NO COMMENT

WASHINGTON, June 7 (AP)—The State Department had no comment today on reports that Venezuela and Guyana were fighting in the jungle between the two countries. Donald Eller, a State Department spokesman, said that information about the conflict was still unavailable. "With so few details at our disposal," he said, "it would be premature to comment. Certainly we wouldn't want to assign blame to either country without knowing all the facts. Of course, if these reports are confirmed, we would have to take another look at the matter."

He stressed that the United States was opposed to the use of arms in circumstances when a diplomatic solution might be available. In answer to questions regarding a possible Cuban involvement in the conflict, Mr. Eller declined to comment. When asked what would happen if Cuban forces were found to have assumed a direct military role, he said that "the consequences would be extremely serious. But at the moment we're dealing in the realm of the hypothetical."

13

JUNE 8,
PUERTO LIMÓN, COSTA RICA

William Drexell had no sooner arrived in Limón, posing as a businessman with sizable investments in the banana trade conducted out of the port city, than he received Zoccola's message from Venezuela. Relieved to finally learn of his whereabouts, he was nonetheless concerned about the uncertain state of his health. Ordinarily he'd have the utmost confidence in Zoccola, but how well he'd be capable of functioning with a recent knife wound in his belly was another question entirely.

Yet he had to admit that he was grateful to have direct information about the Guyanese-Venezuelan conflict.

Ironically, it was Lisker he'd dispatched for the purpose of reporting on the war, and yet Zoccola was much closer to it now.

Still, Lisker, to the rear of Cuban and Guyanese lines, had relayed other information to Triad headquarters that very morning, stating that there'd been a battle between Venezuelan and Cuban forces two nights before —on the sixth. According to his dispatch, only a small contingent of Guyanese had been involved, confirming Drexell's assumption that it was the Cubans rather than the Guyanese who would be doing most of the fighting.

Having installed himself in a Limón hotel, Drexell put

in a call to Hahn and arranged to meet him in Vargas Park at quarter to five in the evening.

At the appointed time and under the baleful gaze of the sloths dangling upside down in the trees, the two met on a secluded bench.

Knowing that Drexell could not abide small talk, Hahn immediately began to tell him what he'd learned since he'd come to Limón. He admitted that while he'd not quite succeeded in pinpointing the Cuban-Soviet staging area, he had a good general idea of where it was. "There's no question it's up north, probably someplace near the coast between the Costa Rican town of Las Palmas and the Nicaraguan border. But where exactly it is I haven't been able to determine."

"What about Hidalgo?"

"I lost him. My contacts here were supposed to be keeping an eye on him, but he somehow vanished. I suspect he disguised himself and walked right past them."

"Well, where does that leave us?"

"Well, you may be surprised to know I've found Mr. Clean."

"Ah," Drexell said in mild surprise. "I thought he was gone for good."

"Not at all. He's right here in Puerto Limón and, in fact, I'm supposed to call him in half an hour."

Maxim Kolnikov—code-named Mr. Clean—had worked for Triad before, supplying information to the Americans during the North African crisis and again during the outbreak of fighting in the Balkans and the Aegean area. As a high-ranking functionary in the GRU, the Soviet military intelligence, he was in an excellent position to collect information of incalculable value to Triad.

In exchange, he demanded not money—although money figured prominently in the arrangement he had with Triad—so much as a constant supply of Western goods: video equipment, tape decks, radios, software, even Rolling Stones and Black Sabbath records; anything, in short, that he could sell at an immense profit on the black market inside the Soviet Union. Moreover, he also had asked Triad for—and received—a ready market for the antiques and old Russian icons he was smuggling out of his country.

While Drexell had approved the original agreement because Kolnikov was such a valuable source of intelligence, he feared the Russian would not last long. Either he would be arrested on charges of spying or of smuggling and profiteering and be executed.

That he continued to occupy such a favored position in the GRU even after he'd begun his illicit trade did not necessarily allay the American's anxiety about him. On the contrary, it heightened it. Drexell had begun to suspect that he was able to survive only because he enjoyed protection from somebody higher up. That in turn might mean that he was a double agent who was feeding Triad with deliberately misleading information.

Then, one day in mid-January Kolnikov had seemed to disappear from sight. He failed to pick up the supply of electronic calculators that had been deposited for him at a drop in Berne. At the same time the information he'd promised regarding Soviet military maneuvers in East Germany never materialized.

Drexell had no choice but to presume him lost. Whether he was a double agent and had been reassigned or whether he'd been exposed and arrested, there was no way of knowing. But he had stopped counting on him as a source of intelligence.

Now Kolnikov had turned up again.

"How did you make contact?" Drexell asked.

"I had him tailed back to his hotel, the Acion, after I saw him meeting with Hidalgo. I thought of having him picked up, but I didn't want to scare him off. So I took the liberty of suggesting a meeting."

"And he agreed?" Drexell asked. Hahn nodded.

Drexell hoped that the Russian could now direct them to the staging area. If, in addition, he could enlighten them as to the Soviet strategy in regard to Guyana, so much the better. For this kind of information Drexell was ready to promise him almost anything. With so little time at Triad's disposal to assemble the guerrilla force in southern Florida and Louisiana, he was hardly about to stand on ceremony. If Kolnikov wanted half of

Triad's contingency funds he'd get it. There would be time to figure out how to make up for the loss later.

As Hahn explained it, the meeting had been arranged for that evening. He and the Russian were to meet in the back row of the Bebedor movie theater.

The Bebedor was showing a Brazilian film, but the print was so bad and the sound so dismal that neither Hahn nor Drexell could tell whether it was a porn film, as it seemed for long stretches to be, or an action film, when it turned to equally long stretches of violence and fake blood.

It wasn't until nearly half of the lunatic action had flickered across the screen that the Russian appeared in the darkness. With a grunt, he lowered himself into the seat next to Hahn and began to dig into a box of peanuts and pop them into this mouth. Hahn introduced Drexell, but Kolnikov continued to ignore them.

"This is a waste of your time," was the first thing he said, in English.

At first Hahn didn't know whether the Russian was referring to the movie, which surely was a waste of time, or to their attempt at using him as a double agent.

The latter turned out to be the case. When he spoke again, Kolnikov said he was afraid that his superior officer in military intelligence—Karel Vladivomivich—had caught on to his duplicity. If that was so, then his career, not to mention his life, was likely in jeopardy.

"If that's the case," Hahn said, "then we can help you to defect."

Kolnikov shook his head. This was evidently not the solution he had in mind. "No. I cannot help you anymore," he declared flatly.

Drexell wasn't convinced. To Hahn he whispered, "He wouldn't be here at all if he wasn't willing to negotiate. Ask him if there's anything we could do that would satisfy him."

Hahn repeated the question.

Kolnikov pretended to think about it, although it was obvious that he knew very well what he wanted Triad to do for him. At last he said, "I wish you to take care of Karel Vladivomivich for me. I will sleep better at nights if he is no longer disturbing me. At night I have bad dreams. In all of these dreams who do I see? Karel Vladivomivich!''

"Are you saying you'd like to see Vladivomivich terminated?" Hahn asked.

Even in the dimness of the movie theater Kolnikov's smile was visible. "Exactly."

"I don't like it," Drexell whispered to Hahn. "If we kill a Soviet agent of Vladivomivich's rank it'll only set off an underground war of attrition. We kill off a GRU man, they kill off a CIA man— It could go on for fucking ever."

Hahn turned to the Russian. "What good would killing him do?" Hahn protested. "Surely *his* superior will find out about your dealings with us if Vladivomivich already knows."

"No, not at all. Karel Vladivomivich is a man who keeps information to himself. He is like a miser hoarding his money. He wishes to have all the credit for arresting me. You kill—sorry, terminate—" he corrected himself with a half-smile, "him now, and it is all over, perfectly solved!"

Drexell began to consider Kolnikov's request seriously. Had he more time to discover where the staging area lay, he would've sent Kolnikov packing, but there wasn't any. Every day the Cubans and Soviets were entrenching themselves more deeply in the Western hemisphere. There was literally no time available to wait for reports from other agents about the location of the Costa Rican staging area.

"Where is Karel Vladivomivich keeping himself these days?" Drexell asked, speaking to the Russian for the first time.

"Georgetown."

This revelation was a bombshell to both of the Americans. By implication, it meant that Vladivomivich was in charge of military intelligence for the combined Cuban-Soviet campaign in Guyana.

Taking him out might very well serve a second purpose of also impeding the progress of the campaign, Drexell realized. Perhaps if the assassination were done with great care, so that the United States would in no way be implicated, it might admirably advance Triad's objectives in the area.

"All right," Drexell said finally to the impassive Russian. "You have yourself a deal."

Kolnikov grunted his satisfaction and rose from the seat. "Tomorrow night, at this hour, we meet at the Osario movie house—the back row, first three seats—and make everything final."

He put special emphasis on the last word.

Once he'd gone, Hahn turned to Drexell and asked him how he intended to realize his end of the bargain.

"I think we'll just have to speak with Mr. Lisker. If he can get out of the jungle and back to Georgetown fast enough, I don't know of any man better qualified to pull off an operation of this kind. Discreet and—"

"Final," Hahn finished for him.

14

James Lisker didn't want to be back in Georgetown. He thought that, all things considered, he preferred the jungle to the rum bars, the stench of mud in the squalid streets, and the choke-and-rob gangs who preyed on the hapless citizens of the place. The only thing that attracted him about returning was the idea of arranging an assassination, and doing it in such a way that no one could link the American government to it.

His orders were to remain quartered in a safe house that was nothing more than an empty flat a dozen blocks from the Pegasus Hotel, until he'd completed his mission.

While it was possible the police were still looking for him, he thought it unlikely; conditions in the city were too chaotic and the government had more political and criminal suspects than it knew what to do with. If he was arrested, it would probably be because someone didn't like his looks rather than because his identity had been uncovered.

If anything, on his arrival Georgetown had been in sorrier-looking shape than when he'd left it ten days before. The debris from the explosions that had destroyed the People's Progressive Party headquarters and portions of the Stabroek Market still hadn't been cleared away. Everywhere there were signs of the martial law in force. Armored personnel carriers with 90mm cannon were everywhere. At all hours of the day and night reconnaissance planes flew overhead, sometimes at an astonishingly low altitude, as if the pilots meant to spy not on the Venezuelans who, after all, were still several hundred miles away, but on the citizens of Georgetown themselves. Detractors of the authoritarian regime of Sydney Walling were convinced that, if given the opportunity, the government men would be more inclined to fight their political opponents in Guyana than the Venezuelans.

When Lisker returned, the *Chronicle* was full of war news. Guyana, the front-page stories proclaimed, was victorious on all fronts, securing their border areas and advancing into Venezuelan territory. A huge battle was reported in the interior; hundreds of Venezuelans, the paper said, had been either killed or wounded, but with only minimal casualties on the Guyanese side. No mention was made of any Cuban involvement.

It was all propaganda, of course, intended to bolster the people's confidence. Lisker had just been in the very place where the battle was said to have occurred—and on the very day the *Chronicle* reported it—but he'd not heard a single shot fired. There were 6,000 people living between the coastal area and the Venezuelan border, impoverished Indians for the most part who herded cattle and did their best to make the inhospitable earth yield crops. None of the Indians he'd spoken to knew of any fighting either.

At the same time the *Chronicle* fulminated against the Americans, the Venezuelans, and unnamed imperialist elements, it also called upon all "peace-loving Guyanese citizens" to thank the Cubans and the Russians for their "moral support." The Brazilians were also extolled for having sold Guyana many of the armored personnel carriers and reconnaissance planes now being put to use against the Venezuelans.

Lisker had not been told exactly why Karel Vladivomivich was supposed to be killed. The instructions he received from Drexell specified only that the assassination should be carried out as soon as feasible, keeping in mind the need for absolute security.

Absolute security meant that he would have to act on his own. With Colin Harris back in the United States enjoying a well-earned rest, his contacts in the capital consisted only of some men who should long ago have come in from the cold—or in this case, from the heat and the rain. They were burned-out cases and not to be trusted with responsibilities any more important than running errands and delivering encoded messages.

Naturally, the best way to secure Vladivomivich's death was to make it look like an accident. But the press of time didn't allow him to contrive such an elegant solution. Moreover, he was under the same constraints as everybody else in the capital, having to contend with the heightened military presence on the streets as well as martial law and a dusk-to-dawn curfew.

About the only aspect of the operation that Lisker found relatively easy was determining the GRU commander's whereabouts. Vladivomivich held a position as a second-ranked military attaché in the Soviet Embassy, recently relocated to a well-guarded compound a few blocks away from the Magistrates Court. Vladivomivich's was a transparent cover that failed to conceal from anyone his role as coordinator of all military intelligence from the front.

But to penetrate the compound was an impossibility; in addition to the local police who guarded the main gates there were several Russian sentries posted right behind the fence. Equipped with AKS-74's, clad in incongruously heavy gray overcoats, they stood miserably in the constant downpours, observing the passage of Guyanese and Soviet officials in and out of the Embassy.

The Embassy itself was monolithic, with white stucco walls and few windows; it was nearly as tall as the spire of St. George's Cathedral. Six months ago the building wasn't there, and its hasty erection attested to the importance the Guyanese government attached to its broadening relationship with Moscow.

But in deference to the sensibilities of the host government, the Soviet functionaries would from time to time leave the compound and travel by limousine—patriotically, they relied on Zim's imported from home—to the government ministries not more than a few blocks away.

From the reports he'd heard, Lisker was given to understand that these visits were a daily occurrence, their frequency hinting at the control the Soviets wielded over Sydney Walling's regime. The way things were developing it might not be too long before the Soviets enjoyed the same power here in Georgetown that they did in Kabul, Afghanistan.

Among those who paid these courtesy calls on Sydney Walling and his coterie of ministers was Karel Vladivomivich. A pale, stooped figure, with sunken eyes and thin dry lips, Vladivomivich did not look like the sort of person who would occupy such an important role in the affairs of state, but there was no mistaking him. The photographs, brought to Lisker by special carrier from Washington, were clear enough to make the identification without any trouble. One had been taken on November 7, the anniversary of the Russian Revolution, and showed him on the reviewing stand atop Lenin's Mausoleum in Red Square. He was flanked on one side by Valeri Marchenko, the Foreign Minister, and on the other by the former head of the KGB and one of the most influential power brokers in the Politburo. It was obvious that he mattered greatly in the scheme of things.

As Lisker watched the Russian leave the compound early on the morning of June 9, it occurred to Lisker that the most expeditious way of killing Vladivomivich was to do it while he was with some of his Guyanese friends. If it appeared to be an attack directed at Sydney Walling's regime, an attack which a Soviet official just happened to be in the middle of, then it would be much harder for Moscow to call the Americans to account for it.

Along with the photographs, Lisker had received information necessary to carrying out the assassination.

Inasmuch as he was a foreigner working on his own, it was vital that he have help from the outside. For an operation of this scale, Drexell had decided to call upon the now-outlawed People's Progressive Party that had recently been defeated twice—once, by fraud at the polls, a second time, by violence at the barricades.

A single phone call composed of one cryptic message ("Greetings from Gaylord") was all that was required for Lisker to set things in motion.

Four hours later, in the middle of the afternoon, Lisker traveled by bus into one of the poorer sections of the city where the houses were raised above the mud on ten-foot stilts.

The house he was looking for was slightly apart from the others, and right by an open sewer that released a stench foul enough to overpower a horse.

The three men waiting for him all wore ski masks and referred to themselves by code names. One asked to be called Jomo, the second Ptolemy, the third David. The first man was black, the others East Indian.

As they talked, babies howled outside, dogs barked furiously, and mothers screamed curses at their undisciplined children, making a raucous counterpoint to the measured tone of their conversation.

Lisker briefly outlined the plan he had provisionally drawn up. "I've learned from our people close to the government that Deputy Minister Virgil Reade is to meet with a Soviet delegation this evening at seven o'clock at the studios of the Guyanese Broadcasting System," he began.

"Wait a minute," Ptolemy interrupted him. "What are you saying about this evening?"

"That's when the attack must take place," he replied.

There was a stunned stilence from the others.

"There's hardly any time," protested Jomo. "We cannot do something like this on such short notice."

"I believe you can."

"But we were not told that there was such urgency," Ptolemy stressed.

"It gives us no chance to betray each other," Lisker said. "From now on we will be together. That way no one will start having second thoughts and decide to call the police.''

"Just the four of us?'' David asked dubiously.

"Just the four of us. I'll share the same risks as you.''

"I don't like it,'' Ptolemy muttered.

"You will when you hear what I'm paying you. And I'm not just talking about cash.''

"What else?'' Jomo asked.

"Arms. A small arsenal that will be delivered to you on completion of the assignment.''

That seemed to change things. Lisker could sense that the atmosphere had been made more receptive by this offer.

"Who are you working for?'' Ptolemy asked. "The British? The Americans?''

Ptolemy was still reluctant to place too much faith in him.

"Whatever I tell you, you wouldn't believe me, would you? I'll show you the cash and I'll show you a sampling of the arms, and you will see that they are very real. Who I happen to be employed by is immaterial.''

"You will excuse us for a moment,'' said Jomo.

The three then retired into the other room and conferred in whispers. After a while they emerged. "All right,'' Ptolemy told him. "We have agreed that we will do this thing for you. When do we start?''

"Why not right now?'' Lisker said.

Now that he had secured the needed manpower, he had one more resource to get hold of—the arms to dispatch Vladivomivich to a better world.

According to the information brought to him by the Triad courier, a small but well-equipped stash of hand-held rocket and grenade launchers, automatic weapons, explosives, and plastique was to be found in a suburb of Georgetown. Lisker had been given the directions to it, and he only hoped no one had gotten to it first. Given the state of affairs in Guyana, a supply of weapons like this would be more sought after than gold.

Ptolemy offered to drive to the arsenal, although this meant that he would have to abandon his ski mask. Since he had decided, however grudgingly, that Lisker could be counted on, he signaled that his companions should do likewise.

The car Ptolemy owned was a big red Buick, vintage 1971. It was battered and in need of substantial repair, and it made its way with difficulty through the narrow streets. Lisker had earlier slid down in the back seat to keep out of sight; a single white man, an obvious foreigner, would be sure to attract attention were he to be spotted in the company of locals.

The drive into the Georgetown suburbs went without incident. It was still two hours before six and those police who witnessed the Buick's passage no doubt assumed that its occupants were in a hurry to get home before the curfew. They continued out on the road away from the city, along the Atlantic seawall. Slogans in strident colors were emblazoned on practically every square inch of it. "WALLING IS OUR SAVIOR!" one declared. "THE NPC WILL LIVE FOREVER!" another said, referring to the National People's Congress, which was now the only legal party in existence.

The landscape they had to pass through was unrelievedly bleak. Cowsheds and derelict water towers, ramshackle houses and emaciated cattle were all that one could see for miles on end. Beyond the seawall the ocean extended to the horizon, a brackish color of brown under sullen skies.

Shortly after five Lisker directed them off the road. Not far away, among a cluster of abandoned structures opposite the seawall, some of which consisted of nothing more than the foundation walls, he found half the arsenal. The other half, according to Harris' message, lay concealed a short distance away. After Ptolemy and his friends had proved themselves in the assault to come, Lisker would reveal its whereabouts to them. For now they would have to settle for the Kalashnikovs and the pair of rockets he was distributing to them.

Their expressions indicated that they were beginning to look upon their mission with far more enthusiasm than they'd displayed earlier. Fondling the weapons they'd just received, they had the rapturous air of men who had just come into an unexpected inheritance.

The drive back into the city was no more eventful than the one out, again because the police probably decided that they were simply on their way home before the curfew, now just forty-five minutes from taking effect.

Lisker knew that the difficult part came next, when they would have to move in the streets in violation of the law.

Storing the larger armaments in the trunk, they parked the Buick two blocks away from the studios of the Guyanese Broadcasting System. Predictably, the security presence was extremely high, given the sensitive nature of this installation. In the event of a revolution or a coup, the studios would be among the first targets to be seized.

The plan Lisker was following had been devised by Triad, but it was only skeletal in nature; it called for a great deal of improvising on his part. According to intelligence gathered in Washington and in Puerto Limón, Vladivomivich would be present at the station that evening for a half-hour while Deputy Minister Virgil Reade delivered a speech to the nation.

By 7:35, or 7:40 at the latest, Vladivomivich and Reade would leave the studios, and that's when the attack would be launched, first with rockets, then with automatic fire. As far as Lisker's companions knew all the victims would be Guyanese. Lisker hoped the Russian would be killed outright by detonating rockets but if he did survive these, Lisker would make sure to take him out in the mopping-up operation.

Until the time for the attack, Lisker and his fellow conspirators would wait in a rug shop, a block away from the station, lent to them by a PPP sympathizer. The shop was shuttered in front, but had the convenience of a rear exit that was seldom used and unlikely to be noticed by a passing patrol.

The time weighed heavily on them as they waited. There was nothing to do in the darkened confines of the shop, which smelled of wool and dust. Ptolemy, Jomo, and David kept an almost religious silence, eyeing Lisker warily as though they feared that, even at this juncture, he might still betray them. Once at six o'clock, then again at a quarter to seven, they heard the sound of footsteps outside the shuttered facade of the shop. It could only be the police and army squads walking the streets at this hour, and the heavy tattoo of their boots against the pavement did nothing to calm their nerves.

At twenty past seven, Lisker struck a match, signalling them to move out.

They left by a rear door. Stealthily, keeping as close as possible to the shadows of the walls, they proceeded to the Buick.

At the car they were alerted to the sudden glimmer of headlights just up ahead. They dropped to the sidewalk, concealing themselves under the car moments before an armored personnel carrier came into view. The carrier passed them and continued up the street. They didn't dare abandon their cover until the rumble of its motor could no longer be heard.

Quickly opening the car trunk, they extracted the rocket launchers and raced the two blocks separating them from the building housing the Guyanese Broadcasting System.

The time was 7:31.

Karel Vladivomivich was growing impatient. He did not understand English well and he found it tedious to sit and watch Virgil Reade's televised address about the conflict with Venezuela. With his aides, he waited in a room for VIP's adjoining the main studio, his hands clasped in his lap like an obedient child. His principal aide, who also served as an interpreter, sat in silence at his side.

Vladivomivich did not stand when Virgil Reade came out to greet him. The Russian was accustomed to being called arrogant; in fact, he regarded it as a compliment. In his position, he believed it to be absolutely necessary to create an intimidating presence.

Reade frowned for a moment, then strode forward to shake his hand.

"I think it went over very well," the Guyanese official said, lighting a cigarette. "With the war going in our favor even the dissidents are quiet."

"Dissidents may be quiet," the Russian noted, "but they are always plotting. You are not doing enough to suppress the opposition. While we achieve success on the front lines, we could find ourselves stabbed in the back here in the capital."

Reade shook his head. This was not what he wanted to hear. "I think you are exaggerating. In any case, this is something we can take up at the cabinet meeting tonight. I assure you that Mr. Walling is every bit as anxious as you to eliminate any saboteurs and enemy agents as may exist."

Vladivomivich looked doubtful. While he would never say so for fear of jeopardizing his future career, he believed that Stalin knew what he was doing when he sent thousands upon thousands to the gulags. Enemies were everywhere, and it was dangerous to rest for even a moment lest they gain the upper hand.

Together Reade and Vladivomivich proceeded to the lobby where they were joined by operatives of the GRU and a guard composed of the People's Army.

At the exit, a pair of Guyanese soldiers saluted smartly as the officials filed out.

Three limousines had drawn up immediately in front of the station building. Two of them were of American make: a 1976 Seville and a 1978 Cadillac. One, belonging to the Soviet Embassy, was a 1983 Zim. All of them had tinted windows.

It was a distance of only forty or fifty feet from the doors of the studios to where the cars were parked, their motors idling.

Lisker and his three Guyanese allies were in the entrance to an alley half a block away from the studio building at the moment Vladivomivich, Reade, and their retinues emerged.

Ptolemy raised the rocket launcher to his shoulder and prepared to fire it directly at the building. Lisker, Jomo, and David took up positions behind him. Just as

Ptolemy stepped out into the street and discharged the rocket a police patrol on a routine surveillance mission spotted them from down the street.

The police immediately opened fire, hitting Ptolemy several times. But the rocket had already gone soaring over the street and impacted against one of the upper floors of the television studios. With a concussive roar and a sheet of flames, the facade of the building fell away, raining burning debris on the Soviet-Guyanese party about to get into the limousines.

From what Lisker could see, several people had fallen, although he couldn't tell whether they were seriously hurt or not. A policeman on a motorcycle just behind the three idling cars had been catapulted from his seat by the force of the blast and lay immobile on the road, blood oozing from his ears. The windows of the limousines had been shattered or else torn completely from their housings.

But there was no opportunity to assess the damage the explosion had caused, not with the fire directed at them from the patrol approaching from down the street.

Ptolemy was critically wounded; blood covered him so copiously that there was no way to figure out where exactly he'd been hit. He thrashed violently, crying out in pain, but he was so exposed to enemy fire that the others couldn't get to him.

With darkness as their only cover, Lisker, Jomo, and David returned the patrol's fire. In the growing darkness it was difficult to discern how many men they confronted, but Lisker judged them to be no more than five.

Taking a live hand grenade from the cache, he hurled it across the street at the nearing patrol. The detonation was followed by an agonizing scream.

Now Lisker and his two companions rushed into the street in the direction of the studio building. But not all the opposition had been taken out by the grenade. At least one member of the patrol had survived. Machine gun fire tore into David from behind, opening the back of his head. He seemed to leap into the air, then toppled over.

Of the three limousines, only the Zim seemed to be functional. Its driver was trying to move it away from the curb. Lisker could glimpse his face, bloody from the cut glass, through the blasted window. Getting a clear shot with his FN Browning, he shot the driver in the temple and the man's head came down hard on the steering wheel, setting off the horn.

In the distance sirens were wailing as emergency vehicles raced to the site of the demolished building. Soldiers and police were running back and forth, shouting orders and, occasionally, shooting into the air. But it was apparent that no one was aware of where the assault was coming from.

Jomo, heedless of his own safety, took up a position between the Seville and the Cadillac and began firing at random at anyone he saw, including those still sprawled out on the ground for safety.

Lisker remained partly concealed behind the Zim, trying to pick out Vladivomivich. But it was Virgil Reade he saw first; he recognized him from pictures he'd seen on wall posters. The man appeared disoriented. He looked about him, but seemed incapable of making up his mind what he should do. When he turned around so that Lisker had a full view of him, it was obvious why he was so confused. His belly had been blown open and he was so traumatized that all he could do was walk a few paces one way, then a few paces back. He might have continued to do this longer if Jomo hadn't cut him down with a well-directed shot into his chest.

Reade staggered, tumbling down into the shards of glass covering the ground. It was obvious that the deputy minister was dead.

An instant later Jomo himself was cut down.

The deaths of Ptolemy, David, and Jomo—strangers to Lisker until that afternoon—were regrettable, but they weren't without benefit. The presence of the corpses of known supporters of the opposition party would provide the government with sufficient evidence to implicate the PPP. Even the Soviets would be inclined to agree that they were to blame rather than the Americans.

Of course, that supposed that he, too, would not be found among the dead.

A pale haze of smoke lingering in the aftermath of the explosion still hung in the air, impairing visibility.

Despite his heightened awareness during the battle, Lisker was almost taken by surprise when Vladivomivich finally showed up. As he'd hoped, the Russian had decided to go immediately to his car. The horn was still blaring, indicating to the Russian that something was wrong.

As he approached the limousine, Vladivomivich held a gun in his hand, but because Lisker was hunkered down on the other side of the Zim, the other man had no way to anticipate the danger he posed. Lisker noticed that he was dragging his left leg, the pants ripped and soaked with blood.

Six or seven feet from the limousine he paused. Lisker assumed he'd caught sight of the dead driver through the collapsed windshield. At the same moment he hesitated, Lisker raised himself erect and shot him twice. The Russian sustained two wounds in the chest, both of them equally fatal.

He was thrown back against the trunk of the disabled Cadillac and lay outstretched on it while he bled to death.

Soldiers, alerted to the gun reports, turned and began to fire on and around the Zim, but there was no longer anyone there to shoot at. Lisker had vanished into the darkness of the Georgetown night.

15

Although nominally a member of the cabinet, Walter Payton, the U.S. representative to the United Nations, was seldom let in on the real intentions of his own government. A former businessman and onetime college president, he was a man whose gracious manners and bearing reflected his great wealth.

He believed in noblesse oblige; his philanthropical bequests were constantly in the news; his most recent was a $1 million donation to the college he'd once headed, to be used for a chair in international studies.

Soft-spoken and possessed of an erudition that some thought wasn't all that desirable in a diplomat, Payton at sixty-six was highly respected in the body that he served and almost entirely ignored by the administration which had appointed him to his present position.

Consequently, he had no way of knowing that one of his government's own agents had just engineered the assassination of a high-ranking Soviet military intelligence official in Georgetown, Guyana. Nor did he realize that this very questionable act was perpetrated to save the neck of a Soviet double agent in Puerto Limón, Costa

Rica. And most certainly he was ignorant of the administration's secret plan—now being carried out by Triad —to employ a clandestine guerrilla force against a Cuban-Soviet staging area in the northern wastes of Costa Rica. Had he been aware of such risky maneuverings, he would have been appalled and probably quit his post.

Adlai Stevenson, during the Bay of Pigs invasion, had been misled by the Kennedy administration he represented in the UN, and had vigorously denied that the U.S. was in any way responsible for the abortive effort to overthrow Castro's regime. Unknown to him, Walter Payton was in danger of being caught in a similar situation.

In spite of a bad cold that had clogged his nose and subjected him to a low-grade fever, he still felt compelled to appear before the Security Council at an urgent session scheduled for four o'clock this afternoon to take up the matter of the widening escalation of the conflict between Venezuela and Guyana.

Both countries had demanded the session. Each, now unexpectedly, was accusing the other of having launched the war and each expected to be supported by the community of nations in the debate that would inevitably ensue.

The irony of the situation was that nobody could say for certain just what was going on in the interior; there were varying accounts as to both the extent of the clashes and the numbers of troops involved. Because of the area's inaccessibility, at this point one country's claims had practically as much validity as the other's.

Although Payton had been shut out of the secret deliberations going on in the White House, he had been provided with some information which was otherwise unavailable to the public, most of it derived from CIA and NSA sources. The most accurate reports owed their origin to a spy plane known as the SR-71, developed by the same people responsible for the controversial U-2 plane.

An astonishing piece of machinery, the SR-71 could

fly at altitudes in excess of 80,000 feet and fast enough to traverse the distance between New York and Los Angeles in an hour.

The photographs the spy plane had come back with had proven better than the satellite reconnaissance, and while they were not quite as clear as National Security Agency photo analysts would have liked, they did reveal that combined Guyanese and Cuban forces were making significant headway in the fighting, crossing the border into Venezuela at several points. Units of the Venezuelan army had fallen back to defensive positions just east of the Guyana Highlands—Venezuelan territory, in spite of the name. Whether any Soviet troops were directly involved in the fighting the analysts were unable to tell.

Up until that morning, authorities in Caracas had maintained that their forces were repelling the enemy and that it was expected that a drive on Guyana itself would presently be initiated to regain the parts of Guyanese territory that Venezuela had always claimed for itself. Instigated by Venezuela, relations between the two countries had been broken off the night before.

But the Venezuelan state radio was now accusing the Cubans of being directly involved in the war, and for the first time since hostilities began, it was now saying that the Cubans were doing the fighting for the Guyanese. The suggestion that Cuban troops were acting as mercenaries might have been made to prepare the Venezuelan population for the worst. If the government in Caracas was forced to acknowledge defeat on the battlefield, then it wanted it known that it was the Cubans, not the Guyanese, who had managed to best them.

Such was the state of affairs in the region when the Security Council convened, twenty minutes later than scheduled. The reason for the delay was last-minute haggling over the working of a Peruvian-sponsored resolution calling on the immediate cessation of hostilities and a mutual withdrawal to internationally recognized frontiers. The resolution made no attempt to lay the blame with either party to the conflict, as this was the only way to get it passed.

That part of the resolution was bland enough; it was the second paragraph that was the subject of acrimony.

It read in full: "The Security Council further calls upon all outside forces to refrain from aggravating tensions in the border area between Guyana and Venezuela."

While the resolution did not specify which outside forces it meant, the implication was clear: since no one was accusing Venezuela of relying on third-party help, it could only be referring to Guyana.

The United States supported the resolution in toto, but Guyana, with backing from Brazil, one of its main arms suppliers, as well as from Cuba, the Soviet Union, the Eastern Bloc, and several Third World states holding temporary seats on the Security Council, opposed the second paragraph.

Although private negotiations in the hallways of the UN had been continuing since that morning, by the time delegates gathered there was no indication that any compromise had been reached. In fact, the opposing parties were farther from agreement than ever.

A second resolution, sponsored by Poland, was also being circulated. This resolution demanded an immediate withdrawal of Venezuelan forces from Guyana and called upon the Secretary-General to form a fact-finding committee to investigate that country's "territorial aggrandizement."

As the U.S. would automatically veto it, this second resolution had no chance of passing. Payton recognized it as a propaganda ploy, a gesture by the Soviets to show their support of Guyana, a country that might soon become one of their client states.

While neither Guyana nor Venezuela occupied a place on the Security Council at this time, both countries, because they were parties to the conflict under debate, were invited to attend the session and address the body.

The delegate from Guyana—a balding, overweight

man with bad eyesight—was asked to speak first. Not unexpectedly, he chose to denounce Venezuela and demand an end to what he called an unprovoked invasion against his country. "It is well known," he said, "that since the termination of the Port of Spain Treaty, Venezuela has expressed its intentions of seizing five-eighths of our country and that it has continually, and arrogantly, rejected all efforts to reach a peaceful solution."

In addition, he said that he held the United States responsible for encouraging Venezuela's imperialist designs.

The delegate from Venezuela—a much younger man who had once served as ambassador to the United States —charged that it was Guyana which had opened the hostilities to divert the attention of its own people from the desperate economic plight into which the country had fallen. He raised the subject of foreign intervention, but did not mention Cuba or the Soviet Union by name.

It was left to Payton to do that. When he took the floor it was to declare that the United States consistently sought a peaceful solution to international conflicts, and it viewed the present situation in the border region as an especially dangerous one.

"What we are witnessing is not some obscure, localized war over a mass of jungle unknown to most of the world. Rather, we are seeing a serious border dispute being exploited by forces outside the hemisphere to advance their own malevolent aims."

Directing his gaze at the Soviet delegation, he continued, "I am not going to beat about the bush. I think that all the delegates are very well aware of to whom I am referring. The United States has incontrovertible evidence that Cuban troops are actively engaged in the fighting now occurring between Guyana and Venezuela. It is an established fact that it is these troops, not units of the Guyanese armed forces, that are responsible for prolonging this war. The denials issued by the Georgetown government, that no foreign troops are involved, are absurd."

He thereupon instructed his aides to mount half a dozen photographs on a mobile cork board wheeled in for the occasion. All but two of the photographs had been recorded by the SR-71's camera equipment; the remaining two were taken on the ground by James Lisker, although Payton was not aware of their source.

Although only those delegates seated closest to the photographs were capable of seeing them clearly, the purpose of this demonstration was less to convince the members of the Security Council—whose minds were for the most part already made up—than to capture the attention of the international press in a way that most sessions of the Security Council could not.

Using a pointer, Payton described each photograph, indicating Soviet-built BTR personnel carriers, Soviet-built Hind helicopters, Soviet-built amphibious equipment, and Soviet-built T-55 tanks.

Impressive as this evidence was, Payton recognized that a mere enumeration of military equipment in Guyana did not in itself constitute proof of Cuban involvement. While troops could be made out in the two photographs Lisker had taken, who was to say that they were Cuban and not Guyanese? Nonetheless, he declared categorically that Cuban troops were directly engaged and had, in violation of all the relevant international accords, crossed the Venezuelan border. "There can be no doubt," he said, "that this constitutes an invasion for the purpose of territorial aggrandizement."

However, Payton deliberately refrained from accusing the Soviet Union of introducing its own forces into the area. Instead he contented himself with a more general indictment, asserting, "It is no secret to anybody in this chamber that the Cubans do not act except at the Kremlin's behest. Having secured a base on the island of Cuba in 1959, the U.S.S.R. has for the last two and a half decades followed a policy of sowing discord and death throughout the Caribbean basin. Encouraging insurgencies in Central America, the U.S.S.R. has now set its sights on South America, choosing an impoverished totalitarian state where the people do not have a say in their own government as its next base of operations. Through the Organization of American States, the United States, together with the free nations of the Western Hemisphere, will, I assure you, act decisively to end this flagrant violation of the security and peace for which the U.S.S.R. and its client, communist Cuba, will be held completely responsible.

"The United States therefore appeals to the United Nations to take whatever measures are necessary to end this aggression and bring this unhappy conflict to a close."

His remarks were greeted by applause from delegations friendly to the United States, but fully half of those gathered in the room reacted only with stony silence.

Valeri Marchenko, the Soviet Foreign Minister, was acting as the head of his delegation, and he was given the right to respond to Payton's statement.

An imposing man, built like a peasant, with deep-set eyes and a rugged countenance, he slipped a pair of glasses on and riffled through some documents on his desk before addressing the Security Council.

"The insinuations that have just been made by the representative of the United States," he began, "are baseless and reprehensible, an insult to the intelligence of all peace-loving peoples. There is absolutely no truth to the ill-considered remarks we have just listened to. The U.S.S.R. respects the rights of all nations to live in peace and does not interfere with their internal affairs.

"On the other hand, the U.S.S.R. supports all movements of national liberation aimed at restoring justice and security to their lands. When reactionary and imperialist forces challenge us, we will not hesitate to meet that challenge. The people of Guyana have made their choice and democratically elected a man to lead them. This man is well known to you. He is a heroic figure in his own country, a socialist who intends to protect his country from antidemocratic elements which are guided by imperialist and corporate interests in the United States. This man is Sydney Walling.

"Time and again the U.S.S.R. has announced its support for the people of Guyana and for their leaders. We would be remiss if we did not come to the aid of the Guyanese in their time of need. But you have only to listen to Prime Minister Walling to know that the Guyanese are capable of defending themselves against the unprovoked aggression directed by the Venezuelan government with the backing of the United States.

"Accordingly, the U.S.S.R. has not, and will not, intervene in the conflict. But neither will the U.S.S.R. or any other socialist country stand by and not render to the Guyanese people the moral and strategic support that are required to repel the aggression. For that reason we will continue to look with favor on any requests for matériel assistance that may be presented to us by the government of the sovereign state of Guyana. This is our right, this is our obligation.

"But I must also warn the United States and the puppet government that currently occupies power in Caracas that the U.S.S.R. cannot allow this aggressive war to continue. We demand that all hostile forces pull back from any Guyanese territory and that an international peace-keeping force be dispatched to the area to insure that Guyanese territorial sovereignty is never again violated. Should the imperialist powers persist in their folly, the U.S.S.R. will respond firmly and decisively. Make no mistake of this."

The Foreign Minister's statement was along the lines that Payton, and indeed most of the other delegates, had been expecting. It was interesting only in that he refrained from saying how the Soviet Union would react should the conflict continue. His restraint was probably due to the fact that the old men in the Kremlin had yet to figure out what they would do in such a case.

Ironically, while Marchenko was calling for Venezuela to withdraw its troops from Guyana, those troops were being driven out, back across their own border. If anything, the call should now have been for the Guyanese and their Cuban mercenaries to be withdrawn from Venezuelan territory. Marchenko was undoubtedly as much aware of what was actually occurring between the two warring states as Payton was—maybe more so, given the numbers of Cuban troops and Soviet advisers in Guyana. At the moment he was speaking only for public consumption; the very last thing that the Soviet Union wanted was an international peace-keeping force in the area, not so long as the Guyanese and the Cubans were gaining the advantages they were.

CUBAN INVOLVEMENT PROVEN,
CARACAS SAYS

Special to the New York Times

CARACAS, June 11—Four Cuban soldiers, captured in the Guyana Highlands of Venezuela by
Venezuelan forces, were presented to the public on
nationwide television last night. The four Cubans,
all said to be in the infantry, were taken after a battle in which ten Cubans and six Venezuelans were
reportedly killed. The battle, according to a spokesman for the defense ministry, occurred on the
Venezuelan side of the border, approximately fifty
miles from the disputed frontier between Venezuela
and Guyana. The captured men appeared in good
condition although one wore an arm in a sling, evidently the result of a shrapnel wound.

One of the Cubans read from a statement, declaring that he and his companions had been part
of a large force, numbering 4 to 5,000, that had
been flown in to Guyana to aid that country in its
war with Venezuela. He said that until recently he
had served with the 15,000-man contingent of
Cuban forces based in Angola. He added that he
and approximately 500 other soldiers had been
transported by ship from Angola to a base on the
coast of Central America. He said that neither he
nor his companions were certain of the exact location. He was led to believe that the base was somewhere in Nicaragua, whose Sandinista government
has expressed sympathy for the policies of Fidel
Castro's government.

The Cuban said that he and the other captured
men had been well treated by the Venezuelan army
and that their only wish was to return home to their
families. "We have been away much too long," he
said.

The public display of the Cubans was meant to
underscore Venezuela's contention that much of

the fighting is being conducted by Cubans, not Guyanese.

The war, which broke out earlier this month, culminates years of unsuccessful negotiations over the demarcation of the border between the two countries. Venezuela has repeatedly asserted that five-eighths of Guyana should be turned over to it.

16

JUNE 16,
THE GUYANA HIGHLANDS
OF VENEZUELA

In the five days since Zoccola and Adrienne had come to
the tourist camp on the banks of the Carrao River, the
war had come increasingly closer. Battles were now raging less than ten miles away and, because of the critical
nature of the situation, the commander of the Venezuelan forces in the area had decided to pull out.

It fell to Lieutenant Luis Zummullo to deal with his
American visitors.

"You have had a good time here, no? Very good!" he
said as he met with them outside their cabin.

And the truth was that, even with the proximity of the
war and the shelling which went on day and night and
a few miles upriver, they had had a good time, like a
couple on their honeymoon. There had never been any
question of Adrienne's visiting Angel Falls, as the area
around the falls was off limits to civilians. So they'd remained on in the tourist camp, spending all their time
together.

During that period Zoccola had made three phone
calls back to Caracas, pretending to be one of Adrienne's kidnappers. His demands had grown more pre-

posterous with each call to insure there would be no possible way the bodyguards could fulfill them.

But now, with their forced departure, it appeared as though Adrienne would have to "escape" her kidnapper whether she wanted to or not.

"We are evacuating by airlift any personnel not required on the battlefield," Lieutenant Zummullo announced. Gazing up at the sun, which was almost at its zenith, he said that they should be ready by midafternoon, when the transport plane was scheduled to arrive.

"And what about you, lieutenant?" Zoccola asked.

"I stay with my unit," he replied proudly. "We are making first a reconnaissance mission, then we are making a strategic withdrawal to more defensive lines fifteen kilometers from here."

"Would it be possible for me to accompany you?"

Adrienne gave him a questioning look. She'd expected Zoccola to return to Caracas with her.

The lieutenant seemed no less surprised.

With a shrug he said, "It is your life, señor. If you would like, you can come with us, but it will be tough going."

Alone inside the cabin a few minutes later, Adrienne reproached him violently. "You're not well, John. It's madness to go out there. What can you possibly hope to gain by it?"

"I'm the only person Triad has on the ground in the war zone," he replied. "I can provide Drexell with information that he's never going to get from satellite photos or broadcasts coming out of Georgetown or Caracas."

Adrienne shook her head, obviously unconvinced. "That's not the real reason and you know it. You're trying to prove something, to yourself or to your mysterious friend Drexell."

Zoccola realized he'd confided more in her than he'd meant to. Not enough so that she knew anything important about Triad or its operations—nothing, certainly, that would compromise his position—but she now had a much better idea of what he did than she had on the day they'd first arrived here.

"Prove what?" he demanded, angrier at himself than he was at her because he sensed that she was right.

"Prove that you can make up for running out on him for the sake of a woman."

He refused to pursue the argument further. "I'm going and that's it. This discussion is finished."

But she wasn't through. "I think I know why you spent so much time befriending Luis these last few days," she said thoughtfully. "You were planning on this venture all along, weren't you? You figured if he liked you, he'd take you with him without looking too deeply into your credentials."

"You wouldn't be thinking of telling him that I'm not what I seem, would you?"

"I'd love to because it might be the only way to save your ass. But I won't. I have no real claims on you," she said frankly.

Despite her attempt at calm, she was breathing hard. Inside, she was upset and hurt because he hadn't told her of his plans, and now she was worried that in the next day or two some Cuban marksman might come along and riddle him with holes.

He wasn't able to calm her down by the time the transport plane—a Spanish-manufactured C-212 Aviocar—was ready to take on passengers at the Canaima airport later that day.

It was only at the last minute, when she was about to ascend the ramp into the plane, that she seemed to have a change of heart. Throwing her arms about Zoccola, she kissed him hurriedly as if she couldn't trust herself to really leave him. "Take care," was all she whispered into his ear.

Then she was gone in a blur of blue dress and beautiful tan legs, into the darkness of the transport. He continued gazing at the doorway as if to memorize her and the last look she had given him.

"I'll see you in Paris next time!" he called as the door

was pulled shut, but with the thunder of the Aviocar's engines, she probably didn't hear.

After the noncombatants had been airlifted out of the area, the Venezuelan forces based at the tourist camp consisted of less than 100 troops. Of this number, twenty men were put under the direct command of Zummullo, whose mission it was to reconnoiter the headwaters of the Carrao and probe Cuban positions there.

"We don't know exactly where they are," the lieutenant explained to Zoccola. "We need to target them for our air force."

Once this mission was completed, he went on, his men would pull back with the others to more secure defensive positions while Venezuelan air power was used against the enemy.

The patrol left the tourist camp, now a ghost settlement of cabins, and headed out along the Carrao. As they continued in the direction of the frontier, the sound of artillery fire grew increasingly loud. Puffs of smoke could be seen rising above the jungle in the distance.

At one point they spotted the wreckage of a Spica gunship in the river; it made for a surrealistic sight with its white hull upended and its conning tower protruding above the surface. A Cuban bomb seemed to have been responsible for sinking it, and its gaunt presence was evidence of another battle Venezuela had lost.

Zummullo's unit had advanced only six miles upriver when they spied a patrol approaching through the brush from the opposite direction. They had found the Cubans.

Lieutenant Amado Silvas regretted one thing in life, which was that he had been born too late to have fought with Fidel against Batista, too late to have gone to the mountains of Bolivia and served under Che. In Angola he had fought no one, neither the imperialist-supported rebels nor the South African troops who regularly attacked guerrilla strongholds beyond their borders. Instead he'd been part of a garrison in Calenda assigned to protect oil fields—oil fields operated by Gulf Oil of America.

He could not understand how such a thing had come to be—that communist troops were guarding capitalist wealth for a socialist country.

But now, in the jungles of Venezuela, it was entirely possible that he would have his moment of heroism. Here, there was no mistaking that he would be advancing the cause of revolution and freedom.

Eight men were under his command, and they were on patrol, searching for the main body of Venezuelan troops. The maps of this region, prepared in Havana, were of scant assistance; in point of fact, Lieutenant Silvas was lost. He was not overly concerned, though; if necessary, he could resort to radio contact to establish his bearings.

He ordered his men to halt while he determined his next course of action. The muddy waters of the Carrao were just visible between the foliage of the trees.

Suddenly to their left they heard the sound of rustling leaves and the crackle of plants underfoot. Silvas silenced his men and directed them to drop to the ground, from which position they raised their weapons, training them toward the unknown disturbance.

A moment passed before the first Venezuelans came into view.

Silvas gave the command to fire.

Two Venezuelans immediately crumpled, but the others behind them immediately took cover and began to return the fire.

Silvas realized he'd acted precipitately, that if he'd waited the ambush would have had a greater chance of succeeding.

Not wishing to allow the advantage to pass into the hands of his enemy, he led half his men around in a half-circle in hopes of taking them from the rear. This meant trying to move quietly through almost impenetrable vegetation while three of his men were left behind to continue a diverting barrage.

But the Venezuelan contingent was larger than he'd anticipated.

Several machine guns and automatic weapons opened up on the Cubans as Silvas' men attacked the Venezuelans from the rear. Silvas was the first one hit. He flew up in the air, then flopped clumsily back down again, his body torn and blood oozing from every part of him like sweat. He knew he was dying, but he wasn't ready for his life to end; he had accomplished so little.

The pain was unbearable, and now he wanted to die quickly. As he waited, with his eyes close to the ground, he watched a throng of large, multilegged insects coming toward the blood he had shed on the jungle floor. It was the very last thing he saw.

Of the four men he'd led into battle, three others were cut down while the fourth escaped and returned to the others. Without their leader, they broke rank and plunged deep into the jungle rather than continue to fight.

Lieutenant Zummullo was ready to pursue them, but by the time he'd managed to mobilize his men, the Cubans were gone. Zoccola was just as happy; there was no sense expending excess energy to wipe out a small patrol when the first priority, now that they had an idea where the Cubans were, was attaining a secure redoubt.

While there was no more excitement that day, the night offered its own surprises. All up and down the Carrao River Cuban guns began to open up against Venezuelan positions, and the walls of banana and palm trees along the banks assumed an eerie glow from the explosions. In the far distance the great craggy peak of Auyán Tepuy Mountain was cast into ghostly relief by the explosions.

The din was terrible. Zoccola knew that if he spent enough time with the explosions he could get used to them, but for the present, he found sleep impossible.

Just when he'd drifted off, another shell would come whining in somewhere upriver and again thrust him into unwelcome consciousness.

An hour before dawn, when the sky was a melancholy cast of gray, Zoccola was awakened by Zummullo. "I've just received orders by radio to move out," he declared. "We are to go back downriver to link up with the rest of our men."

Something more seemed to be weighing on his mind; the lieutenant's face was drawn and for the first time since Zoccola had met him, Zummullo looked dejected.

"What's wrong?" Zoccola asked.

"My commander tells me that he monitored the radio broadcasts out of Caracas. They are speaking of reverses in the field, which means that things have become very bad. Ordinarily the government would not make such admissions."

No sooner had they begun on their way forward than a jet fighter swooped over their heads and after a minute's pause dropped several bombs into the jungle about ten miles away. At first the Venezuelans were cheered, thinking that the plane was one of theirs and that the bombs were falling on the Cubans. But Zoccola knew as soon as he saw it that there was no cause for rejoicing; the war plane was a MiG and presumably it was attacking what few Venezuelan units remained in the forward area, cut off from their main force.

Zummullo's men now faced a trek of some fifteen miles to reach the Venezuelans' newly consolidated forward positions fifteen miles up the banks of the Carrao. It was quite a stretch of territory to cover, especially when the enemy, increasingly in control of the area, was interested in killing you.

U.S. TO SEND ADVISORY FORCE TO VENE-ZUELA

WASHINGTON, June 13 (UPI)—A senior official with the State Department said here today that a special U.S. military advisory force would be dispatched to Caracas within a very few days. The official, who refused to be named, told reporters that the force would be small, "no more than 500 men," and that its primary objective would be to assist the Venezuelan army in its struggle against Guyanese armed forces. Cuban troops are also said to be heavily involved in the conflict, which erupted seven days ago over a disputed border. "We would hope that the advisory force will not have a combat role," the official said. He added that in accordance with the War Powers Act, enacted by Congress to avoid another situation like the Vietnamese war, the President would send a letter to Congress specifying the nature of the involvement. After 90 days Congress has the right to order the President to recall the troops or else make a formal declaration of war.

STATE DEPARTMENT REFUSES COMMENT

WASHINGTON, June 13 (Reuters)—Donald Eller, a State Department spokesman, refused comment on a report that the United States might shortly send a military force of 500 to 1,000 men to Venezuela to offer technical and strategic aid to that country in its war with Guyana over territory claimed by Venezuela.

CARACAS BREAKS RELATIONS WITH HAVANA

(KCET NOW electronic magazine)

CARACAS, June 13—The Venezuelan government formally broke diplomatic ties with Cuba, asserting that there was incontrovertible evidence Cuba was involved in helping Guyana in its war with Venezuela. A spokesman for Fidel Castro said in Havana that the Venezuelan decision was "regrettable and misguided." A Cuban interests section will remain in the Czech embassy in Caracas.

GEORGETOWN REPORTS ADVANCES

GEORGETOWN, June 13 (Agence France Presse) —In a radio broadcast here today, Prime Minister Sydney Walling declared that the Guyanese armed forces were successful on all fronts and that Venezuelan troops were in retreat. In another development, a spokesman for the Guyanese Defense Forces said that the Guyanese army was pushing into Venezuelan territory in the the direction of the Jobo oil fields in the northeast of the country. The push, he said, was necessitated by tactical demands and did not represent any territorial designs on Venezuela. At the daily press briefing, the military spokesman said that Venezuela had sustained the loss of 235 dead and in excess of 600 wounded in battles yesterday compared to losses of 78 dead and 128 wounded on the Guyanese side.

"Our only intention is to punish the Venezuelans for inflicting this conflict on us," the spokesman declared. "We are of course interested in bringing hostilities to an end as soon as our military objectives are achieved." Once again he denied that any Cuban or non-Guyanese forces were involved. Statements to the contrary he dismissed as "propaganda."

VENEZUELA ACKNOWLEDGES SETBACKS

CARACAS (DPA)—A press liaison with the Venezuelan military admitted that Venezuelan troops had suffered setbacks on the battlefield in the Guyana Highlands, on the Venezuelan side of the Guyanese border. While refusing to divulge casualties on either side, he maintained that the Venezuelan forces were regrouping and that the reverses were temporary. "We are holding our own and we will soon be in a position to recover the territory now occupied by Cuban mercenary forces."

OAS TALKS ADJOURN WITHOUT ACCORD

Special to the New York Times

SANTO DOMINGO, Dominican Republic, June 13—Representatives of the Organization of American States adjourned at least until the weekend after failing to agree on a resolution calling for an end to hostilities between Venezuela and Guyana. In spite of personal appeals from Secretary of State Jeffrey Schelling, the representatives meeting here could not agree on a compromise resolution which would condemn Cuba and the Soviet Union for violating hemispheric security and peace. The main stumbling block appeared to be Brazil's opposition to the resolution. Brazil has supplied arms to Guyana in the past although Juan Rios Aquilla, the Brazilian delegate to the OAS, has repeatedly said that no further arms were on order for Guyana and that his country prefers to remain neutral in the conflict.

17

A soft evening breeze wafted in through the window of William Drexell's room, carrying with it the stench of oil and diesel fuel. He was staying in a pension overlooking the port area where a small armada of black-hulled freighters was waiting to be loaded before turning back into the Caribbean.

He was spending the early evening hours perusing a series of photographs that had been developed in Washington, at National Security Agency headquarters, and rushed by plane to San José's Juan Santamaria Airport several hours previously.

The photos in question had been taken the night before by the SR-71 in a series of overflights above an area over 100 miles to the north of Limón. After arriving in San José, they'd been conveyed to Limón by way of a small Cessna jet to avoid attracting unnecessary attention to the mission.

When he first saw them, Drexell realized immediately that these photos provided the first solid evidence of the staging area that the Soviets and their Cuban allies were using as a base of operations for their war effort in Guyana.

As for Maxim Kolnikov, the man who'd finally identified the staging area's location for them, he had been pleased by the way Triad had brought off its side of their agreement for the information. With Vladivomivich so promptly disposed of in Georgetown, he no longer felt in danger of losing his job, let alone his life. Far from disappearing, as Drexell had suspected he would, he could now be regularly seen in the cafés and restaurants of the city when he wasn't enjoying his daily afternoon immersion in the swimming pool of the Club Miramar. In his delight at the death of his superior he was radiating good health and, like some machine politician in America, seemed ready to greet everyone he encountered with a vigorous handshake and a hearty slap on the back.

But now that they'd pinpointed the secret base from which transport helicopters and jets were routinely departing for Guyana, Kolnikov was no longer of immediate concern to Drexell.

The photos—there were 500 in all—revealed a base far larger and better equipped than Drexell had imagined.

Earlier in the afternoon, he had spread the documentation out on the tiled floor of his room, arranging and rearranging the photos almost as if he were engaged in an odd game of solitaire. After an hour spent this way he was joined by Jerry Hahn.

Drexell invited Hahn to have a look at the photos himself, and the other man went through them slowly, astonished that the staging area was as large and well-equipped as the photos showed it to be.

Hahn himself had just come from a camp ten miles north of Las Palmas, near the Costa Rican border with Nicaragua; it was there that the American expeditionary force authorized by the President was in the process of being assembled. Throughout the preceding week more than 250 men had been arriving in Costa Rica from

Florida to take part in the sabotage operation to be launched against the staging area. Their presence in the country was a violation of innumerable international accords and would be strongly protested by the Costa Rican government should it ever become known.

As it was, sympathetic elements in the local government, particularly in the Interior Ministry, had been made aware of the operation—though only in outline— and they had agreed to put their jobs on the line for the sake of eradicating unwelcome communist intervention in their nation. But if news of an American involvement leaked out, then even they would have no choice but to make representations to the U.S. government demanding an immediate evacuation. And that would be the least of it; the international outcry that such a disclosure would trigger would constitute a costly setback for the administration which would in turn produce much unfortunate domestic fallout. Worse from Drexell's point of view, such a revelation would cripple the ability of the United States to counter the growing Cuban and Soviet threat to the Southern Hemisphere.

But there was another even more gloomy possibility: the operation could turn out to be another Bay of Pigs, a catastrophe that would go down in history as one of America's greatest foreign policy failures. Instead of being seen as a mission to undercut communist influence, the operation could very well be viewed as a last-ditch attempt by the U.S. to restore discredited right-wing regimes to power in Central America.

For, regrettably, the truth was that many of the men who were recruited for this operation and smuggled into Costa Rica, posing as tourists, as refugees from Nicaragua and El Salvador, even as migrant workers, had formerly been associated with the right before being forced into exile when their causes were lost in their home countries.

But Drexell had needed trained men in a hurry—men who were not part of the United States armed forces, men who were anticommunists, men who would not mind the risks entailed in participating in an operation of this kind—and so he put aside his reservations and approved their enlistment. If a potential recruit could handle an automatic, had a Hispanic background, suffered from no physical impairments, and exhibited no outward signs of mental derangement, he was allowed to volunteer. It was something like the French Foreign Legion; no questions were asked about a man's past.

Having spent the last two days at the jungle assembly point, Hahn was able to report that preparations for the operation were proceeding practically without incident. The only hitch seemed to be that there was some difficulty getting arms and supplies in.

"Part of the problem is just physical," Hahn told Drexell. "We have a dozen trucks going back and forth every day and with the rain and the uncertain conditions of the roads, they keep breaking down. In the best of all possible worlds we'd have a mechanic in every truck, but we don't have that luxury. The most competent mechanics are needed at the assembly point.

"The other part of the problem is that we can't afford to put more than a dozen or so trucks into operation at the same time. It's bad enough as it is. People are already starting to wonder what they're carrying, and while we've spread rumors that a big prospecting enterprise is gearing up in the jungle, there's no way to avoid drawing attention to ourselves."

Drexell had anticipated that a problem of this sort would arise. Had they the luxury of a couple of months, this operation—code-named Sunbaker—could have been executed far more proficiently. With the absence of time, they had to improvise quickly and resort to papered-over solutions when more substantial arrangements were unavailable. "What's the status of the operation then? What kind of numbers are we talking about?"

"I'd say fifty percent of the arms we need are in place and sixty percent of other supplies—fuel, medical facilities, troop transport vehicles, and the like."

"That's not too good, Jerry. We have to move out soon." He glanced at his watch. "In fact, we're going to move out in eight hours' time, at one."

It wasn't so much surprise that registered on Hahn's face as horror. "Wait a minute, you're telling me you're going into action at one *this morning*?" It wasn't that Hahn balked at the danger but rather that he liked to prepare himself, reflecting fully on a situation before plunging into it. Drexell was denying him the one thing he would like most to have: time to think things through.

"That's correct," Drexell confirmed sharply.

"But I told you we're not ready."

"I am aware of that. But we have to weigh the risks. If we wait much longer, we're likely to be discovered and we'd have to abort the operation before it could get under way. And given how many people are aware of Sunbaker's existence—as you say, even the peasants have been watching the trucks coming and going every day—the odds grow increasingly against us with every passing hour. We *are* in a condition to go, aren't we?"

"It could be done," Hahn said grudgingly, "but at a considerable handicap."

"Remember, our objective isn't to destroy the Soviet staging area or to deliver a military defeat to them. With what we've got that'd be impossible. We're just aiming to cripple the opposition's military and transport capacity, slow them down, force them to come out of cover. If we slow them down enough, we've got a chance to alter the outcome of the war with Venezuela."

Of course Hahn was well aware of the purpose of the mission, but Drexell was anxious to dispel any illusions that he might harbor in his mind about it. The men that composed the expeditionary force were fanatics in many cases—especially the former national guardsmen who'd fought under the late Nicaraguan dictator Somoza—and it was possible that in the heat of combat they might get carried away. It was important that he and Hahn control their zealousness so it did not jeopardize the success of Sunbaker, and he was anxious that Hahn not lose sight of this.

Hahn continued to argue for a delay of at least four days so that the force could be brought up to greater combat strength.

"I've made my decision," Drexell said. "There's nothing further to discuss. In half an hour there will be a chopper waiting to take us up to the assembly point."

"Has Lisker been told of the change of plans?" Hahn asked. It was his understanding that Lisker would be joining them to share the leadership role with Drexell.

"Jerry, that's another matter I'd like to talk to you about."

Hahn's features tightened. "What do you mean?"

"I'm afraid Lisker hasn't been able to get out of Georgetown. The police are cracking down and the airports are being scrupulously watched, so he won't be here in time to help us with Sunbaker."

"Who have you got in mind to replace him?"

Drexell looked at Hahn without speaking.

"You can't mean me?"

"I do, indeed," Drexell said roughly.

"You forget I'm your political adviser, sir. I am not a military man. It's one thing to go out in the field every once in a while, but to take a group of men and lead an attack . . . Why, it would be madness. I haven't the experience to pull off something like that."

"You're frightened, scared shitless?" Drexell said calmly.

"Bet your life I am."

"I like that. It's a good sign. Don't like a man in my command who isn't at least part scared. You'll get over it once the fighting starts. Too many other things to do to stay scared. *Really* scared is what happens when the fighting's all over."

"I can't do it, I won't do it," Hahn said. "You'd be risking Sunbaker's success if you put me in a position like that."

"You think I don't know what I'm doing?"

"Not in this instance."

"You're refusing to carry out the order."

"Triad's an intelligence group, not the Army. I'm a volunteer, not a recruit. I can walk away any time I choose," Hahn said quietly.

He got up from the bed where he'd been sitting, paused a moment, then opened the door to the room and went out. He stood in the hallway without closing the door.

Meanwhile, Drexell had returned to the floor where he began to scrutinize the satellite photos again. He waited for the sound of the door closing, but it didn't happen.

More than a minute went by. Drexell didn't look up, but he was sure that Hahn was still just outside the room.

"Are you going or not?" he snapped.

The door closed.

Drexell looked up. Hahn was standing stiffly just inside the room, looking like a man facing a firing squad.

"You really think I'm capable of it?" he asked wearily.

"I said you were. You think I'd lie to you just to make you feel good?"

"You could be making a big mistake."

"I could be doing a lot of fucking things," Drexell muttered. "Now are you staying or going?"

Hahn stepped away from the door. He was staying.

The Soviet-Cuban staging area in Costa Rica was situated eight miles west of the Caribbean coast and less than twenty miles south of the Nicaraguan border.

There were docking facilities on the coast capable of handling as many as three tankers and several smaller craft. As of twenty-four hours earlier, two large vessels were berthed in the small military harbor: a troop transport ship—the one that the U.S. recon satellites had lost track of in its journey from Angola across the Atlantic —and a freighter flying a Liberian flag that Drexell believed was intended to ferry weapons and supplies to Guyana.

In addition, patrol boats and trawlers fully equipped with radar were stationed a short distance offshore. While the U.S. spy plane had picked up no sign of submarines, Drexell suspected that a couple of them were in the vicinity as well, carrying out reconnaissance just below the surface.

A road led from the docking facilities to the staging area itself by way of an eight-mile stretch of asphalt. The road ran through a river valley that was flanked by hilltops on which antiaircraft guns and mortars had been mounted. The road, if it existed at all three months ago, would have been nothing more than a narrow dirt walkway for the few Indian inhabitants of the area. Now the way had been expanded by Soviet and Cuban engineers so that it could accommodate T-54/55 tanks, half-tracks, and Soviet TR-64 armored personnel carriers, some of which the photographs showed proceeding from the shore inland.

The main installation eight miles in the jungle was sufficient to hold two battalions, with ten barracks buildings, each 150 feet in length, a vehicle storage area, and an elaborate vehicle service area. There was also a ground-force training area—with a Soviet-style obstacle course—and a parade field with a reviewing stand.

From the photographs, it was obvious that expansion of the installation was continuing; foundations were being laid for dual-bay garages and for still more barracks; bulldozers were visible in a number of locations throughout the installation.

A whole swath of jungle had been cleared to provide for an airfield parking apron. The airfield itself measured 6,800 feet in length and it had already been blacktopped. An airfield this long was perfect for use by MiG-21's. Fuel storage areas lay at opposite points on the perimeter of the field with fuel lines extending from them so that planes could be serviced and refueled.

There were nearly two dozen revetments—storage

points—marked by white tarpaulin covers under which tanks were concealed. Other tanks had been parked in armored storage areas.

More easily determined were the number and type of aircraft available. There were eight MiG-21's (code-named Fishbeds) and a pair of MiG-23's (Floggers), along with a number of Hip and Hind helicopters used, respectively, for assault and transport.

In another month the installation would probably be completed and made so impregnable that the kind of sabotage envisioned by Operation Sunbaker would be out of the question. Even now, with the base half finished, the enterprise was a formidable one.

The men attached to Drexell's force at the assembly point near Las Palmas, forty miles away, had no idea how formidable. It was better, Drexell thought, that they didn't know.

At ten-thirty P.M.—minutes after Drexell and Hahn had arrived in camp by chopper—a general alert was issued. The mercenaries filed out of their tents and, with a surprising lack of noise, began to gather up their arms and supplies. A little after eleven they proceeded in an orderly fashion to the motor launches awaiting them at the banks of the Rio Moreno, executing procedures that they'd been rehearsing for several days in the broiling sun. If they felt any displeasure at the suddenness with which they'd been mobilized, it did not reflect itself in their faces. Quite the contrary; there was an air of expectation, a surge of joy that the waiting was over and that they would finally see action. The great majority of this 250-man force had been waiting for action not just for these couple of weeks in Costa Rica. They'd been marking time in cities and training camps in the United States for years.

Into the score of boats the men loaded the supplies, arms, and explosives. They did so in virtual silence, and with great efficiency. The entire operation consumed no more than an hour.

The motor launches did not deserve to be called

motor launches at all, since they were actually long dug-out canoes with outboards attached, purchased cheaply from the local Indian tribes, who appeared to believe that they were to be used by these strangers for prospecting. But the craft would serve their purpose well enough, which was to take them several miles upriver in the direction of the coast. In less than four hours, Drexell would have them debark and set out for the staging area, a march of almost twenty miles through the jungle.

At quarter to twelve, Drexell gave the order to move out.

The first trickle of dull gray light revealed a lush forest full of greens and yellows standing on either side of the river. Birds shrieked overhead. Dawn was perhaps an hour and a half away.

Standing in the prow of the lead boat, Drexell viewed the inky terrain through a pair of all-weather binoculars. Behind him, stretching all the way to a bend in the river, twenty launches, each with its own contingent of mercs, maintained a slow but steady speed, their motors puttering feebly so as not to create too great a disturbance. They'd been traveling now for nearly four hours.

At last Drexell saw what he was looking for. He tapped Hahn on the shoulder, pointing to a small inlet a quarter of a mile downriver. There, beneath a palm, stood two Indians wearing clothes that would not have looked out of place on the streets of San José.

"Who are they?" Hahn asked.

"Friends," Drexell replied.

Hahn regarded him skeptically. He had been told nothing about Indians being involved in this operation.

When they came abreast of the Indians, Drexell ordered the navigator to steer inland. The other boats would follow in turn.

Hahn noticed that the Indians didn't appear in the least surprised to observe this makeshift flotilla putting ashore. Stepping off the boat as soon as it was beached,

Drexell approached the Indians. Between them, they knew enough Spanish to hold a limited conversation.

"The way is clear," the older of the two Indians said. "Earlier we found a patrol. The patrol is no more."

"I'm grateful to you," Drexell said.

The Indians nodded and vanished so rapidly, so completely, into the undergrowth that they might not have ever been there.

While they conversed, the mercs followed Drexell's example, one by one drawing up their launches on the shore and disembarking. "They hate the Cubans," Drexell explained to Hahn, "and they're none too fond of the Russians either. Nothing to do with ideology—they just didn't care for the idea of two full battalions and a shitload of tanks and airplanes occupying their land. Under the circumstances they're our natural allies."

"What did they do, gun down a Cuban patrol?" Hahn asked.

"I doubt they were quite so noisy about it, but I'm sure their methods are equally as effective as bullets."

"But how did they know we were coming tonight?"

"I telegraphed our man in Las Palmas this afternoon and he relayed my message to the Indians. All very simple."

That was all the clarification Hahn was likely to obtain for now as Drexell turned his attention to the debarkation of his troops. It was a time-consuming and arduous process, offloading the equipment and the arms and then packing them so they could be transported the distance required.

By the time they were ready to set out, the sun was already beginning to beat down on them. Two hundred fifty men bristling with NATO surplus M-14's, they made an improbable jungle caravan.

Drexell respected the M-14—it was reliable even in dusty climates and possessed excellent long-range accuracy—but he would have preferred the M-16. The problem with the M-14, demonstrated in Vietnam, was that its stock could be easily cracked and the barrel, with its flash hider, was so long that it could end up becoming entangled in underbrush.

Nonetheless, the government had some 700,000 M-14's in storage and if that was what was available that was what he had to live with.

In addition to the M-14's, the force was equipped with 9mm MAT 49's weighing in at almost nine and a half pounds, with a cyclic rate of 600 rounds per minute; rocket grenade launchers; explosives; and an assortment of light arms including Galil assault rifles and 9mm Uzis.

They hadn't gone very far into the jungle before they came upon the bodies of the patrol the Indians had ambushed. There were more than twenty bodies scattered about the trail. They lay in contorted postures, their faces frozen in agony. In some instances they had been disemboweled and their entrails placed beside them. One had lost his head and other bodies bore the signs of hand-to-hand struggle, their trunks crisscrossed by gashes that could only have been caused by scythes or very long blades.

From what Drexell could see, they were all Cubans save for one whose features were unmistakably Slavic. There was no identification to be found on any of them.

Although the men in his force were accustomed to savage fighting and had even committed atrocities themselves under the banner of patriotism, many of them were still sickened by the spectacle that greeted them, but not one of them showed a visible reaction to it.

Still, many made remarks that exhibited no respect whatsoever for the dead; they particularly seemed to enjoy the sight of one Cuban soldier, his mouth gaping open to accommodate his severed genitals.

"Some friends," Hahn muttered, shaking his head in wonder.

"Better them than us," Drexell replied.

He was under no illusions that they'd meet with no further opposition along the way. That was why he had sent fifty men ahead as a diversionary force, to confuse the enemy and distract it from the main thrust of the American attack.

The remaining two hundred he divided in half. The first group, under Hahn's command, was to take a route through the underbrush that would put them on the southern perimeter of the Soviet base not far from the vehicle storage area; the other group, Drexell's, would advance in the opposite direction until it reached the northern perimeter, where the airfield was situated.

When they got to within five miles of the base, they would have to hack their way through; the denseness of the jungle was as much a part of the Russian and Cuban defenses as their barbed-wire fences. Drexell calculated that they'd arrive at their respective destinations just before twilight. Once darkness fell they would strike.

18

A light spring rain was falling on Moscow, but it did not seem to be doing anything to deter the crowd lining up for a view of the embalmed body of Vladimir Lenin. They stood there—Georgians, Byelorussians, Ukrainians, Kazakhs, and Uzbeks. These were people for whom the whole mythology of the Revolution still held meaning.

At precisely three o'clock, when the clock on Spassky Tower intoned the hour with a clanging of bells, four goose-stepping soldiers, rifles slung over their shoulders, came marching out of the Kremlin and, advancing across half the length of Red Square, proceeded to take their place at the mausoleum, relieving the honor guard already there. There were tears in the eyes of many of the Russian peasants who witnessed this ceremony.

A minute later two of the traffic police, clad in drab overcoats, put their whistles to their lips and stepped forward to halt the sparse traffic. Presently a black Zil limousine, its windows tinted, appeared from behind St. Basil Cathedral and sped across Red Square in the direction of Nikolsky Tower a short distance beyond the mausoleum. It then turned and went through the gate at the base of the tower and disappeared from sight.

As every government functionary and diplomat tended to rely on limousines like this, there was no way to tell who might have been riding in the Zil. In this instance it was Bunker Knight, the American Ambassador to the Soviet Union.

There'd been no advance warning that he was to attend this meeting. Only forty-five minutes earlier, Knight had been informed that the First Secretary wanted to speak to him.

Knight was a career diplomat who'd served in Riyadh, Paris, Vienna, Cairo, and Brasila. He'd earned a reputation as an expert in Soviet affairs and was widely credited with expanding U.S. business interests in the U.S.S.R. during the era of détente. A man of sixty-eight, he was rather donnish in appearance. He was white-haired and had a grave, dignified air that tended to make people self-conscious in his presence.

As ambassador, Knight was in the habit of meeting routinely with various members of the Politburo and bureaucrats of all kinds from the ministries of foreign affairs and trade, but he'd rarely spoken with the First Secretary. The last time he'd seen him was at the wedding of Foreign Minister Marchenko's daughter, held in one of the ballrooms of the Cosmos Hotel. On that occasion Kadiyev had been friendly enough and more animated than Knight remembered him as being. There was nothing about his manner to suggest that the fighting in Albania or the deterioration in East-West relations then taking place disturbed him in the least.

Although Marchenko was now in the United States representing Russia in the fruitless UN talks on nuclear disarmament, Knight did not expect that in his absence he would be summoned before the First Secretary himself.

The office in which Kadiyev had chosen to receive the U.S. ambassador was one Knight had never seen before. It overlooked the Cathedral of the Assumption and the small single-domed Church of the Deposition of the Robe. Beyond, Knight could make out the Kremlin wall, parts of which were up to sixty-five feet high.

The office itself was simply appointed, with a beige-topped desk, three upholstered chairs, and walls paneled with dark wood. An oil portrait of Lenin was mounted just above the desk. To the American Ambassador's eyes, the great revolutionary looked wistful, as if he would rather be somewhere far away, perhaps on the beaches of the Crimea.

Besides Knight and the First Secretary, there were four other men present for the meeting, including the interpreter, a sullen-looking young man who appeared to have been taken from his studies at Lermontov University across the river. The other three Knight recognized from various ceremonial events, but he'd had an opportunity to meet only one of them personally: Grigory V. Romanov, who while still in the Politburo no longer loomed as a possible candidate for the position Kadiyev now held. Next to him was Viktor Grishin, head of the Moscow party organization and also a Politburo member, and sitting to his right was Marshal Sergei L. Sokolov, First Deputy Defense Minister.

A heavy crew, Knight thought as he took a seat. A cup of coffee was offered to him, but he refused.

A trail of smoke partially obscured the First Secretary's face. Already the ashtray was littered with cigarette butts. Knight noticed that they were Marlboros, perhaps the version of Marlboros licensed by and produced in Bulgaria.

After the most perfunctory formalities, Kadiyev addressed himself to the subject at hand. He drew out a document, which he read from in a monotone; to Knight it was like listening to the voice of a radio newscaster coming from the next room. It was all Knight could do to pay attention. The interpreter's rendition of the First Secretary's remarks was only slightly less enervating.

"The Soviet Union," Kadiyev said, "regards the action of the United States in sending troops into Venezuela to be a provocative act and a gross violation of the spirit of détente. The Soviet Union strongly protests this move by the United States to interfere in the internal affairs of another sovereign state on the pretext of coming to its rescue. The government of the U.S.S.R. will not hesitate to repel any attempt to impose a solution on either Venezuela or Guyana. Such a solution must come from the relevant peace-keeping bodies. Attempts to adjust the border between Venezuela and Guyana that do not take into account the interests of all concerned parties are unacceptable to the Soviet Union.''

Knight understood this to mean that the Soviet Union regarded itself as one of the concerned parties. Obviously Kadiyev feared that the introduction of a U.S. military force into the area might alter the course of the war and undermine the successes thus far achieved by Cuban and Soviet troops on the Guyanese side.

In spite of his growing impatience, the U.S. Ambassador held his tongue, but his fixed expression and the tense way in which he maintained his posture in the chair—an antique from the time of Catherine the Great—could leave no doubt in his hosts' minds as to what he was thinking.

"Accordingly, the Soviet Union wishes it known that should unwarranted U.S. interference in this dispute continue, we will not hesitate to take urgent measures to end this interference. Any threat directed against the will and sovereignty of the Guyanese people will be regarded as a threat directed against the Soviet Union, and the government of the United States must be prepared to face the consequences.''

Knight waited for more, but that was apparently all there was. Kadiyev handed the formal protest to him across the table and looked at him as though he expected him to applaud.

What the Soviet leader seemed to be implying was that in the event that Guyana suffered a loss in its war with Venezuela—a loss that might lead to the overthrow of the government of Sydney Walling—then the Russians would retaliate in any part of the world that suited them.

It was Knight's conviction that he was bluffing.

"I must categorically reject this protest, Mr. Secretary," he said. "The United States is not interfering in the internal affairs of either Venezuela or Guyana. If American advisers and technicians are currently in

Venezuela, they are there at the express invitation of the legal representatives of the Venezuelan people." Knight paused to allow this to sink in. A man who seldom allowed emotion to intrude upon his professional obligations, he maintained a quiet, even tone as he continued speaking. "May I remind the government of the U.S.S.R. that were it not for the fact that the Guyanese have sought to use Cuban troops to fight their own war there would be no need for any American advisory presence in Venezuela at all. It is the Soviet Union, and not the United States, which is responsible for inflaming a tragic state of affairs. Should the U.S.S.R. remove itself from the conflict I believe that it would soon come to an end. It is the U.S.S.R., not the United States, which refuses to allow the two parties in the conflict to settle their differences on the negotiating table."

With that, he got up and stalked from the room, leaving the official protest lying on the table behind him.

19

It was in some respects ironic that the war raging in the frontier regions of Guyana and Venezuela might very well be decided here, in the jungle of Costa Rica.

William Drexell had established positions fifty yards away from the northern perimeter of the Soviet staging area, on a hill that offered a commanding view of the base. That it was poorly patrolled surprised Drexell, but he recognized that his force might still be discovered at any time prior to the launching of the attack.

The base, now that he could get a good look at it, appeared much larger than it had seemed in the reconnaissance photographs. In the gathering twilight, the airfield and the taxi apron appeared to stretch for miles, the gleaming metal surfaces of the MiG's and transport and assault helicopters reflecting the setting sun, which had turned a fiery shade of orange. Drexell estimated their time of attack to be 9:30, when there should be just enough darkness to provide cover for them.

He had received earlier confirmation from Hahn that his group had reached the southern perimeter and had secured positions nearby. The confirmation was a short burst of code transmitted over two-way radio, nothing more. Drexell wished to confine radio contact to a minimum to limit the possibility that some alert Russian engineer monitoring radio traffic might become suspicious of the American messages and initiate an investigation.

Bearing out Drexell's fears, the third prong of his expeditionary force, consisting of fifty men, had been sighted twelve miles from the base by a Cuban surveillance team. A brief engagement—marked by repeated bursts of automatic fire and detonations of grenades—had occurred, with minimal losses on both sides, before fighting had broken off. Drexell's men had staged what was meant to look like a panicky retreat and disappeared into the jungle. This diversionary clash had taken place just an hour and a half ago.

Thinking that they had routed the enemy troops, the base's command had then decided to round them up. Accordingly, more than a hundred Cuban troops had been sent out to participate in a search for them.

This only made it easier for Drexell, for now there were that many fewer troops to contend with at the base.

As agreed on beforehand, the primary targets were the installations: the vehicle storage area to the south, the fuel supply, the tank storage area in the center, and the planes parked on the runway to the north. The idea was to sow confusion and to wreak as much damage as possible. Drexell was anxous to minimize the possibility of a direct clash with the Cubans and any Russians that might be on the base. Two hundred lightly armed men pitted against two full-strength battalions did not represent odds that he considered favorable.

Moreover, the strike would have to be fast. The longer it dragged on, the greater the prospect that the defenders would be able to mobilize themselves and eliminate them.

It was 9:15 when a convoy of supply trucks appeared on the newly blacktopped road leading from the port area to the main base. The road was so narrow that the trucks had to proceed in single file.

There were eight trucks in all, and except for a single 122mm self-propelled howitzer out in front, they were undefended. Although there was still a band of light along the western horizon, Drexell decided that this was too important an opportunity to pass up. He sent word by messenger to those manning the grenade launchers that the trucks were to be targeted.

In approximately five minutes the trucks would pass directly beneath their positions, at which time his men would launch a succession of grenades into their midst. The lead truck and the self-propelled howitzer were the most important targets, while the last truck in the convoy was almost as important; taking it out would block the road in the opposite direction, leaving the vehicles in between completely trapped.

But the attack would have to come simultaneously with that launched against the base itself. Already men with rocket grenade launchers had trained their weapons on the fuel tanks and pipelines extending out onto the airstrip. They waited for Drexell's signal to fire.

First, though, it was necessary to inform Hahn's contingent that the attack was to occur ten minutes prematurely. He used a burst transmission: a preset message that spurted out so fast it was impossible for the enemy to pin down the location of the sender with direction-finding equipment.

Drexell waited a moment before he heard the confirming signal from Hahn. Once again, he hoped Hahn would prove that his confidence in him was not misplaced.

Then he raised his hand so that the men with the grenade launchers could see it. An instant later he brought it back down.

The attack had begun.

A dozen grenades soared aloft, and a moment later several explosions ripped through the carriages of the truck convoy, igniting still more explosions as their highly combustible contents began to go up as well. The din was unrelenting.

After an interval lasting no more than a few seconds, rockets, also launched by hand, trailed through the air in the direction of the tanks and pipelines at the edge of the airfield—half a mile downrange from their positions. One failed to do more than tear a hole in the side of a cylindrical tank, but a second penetrated further, touching off an explosion that soon had half the tarmac in flames.

It didn't take long for the defenders to respond. Tracer bullets arced through the darkness, every fifth bullet a luminous yellow. But it was apparent from the way these bullets were aimed that the Cubans had no real idea where the attack was originating from.

But Drexell's mind was elsewhere. "What's taking Hahn so goddamn long?" he muttered, seeing that no assault had begun from the southern sector.

What Hahn was doing was waiting for two weapons platforms to be brought into position. They were both equipped with Browning .30-caliber machine guns and Oerlikon 20mm belt-fed cannon. However, it had proved impossible to deploy them quickly by pushing them, given the steep incline.

Once the firing on the other side of the camp had broken out, however, Hahn ordered every available man to drag the platforms up the slope.

Apparently no one at Hahn's end of the base was expecting a strike against the vehicle and tank storage area. For the ten tanks, five armored personnel carriers, and pair of ZSU-57-2 self-propelled antiaircraft guns parked on the field, only six sentries had been assigned to guard duty.

To the man acting as his liaison, Hahn said, "Give the order to open fire with everything we have. I want a concentrated fire on the vehicles, the rockets should be directed at the garages and the fuel dumps."

The message was swiftly relayed. A half-minute later, inaugurated with a salvo from the Oerlikon, the battle was joined.

Three tanks instantaneously burst into flame as armor-piercing rockets smashed into them. The sentries were suddenly running amok, totally confused as to what they should do. One of the garages was hit repeatedly by fire and its roof soon crumbled, allowing poisonous smoke to escape into the air.

When Hahn gazed across the length of the camp to its far end, he saw that the whole sky was alight with the detonation of shells and rockets. But the chaos prevented him from seeing how Drexell was faring.

Through his binoculars Drexell could observe the panic that seized the Cubans as they sought first to identify where their attackers were positioned and second to contain the flames threatening to engulf the northern half of the installation.

A company of soldiers was drawing out a tangle of hoses with which to fight the blaze. An elite group of Drexell's sharpshooters dug in at a forward position halfway down the hill and opened up on them. The withering fusillade felled eight or nine Cubans before the others abandoned their hoses and fled back to the temporary sanctuary of their barracks.

Now directing his attention to the road, Drexell saw that his ambush had succeeded beyond his expectations: of the eight trucks two had been completely obliterated, another two lay crippled, and the remaining four were paralyzed, stuck between the wrecks of the lead vehicle and the last. The self-propelled 122mm howitzer was still in action, however, and its gun swiveled about until it was trained on the hill. The first shells landed harmlessly on the verge of the hill far below Drexell's men, but that was only because the gunner had yet to find the proper trajectory.

Eventually he corrected his aim, and one shell impacted just a few feet below the line of Drexell's sharpshooters.

When the smoke cleared, five of the sharpshooters lay dead or critically wounded, and one man was stooped over, clutching his ruined stomach. His face held an expression of incredulity and numbness, not pain. Next to him another man kept reaching for a leg torn off by the force of the blast but he seemed unable to summon enough energy to recover it. A copious trail of blood streamed from the stump and drained over the face of a third victim who, while still half alive, seemed not to notice the hot blood soaking him. It seemed possible he would die of drowning in another man's blood before his own injuries carried him off.

In the meantime, the surviving sharpshooters had scrambled to safety on higher ground, and not a moment too soon, for the howitzer continued to fire at the spot they had abandoned, pounding the slope until it was as pocked with craters as the moon. Even if the shelling took no more lives, the fire was having a crucial effect because it was keeping the attackers from consolidating their position over the road.

Under the command of Captain Jaime Santiago, a brigade-strength patrol had for several hours been searching for Drexell's diversionary force. At the time the attack came on the staging area they were already returning to the base. They were less than a mile away when they heard the first explosions.

Santiago, a burly but quite handsome man with several decorations to his credit, immediately contacted headquarters by radio and was told that a siege was under way. At that point there was no way of determining the size of the invading force; the only thing that could be established with any certainty was that the attack was coming from both north and south. The central command post, situated in the middle of the base, was still secure.

There was no way of returning to base except on foot, which served to delay their rescue efforts. It required nearly twenty minutes before they came within sight of the staging area.

Santiago's force however, did have the advantage of surprise. By chance their route took them straight into the rear of Drexell's force.

Drexell was as surprised as anyone by the attack coming from the rear. He'd been concentrating his entire attention on the impact his attack was having on the base. Now he was forced to order the men in forward positions to redeploy themselves. They wheeled about and rushed to meet the Cuban advance.

But already the Cuban patrol was laying a barrage down against the body of combined Nicaraguan and Honduran troops that was protecting the rear of Drexell's force.

Eight men were cut down immediately. Their companions spun around in an effort to thwart the Cuban advance, but they, in turn, were riddled with bullets and died cursing their ill fortune.

Those who hadn't been struck retreated farther back down the slope in an attempt to regroup. Santiago then led his men in a bayonet attack, bringing the two forces too close together for either to use firepower.

A Nicaraguan was caught in the gut by a bayonet and impaled. The Cuban antagonist couldn't extricate it quickly enough to avoid a second Nicaraguan, who jabbed him repeatedly in the ribs before slashing his neck. The Cuban fell over the body of the man he'd just killed and lay still.

Santiago was in the thick of the fight, using a Czech-made 9mm gun with a spiritedness that heartened his subordinates. He seemed oblivious of any danger. A bullet whipped by his ear and tore a part of his lobe off. He put his hand to it and took away a great deal of blood, but after staring at it for a moment, he just laughed and went back to the fighting.

The Cubans drove into the rear of Drexell's unit with a frenzy that caused the mercenaries to fall even farther back down the slope. Soon the ground was so littered with corpses that men on both sides stumbled continually over the remains of the dead.

Santiago was beginning to savor his impending victory when the self-propelled gun still functioning on the road blew his body in half. There was no way that the gunners below could know that the Cubans had for the most part retaken the hill that Drexell's sharp-shooters previously occupied.

The death of the Cuban leader, however, in no way changed the fact that Drexell's force could no longer sustain itself against the pressure the Cubans were applying. There were not enough men available, nor enough firepower, to throw back the attack with any hope of success.

Drexell, ignoring the danger he was exposing himself to, plunged in among his men, instructing them to stage an orderly retreat. It was vital that they avoid panicking.

Finding shelter behind a palm at the side of the hill, he radioed his reconnaissance unit.

"Sigma Eight, come in."

The voice on the other end was barely audible through the crackling interference. "This is Sigma Eight," came the reply, the sound of explosions and heavy shelling detectable in the background.

"Where are you, Sigma Eight?"

"Coordinates point-zero-zero-one-six."

These coordinates were useful only to Drexell; they referred to a map of the area which the Cubans had no access to. He didn't even have to get out the map to know that the recon patrol was halfway between the port and the base. "What's happening there?" he demanded.

"Egress is being cut off along the road by relief forces sent up from the port. Looks very tight around here."

"Thank you, Sigma Eight. Continue on to Michigan Point."

Michigan Point was the code name for the port area.

Now he signaled Hahn—again with a burst transmission—alerting him that they would now initiate the second phase of Operation Sunbaker. With all routes of escape being cut off, Drexell had decided that this would be the best opportunity to escape. But escape was not the only thing that he planned. His objective was to turn this action into yet another attack—this time on the port facilities eight miles away.

No one was more relieved than Hahn when the signal came. While his force had managed to knock out well over half the tanks and other armored vehicles, his position had been exposed to such heavy bombardment from artillery and rockets on the base that he was forced to issue orders for a strategic withdrawal even before Drexell's retreat.

If he had one wish that could be granted now, it would be for James Lisker to be here. Lisker would know what to do in a situation like this; fighting his way out of this kind of mess was his specialty. But Lisker was trapped in Georgetown, and he, Jerry Hahn, was here and would just have to deal with the situation the best he could.

By now the weapons platforms had been demolished; the men who'd operated the Browning and the Oerlikon cannon lay draped over their weapons, blood-soaked and lifeless.

The fear that Hahn was sure he'd fought off was back, the exhaustion that he'd suppressed was reasserting itself; it was all he could do to stay awake.

His liaison stood before him, waiting for his command. They were now at the bottom of the slope from where they'd mounted their attack. The hill concealed them from the base for now, but with their location discovered by an advance patrol, there was no way they could long remain where they were.

Of the 100 men he'd begun with, Hahn now had fewer than sixty he could rely upon. Ten were too badly wounded to be ambulatory.

Hahn could not imagine conducting a second military operation tonight, but he understood that if Drexell had ordered phase two to be put into effect, it must mean that there was simply no other choice. If they did not leave by sea in craft seized from the Cubans and Russians, then they would not leave at all.

• • •

Boris Galanskov, commander of the naval docking facilities, was not a decisive man. Had he been, he would have occupied a position in the Black Sea or Baltic fleet to which some degree of prestige was attached. But because he had exhibited little initiative, and less wisdom, in his choice of friends in high places, he'd been consigned to what was, almost in literal fact, a backwater.

The attack on the staging area could not have come at a worse time for him; he was suffering from cramps and intermittent diarrhea. During this emergency, it was all he could do to restrain himself from bolting to the bathroom and remaining there until his nausea passed.

Maybe, he thought, his nausea would never pass.

His aides, he suspected, were more competent at dealing with a situation so fraught with danger than he was.

Up until now his sole responsibility had been to supervise the loading and unloading of war matériel and troops; the last thing he was expecting was a full-scale assault on his installation.

Alerted first by the explosions, then by direct communication from base headquarters at the inland staging area, he'd ordered a pair of T-72 tanks and an APC with heavy KPV machine guns and a 7.62mm gun to be brought up a mile from the port and a roadblock established.

Two hundred troops were dispatched to fortify this position while an additional fifty were charged with scouting the neighboring terrain to see whether the enemy was attempting to bypass the roadblock.

He was dubious as to how effective such measures might be. It did not require a great deal of imagination to institute such precautions, but it was all that he could think to do in the absence of more precise information.

The quarters from which he directed the defense measures were utilitarian, even stark, consisting of a bare minimum of furniture, surrounded by walls of aluminum and tin that made a hell of a noise every time the rain came down hard on them.

A detailed isometric map of the area was now laid out on the central table. His aides—six ambitious men of whom at least two were GRU operatives assigned to spy on him—clustered around the map, studying it intensely as though it might hold the answer to their problem.

Every few minutes the radio operator ran in from the room next door to announce the latest message from the main base.

"Where is the enemy—that's what I want to know," Galanskov demanded of the operator. "If we don't know where the enemy is, how can we prepare to oppose him?"

The radio operator shrugged; this was not his province. All he could do was repeat what he'd heard: "It is thought that the enemy is advancing along the main road linking the base to the port."

"If they are, why haven't we seen them yet?" he demanded.

But the radio operator couldn't tell him. His only recourse, it seemed, was to wait.

Drexell's force was nowhere near the road. He'd chosen a route that took his men deep into the jungle in anticipation of a Soviet blockade. This detour resulted in a delay of two hours, since it meant that they had to hack their way through a dense nighttime forest to the accompaniment of birdcalls and the derisive screeching of the monkeys. The men had to make do with flashlights to see; using flares was too likely to reveal their position.

Eventually they were rewarded for their efforts. Emerging from the forest, they found themselves on a rise that yielded a view of the Soviet-built docking facilities. The docks jutted out a considerable distance into the murky waters. Bright red beacons burned into the night while ribbons of smaller white lights demarcated the lengths of the docks.

Starkly outlined was the transport ship the SR-71 had photographed. It had a landing platform of the Ivan

Rogov class capable of carrying an entire marine battalion as well as forty tanks and support vehicles. The freighter flying the Liberian flag was gone, but in its place was a Kresta II class guided-missile cruiser and a Moskva class antisubmarine cruiser and helicopter carrier. A patrol boat—a Grisha II class corvette used for antisubmarine reconnaissance—could be seen some distance out in the harbor. Beyond the security fence surrounding the port area, a rocky beach extended in both directions.

While Drexell had scrupulously studied the maps of the area that were put at his disposal, including an isometric map fashioned by computer at Triad headquarters, there was really no way he could have anticipated ending up where he was. He would now have to move his men along the beach to the southern perimeter of the port.

Nonetheless, as far as he could tell there would be no opposition up to the point of the security fence.

He directed his men to descend the slope and traverse the beach, keeping low, well out of the way of the searchlights. When they reached a point within firing range of the docks, they halted and the rocket launchers were brought up.

Drexell intended to use much the same strategy that he had when he'd hit the base: softening up the positions with rockets and grenades at the same time spreading such panic that the enemy could not easily mount an adequate defense.

It was eerily quiet; the only noise they could hear was the chatter of monkeys from the nearby jungle.

The dial of Drexell's watch was a blank. He pressed a button and watched the green phosphorescent digits spell out the hour, 2:14. He hadn't realized that the operation had taken this long. There was no question that he would have to get his men well away from this part of the coast by dawn. More than either the Soviets or the Cubans, the approaching sun was their enemy.

He'd instructed the men wielding the hand-held

rocket launchers to fire at timed intervals of ten seconds.

"When you see my flare," he told them, "fire away."

As soon as the first flare burst, turning the sky a garish color of red, Boris Galanskov rushed out of his headquarters to see what had happened.

Observing the flare, he realized that this was a signal for an attack and that the attack was about to come from a direction altogether different from the one he'd been expecting.

In fact, he had been under the impression that the invading force was still bottled up somewhere between the staging area and the port. While confirmation of this had been impossible to obtain, he hadn't heard any reports to the contrary.

Too late Galanskov ordered the positions along the beach reinforced.

The first rocket came down on the Ivan Rogov class ship, striking its port side, and sending a geyser of flame spurting up from the forward deck.

Galanskov stood mesmerized outside his headquarters as a second rocket impacted further amidships. A third missed it completely, coming down on the docks, which simply crumpled and fell piecemeal into the surrounding water.

More rockets, too many for Galanskov to count, continued to come down. The guided-missile cruiser berthed next to the transport ship was hit. In flames, it began listing badly, threatening to sink.

Alarms were shrieking, emitting prolonged whoop-whooping sounds that intensified the madness of the scene.

Soldiers were rushing back and forth, the gunfire was growing more intense, and yet Galanskov couldn't seem to move. He wondered where on earth his aides were. He finally managed to collect himself sufficiently to walk back into his headquarters and ask the radio operator what news he had had from the base. In the back of his mind, he did not know what possible good such knowledge could do him now. It hardly seemed possible that the partly decimated base could send reinforcements.

"The enemy still has not been located," the radio operator said, apparently in complete seriousness.

"You goddamn idiot, they're right outside!" Galanskov shouted.

Just at that instant another rocket whined in and exploded so close that the walls of the headquarters trembled and Galanskov was nearly knocked off his feet.

They soon discovered that the rocket had destroyed the generating system; the power for the radio was dead.

Galanskov realized that they were completely isolated.

Drexell's men moved quickly, zigzagging across the mud and sand of the beach, sometimes slipping in the ooze, while automatic fire tore into the beach all around, kicking up clouds of choking sand.

But soon they reached the security fence and began cutting their way through it.

No Cubans were in evidence; the defenders were all Russian.

They put up a valiant struggle, but with so much of the port area in flames, it was all the Russians could do to devote these meager forces to repelling the attackers.

The invaders, on breaking through the fence, used their firepower indiscriminately. These men were ruthless; mercy was an alien concept to them. They'd been taught to hate communists and now that they thought they had a chance to avenge their grievances, they went all out.

Hurling grenades into the darkness, they gave no consideration as to where the grenades might be going. It wasn't unusual for them to end up killing their own men this way.

Once they'd succeeded in pushing back the defenders, their objective was to seize one of the ships and put out to sea, but Drexell realized that they were a long way from that point. Although he expected casualties to be heavy on both sides, what concerned him most now was the question of what had happened to Hahn's unit.

Hahn had not imagined that it would take him this long to get within sight of the docking area. He'd led his force—or what remained of it—on a route parallel to the one that Drexell's had followed, but on the opposite side of the road. With so many wounded in his ranks, his progress was even further retarded. There were moments when he didn't think he would make it at all, that he would find himself stranded in hostile territory with no hope of ever escaping.

The first sign he had that he was close to the port was the sound of the detonating rockets. The men straggling behind him paused and listened to the uproar with great satisfaction.

With renewed energy, they plunged on until they could glimpse the crimson sheet that the sky had become from the fires springing up throughout the docking area.

To announce their presence, Hahn directed five men to deploy themselves as close as they could to the port—a position midway down a slope overlooking the boats berthed there—and use the last of the rockets against any target that still remained intact.

This part of the operation called for improvising, and Hahn only hoped that he wouldn't make a mistake that would result in the deaths of the men fighting with Drexell.

The first two rockets struck the Moskva class anti-submarine cruiser. Even from his vantage point, Hahn could see men emerging from belowdeck and leaping into the water in anticipation of the whole ship's blowing to kingdom come. But this failed to happen.

In any case, the water didn't provide the sanctuary the sailors hoped. With such vast quantities of fuel floating on its surface, it ignited easily and soon the water had become a boiling cauldron. Those who did not have their skin sheared off by the blistering flames or who did not suffocate for lack of oxygen, simply drowned.

Mortars and howitzers were now being moved up to the southern edge of the base by Soviet troops held in reserve. But they were constrained from using the artillery for fear of shelling their own men. They had no choice but to either wait until the situation resolved itself or to participate in hand-to-hand combat in an attempt to drive off the assailants.

Only one ship was left that hadn't suffered any damage—the Grisha class patrol boat. Flames leaped harmlessly up from the water all around it.

Reassured by the arrival of Hahn's force, Drexell decided that the time had come to move on the patrol boat. Mobilizing a small contingent of Salvadorian and Honduran troops, he led them toward the boat. They had by now secured most of the port area and were driving the Russians back onto the docks themselves. On the bow of the patrol boat, which was tied to a jetty that had been transformed by a rocket into a tangled heap of wood and metal, two Russians were using a twin 57mm Gatling on the invaders. Their fire managed to stall the advance the Salvadorians and Hondurans were making, obliging them to renew the attack by other means.

The attackers hurled grenades toward the turret mount, but failed to silence the guns. Finally, six men decided to knock out the guns themselves. Crawling around the mangled jetty to the other side of the ship, they clambered up the starboard side.

Drexell, keeping apprised by radio of the positions of both his men and Hahn's throughout the port area, took personal charge of the attack on the patrol boat. Taking it over was the most important objective at this stage of the operation.

Stealing toward the turret, the six men came within five yards of it before the gunners detected their presence and swiveled the Gatlings around.

Four of the six men were killed instantly. The other two were able to fire their weapons, felling one of the Russians and leaving the other dangling bloodily over his gun, which spewed the deck randomly with bullets until the life ebbed out of the gunner.

The way was now clear for the rest of the attackers to climb on board. As soon as Drexell had come up on deck he discharged his flare gun so that the patrol boat shone with a sudden strange brightness. So unexpected was the flash of light that the combatants stopped fighting for a moment.

Drexell's purpose was to alert Hahn as to his location and to signal him and his force to join him on board. This Russian patrol boat, he decided, was going to provide their means of escape.

As more and more men came on board, some of them dragging wounded with them, others were sent below to quell any resistance that might develop from the crew belowdeck.

But there was surprisingly little. Several of the soldiers quartered in the cabins below surrendered at the first sign of the enemy. Under the impression that all was already lost and that further fighting would be useless, they were led out onto the bridge, their hands held behind their heads.

The officers, clustered in a knot at the starboard side of the boat, were divided as to whether to try to prevent a seizure of their vessel. For several minutes they laid down a fitful barrage from behind the conning tower.

However, when they realized they were surrounded they, too, ceased firing and gave up.

Drexell knew enough Russian to communicate his orders to them.

He informed them that he wanted them to return to their stations and navigate the patrol boat out into the harbor. When they expressed their reluctance, he pressed his .45 to the captain's temple. This seemed to alter their attitude, but to insure their compliance he sent armed guards along with them.

As he waited, he heard his name called. He looked to see who had spoken and spotted Hahn standing on what remained of the jetty.

As Hahn came on board, Drexell saw that his clothes were in tatters, his face blackened with soot, but otherwise he appeared in reasonable shape. So, Drexell thought, his faith had not been misplaced after all.

The two men began to talk, paying scant attention to the bullets trailing through the air and ringing painfully close on the boat's superstructure.

"We taking this ship out of here?" Hahn asked wearily.

"That's right," Drexell affirmed.

"Not all the men have made it on board," Hahn pointed out.

"Nothing to be done about it. The longer we stay here, the more risk we're taking. Anyone who's still in the area can try to make it back on the launches," he said, pointing to other craft nearby.

While recognizing that this was the only practical thing to be done, Hahn was nonetheless disturbed by the ruthlessness of Drexell's decision.

"And what about those jokers?" Hahn eyed the dozen Russian prisoners lined up on the quarterdeck.

"When we're on our way we'll load them and their command into lifeboats. I have no intention of taking them into international waters."

Their conversation was interrupted by a terrific roar to their right. A fire had apparently made its way through to the fuel supply of the antisubmarine cruiser and set it off, causing the craft almost to break in two. Men jackknifed into the burning waters, their screams drowning out the sounds of battle.

Meanwhile, the boat they were on began to come to life and little by little pulled away from its berth. Sporadic fire from the docks failed to impede its progress.

Drexell knew that if they managed to effect their escape without further interference, they would be well out into the Caribbean, in international waters, before dawn. Only then would he allow himself to rest.

Just as he was about to go belowdeck, two of his men, both wiry Miskito Indians from southern Nicaragua, approached him, holding a man between them.

He was a handsome fellow dressed in whites, and when he looked at Drexell it was with defiance.

"We found him hiding in a stateroom," one of the Indians said.

"I was not hiding. I was sleeping," the man replied petulantly.

"And what might your name be?"

"You may look at my passport. I am a Mexican national. My name is Hidalgo."

Drexell told the Indians to release him. Then, much to Hidalgo's surprise, he reached forward and took his hand.

"You don't know how much I've been wanting to meet you, Hidalgo," he said with enthusiasm. "You and I are in for a very long talk."

GUERRILLA CLASH REPORTED
IN NICARAGUA

MANAGUA, Nicaragua, June 16 (Reuters)—
Reports reaching here from the interior say that a
major battle took place between Sandinista and
Cuban troops and antigovernment guerrilla forces
in an area not far from Nicaragua. Witnesses to the
conflict said that they heard a series of explosions
throughout the night of June 14. They could not
confirm the identity of the attackers, however. The
Sandinista government in Managua denied that
such a clash took place, adding that with the exception of Cuban advisers and technicians, no Cuban
troops were based in the country.

Some sources, who refused to be identified by
name, said that the reported clash occurred not in
Nicaragua, but in the northern tier of neighboring
Costa Rica. A spokesman for the San José government said that as far as he knew no foreign forces
were in his country. "We have heard nothing about
any battle on the night of the 14th," he said.

MOSCOW REPUDIATES HIJACKING CLAIM

MOSCOW, June 16 (UPI)—Tass, the official
Soviet news agency, released a statement today
branding a West German magazine item as "an
outright falsehood and provocation" for reporting
that a Soviet military vessel was hijacked off the
coast of Costa Rica yesterday. The magazine Quick
said that the Soviet Union had established a clandestine base on the northeast coast in a relatively
uninhabited part of the country and that various
destroyers and transport ships had routinely used it
in the last several months. Quick said that the harbor was a supply depot for Cuban troops on their
way to fight in the war now going on between Vene-

zuela and Guyana. A guerrilla force, according to the German weekly, attacked the harbor and seized at least one Soviet ship. In the Tass statement, Deputy Defense Minister Marshal Sergei Sokolov was quoted as saying, "The Soviet Union has no ships of a military purpose anywhere proximate to the coast of Costa Rica. Consequently, it is not possible that any Soviet ship could either have been hijacked or pirated from there."

WASHINGTON DENIES KNOWLEDGE OF FIGHTING

WASHINGTON, June 16 (Combined dispatches)—Donald Eller, a State Department spokesman, said that he had no knowledge of a bitter clash that was said to have taken place in northeastern Costa Rica on the night of the 14th. According to reports, Cuban and possibly Soviet troops might have been involved in the fighting against guerrillas drawn from camps in Honduras. Widespread rumors have been circulating for years that anticommunist guerrillas are being trained by American advisers in that country. "Guerrilla warfare has been endemic in that part of Central America for years," Eller said. "But we are unaware of any major new outbreak." He added that "there is absolutely no truth to allegations that any American forces might have been involved in military engagement in the region."

SECRET PEACE TALKS SAID TO BE UNDERWAY

Special to the New York Times

NEW YORK, June 16—UN officials refused to confirm that behind-the-scenes negotiations were in motion to end the fighting between Guyana and

Venezuela. According to one source, who declined to give his name, both Secretary of State Jeffrey Schelling and Soviet Foreign Minister Valeri Marchenko were actively seeking to lay the groundwork for a diplomatic solution to the three-week-old war. Presumably Schelling is representing the Venezuelan position and his Soviet counterpart the Guyanese. The source, who is close to UN Secretary-General Hueller, said that "With the war bogged down both sides have an interest in seeing the conflict brought to an end so long as neither has to lose face in the process."

20

When Drexell had completed his briefing, an exhaustive summary of Operation Sunbaker, he waited for the President's reaction.

Creighton Turner appeared far less pleased than he'd anticipated. Swiveling back and forth in the chair next to the President, his chief of staff, Morse Peckum, looked decidedly glum.

Only Martin Rhiel gave the impression that he was satisfied with Sunbaker's outcome.

"What were those casualty figures?" the President asked.

"Our losses were forty-three dead, seventy-two wounded, half of those critically."

"That means nearly half your men suffered casualties," said Peckum.

"It was a very difficult mission. Considering the circumstances, I believe we did exceptionally well."

"How many did you have to leave behind?"

"Ten dead, another eight or nine wounded."

"They'll interrogate the wounded," Peckum pointed out.

"We took that contingency into account. But it's not very relevant at this point. The Russians continue to deny that they had a base in Costa Rica. I don't believe that they'll suddenly begin naming us as their attackers.''

"Still, I don't like it,'' the President said, shaking his head.

"Mr. President, Operation Sunbaker was very nearly a complete success. May I remind you that we also netted a top Cuban operative in the process who I expect will be able to provide us with some excellent intelligence in regard to Castro's other activities in the Caribbean. We might even turn him and set him loose again. I don't understand what the problem is.''

Drexell was convinced that once again the President had fallen under the spell of his chief of staff. Morse Peckum was always terrified that an international crisis would get out of hand and result in a precipitous dropoff in the President's domestic support.

"The Cubans are one thing,'' the President said, "but engaging the Russians in combat is quite another.''

It was the thought of Americans and Soviets clashing that really had him worried, Drexell realized.

"If we were to get at the military installations, there was no way we could avoid a confrontation,'' Drexell said patiently. "We were pretty certain Russians were bivouacked there, and it was something we were ready to deal with. I think you have to look at the bigger picture.''

"The bigger picture!'' Peckum screamed. "What bigger picture could there be than Americans and Russians locked in hand-to-hand combat? What's bigger than the possibility of our nuking one another?''

"Not so loud,'' the President said, putting a restraining hand on Peckum's wrist.

"May I remind Mr. Peckum that none of our men were directly involved in fighting with the Russians,'' Drexell said softly. "Hondurans, Nicaraguans, Guatemalans, yes, but not citizens of the United States. It's my opinion that the Soviets will shut up about the incident and get on with the business of setting up shop elsewhere in Central America.''

"It'll take them time," the President said as if to reassure himself.

"Absolutely. I'd say a great deal of time. Time we can use." Drexell paused for a moment before continuing on a related subject. "I understand that Schelling and Marchenko are trying to work out a deal on the Venezuela-Guyana thing."

"It came as quite a surprise," the President admitted. "We've made our good offices available since the start of the conflict, but it wasn't until yesterday morning that we got a call from Marchenko saying he wanted to talk."

While Drexell thought it likely that Sunbaker might have been instrumental in convincing the Soviets to consider the negotiating table rather than the battlefield as a means to iron out a settlement, he refrained from taking any credit. With Peckum's skepticism already poisoning the atmosphere, he decided to watch his step.

"Does it look like they might come to terms?" he asked.

"I spoke to Schelling at noon," the President said, "and he sounds reasonably optimistic. He and Marchenko are talking about a cease-fire and a freezing of all positions on the ground, followed by mutual negotiations over the final adjustment of the border and then a phased withdrawal."

"We're confident that we can announce a cease-fire by tomorrow midnight."

"How will that affect the disposition of opposing forces?"

Rhiel took Drexell's question. "The Venezuelans are still in a defensive posture. But the supply lines of the Cuban and Guyanese troops have been way overextended and the Venezuelans are primed to take advantage of it. If Sunbaker has in fact debilitated the capability of the Soviets to furnish Guyana with additional military matériel and personnel, then I think the Venezuelans are in a better place now than they've been in since the war started. If I were in charge of the Guyanese war machine I'd be looking for a cease-fire before all my gains were eroded."

"Why would the Venezuelans go for a cease-fire now rather than push for a win on the battlefield?" Peckum demanded.

"Because it would take some weeks before the loss of the Costa Rican staging area would make itself felt," Rhiel replied. "The Cubans are crack troops, they could hold out for another month and, frankly, the Venezuelans don't have the strength to sustain the war for that long. Their economy is already in bad shape, the government's position is very shaky, and they're as anxious for an out as the Guyanese.

"And I don't have to remind you that we would probably have to send still more advisers into Venezuela if the war went on."

Peckum eyed the Defense Secretary reproachfully. Their having recently sent even 600 men down to Venezuela had met with an unwelcome response on the part of Congress and the American public. There would almost unquestionably be an uproar if additional troops were dispatched, and the action would throw into doubt the President's assertion that they were only being sent to provide "technical assistance and not participate in a combat role."

In point of fact, 400 American men were now attached to a Venezuelan division actively engaged in the fighting. True, they were in the rear lines, but that could change overnight.

"What do you see happening now, Bill?" The President once again turned to Drexell. Though he basically trusted Drexell, the President still harbored the suspicion that one day he would perpetrate some clandestine operation that would jeopardize his position, perhaps even to the point of precipitating his impeachment.

"If a cease-fire does occur, then I would expect an intensification of the conflict in the next thirty-six hours as both parties try to gain the most favorable positions they can before they have to sit down at the bargaining table. I wouldn't even be surprised if the Venezuelans discover a weakness in the Cuban lines and break through in an attempt to seize a small portion of Guyana."

"And then?"

"Then a series of cease-fire violations until the troops withdraw or we can get a neutral force in there to mediate between the two."

"Well," the President said, "I think we can all live with that. Cease-fire violations are nothing new to us. "We just want to get our boys out in one piece before something happens to them."

21

JUNE 17,
VENEZUELA, THE FRONTIER

From 8,000 feet up, the landscape presented an idyllic image: a sweeping panorama of green, broken here and there by dark waterways, narrow riverbeds, and rapids that suddenly spilled over into surging falls.

John Zoccola was in the rear of a large twin-engine craft, waiting to be fitted into his parachute—a T-10 —by the riggers. Sixty men, all Special Forces "advisers" detached from Fort Bragg under the command of Lieutenant Colonel Ky Lawson, waited in silence to make the jump. Their mission was to secure a base behind Venezuelan lines and to establish communication links with three battalions of Venezuelan marines and infantry that had earlier that morning parachuted more than fifty miles into Guyana. The Americans were under explicit instructions to remain in Venezuelan territory while the Venezuelans pursued a far-reaching, and potentially dangerous, operation advancing well into Guyana. Lawson's men were charged with coordinating communication and support systems from the rear; if it proved necessary, they were also to assist in an orderly retreat should the combined Cuban-Guyanese forces succeed in dislodging the Venezuelans.

The Venezuelans, of course, were seeking a more advantageous position on the ground for future negotiations at the bargaining table.

But there was always the possibility that the cease-fire would not be agreed upon, with the result that the Venezuelan troops might be either cut off or completely destroyed.

It was the responsibility of this Special Forces unit to make certain that this did not happen.

Lawson stepped up to Zoccola and glanced without interest out the open door of the plane, in the direction of the drop zone.

"One thing I can't for the life of me understand is why you want to go back into this goddamn jungle. You just got out of it, didn't you?"

"The people I work for want me to see what happens," he said cryptically. Lawson had been ordered to take Zoccola along on the mission and had been told not to ask any questions about his role. Still, he couldn't entirely suppress his curiosity about this enigmatic stranger.

"You ever do this sort of thing before, jump out of a plane?" he asked.

Zoccola nodded. The truth was he hadn't. He had gotten no farther than practice jumps from towers at the Farm. But this was not something he cared to admit to Lawson.

A captain standing at the forward end of the cabin gave the thumbs-up sign.

The captain began calling out names in the order the men would jump. Lawson and Zoccola were last in line.

The craft climbed higher. A vast overgrown stretch of forest was yielding to a lush valley through which countless streams meandered, some to join larger bodies of water, some to disappear altogether.

Zoccola flexed his legs, checked his static line, and took his place among the men.

The plane was leveling off, making a wide circle before coming in on its jump run.

The first man went, receding fast before the green

Army T-10 opened in a burst of nylon. The second and third men quickly followed him.

Below, purple marker smoke dropped from the plane, was beginning to cover much of the drop zone.

Much farther in the distance, puffs of smoke from antiaircraft guns could be discerned, but the Cuban battery emplacements were so far away that they produced little sound.

Lawson talked while they waited. "Gooks, Guyanese, all the same to me," he said to Zoccola, methodically chewing the same piece of gum he'd been working on ever since they'd taken off from Ciudad Bolívar.

Lawson was a big confident man with the face of a boy from the country who knew a hell of a lot more than he would let on; with his aviator glasses, his polished boots, and his beret, he could not have been mistaken for anything other than a group leader.

He'd served in Nam and in Cambodia and to him, jungles and bush were familiar territory.

Over the land hailer, a sergeant was reminding the men to bury their chutes once they hit the ground so as to cover their trail in the event of aerial surveillance.

The sky was becoming full of green as the chutes opened up.

"You're next, babe," Lawson said.

Zoccola stood for a moment in the opening of the door, gazing out uncertainly.

"You going or you bullshitting?" Lawson asked.

Zoccola decided that he didn't much like Lawson and let himself go.

Falling, Zoccola almost immediately pulled himself up into military tuck position. He counted to two and tugged on his chute. An instant later he felt the shock of the chute coming open.

After checking the canopy for a Mae West or for any blown panels, Zoccola then began to unhook his Stevens system, a cord which could automatically pull the reserve handle in the event that he would have to cut away the main chute.

Then he reached for the steering toggles on the risers

so that he could navigate himself closer to the drop zone. Turning into the wind, he prepared to land.

The landing was soft. Zoccola raised himself from the ground to see Lawson and the captain who'd acted as jump master approaching.

With the last men in the stick safely in the drop zone, the unit proceeded to bury the chutes. It was done efficiently, but even so, anyone patrolling on the ground would have no problem spotting them.

It was now close to noon. If rumors that a cease-fire was in the offing were indeed correct, they might be only hours away from an end to the war.

But the last day of a war could as easily take your life as the first one.

Lawson gave the order to move out. He showed Zoccola the point on the map where they were to establish their base. "What it is is a small Indian vilage about six miles from here. But the word is there's no one there."

"What happened to them?"

Lawson shrugged, exhibiting scant interest. "The Reds scared them off."

As the Special Forces advanced toward the village, the rumble of artillery fire in the direction of the border region grew louder. From time to time Venezuelan F-16's swooped in low over the jungle fifteen miles away and dropped incendiary and cluster bombs on suspected Cuban and Guyanese positions. Flames surged up above the treeline moments later.

When they arrived at the outskirts of the village, they had a view of a cluster of thatched and mud-baked houses, most of them set on stilts fixed in the mud.

Evidently not all the Indians who lived here had been driven away. Those still in evidence gave the Americans stony looks, but otherwise failed to register any reaction. It was as though they'd gotten used to encroaching armies.

One family of Indians they found had decided to make an abandoned Panhard AML armored car their home. To Zoccola's astonishment, the villagers had neglected to appropriate the Draganov rifles and an interesting collection of ordnance left behind in a nearby house by the retreating Cubans.

"What happens now?" Zoccola asked as they studied the indifferent Indians.

"We set up base, we tune in our radios, and we hunker down and wait," Lawson said.

"I'd like to monitor the radios."

"Who are you anyway?" Lawson exploded. "The ambassador says he's got instructions you're to be extended any privileges I can offer. He says he doesn't know why. He says the instructions came from on high. You have any idea where on high means?"

Zoccola raised his eyes to the heavens.

"Nobody's that fucking high," Lawson muttered, but he didn't pursue his line of questioning.

"The radios?" Zoccola reminded him.

"Sure, listen to the fucking radios all you fucking want."

The communications room was set up in one of the huts; it smelled like mud and dung inside, but Zoccola figured that he'd get used to it. He didn't, though; over the course of the day, he kept having to go outside and take a deep breath to remind himself what fresh air smelled like.

From the messages coming over the military bands—decoded with dispatch by a captain who said he had a doctorate in Russian literature—Zoccola surmised that the Venezuelan advance was proceeding well. Relying on satellite and spy plane photographs supplied by their American allies, the Venezuelans had managed to secure a bridgehead in an area where the Cuban lines were stretched to their thinnest, at a distance of twenty miles from where the Special Forces were bivouacked. Apparently the strike had come so unexpectedly that the Cuban and Guyanese forces had yet to mobilize sufficiently to counteract it.

So far no request for any assistance from the Americans had materialized.

One radio was tuned to a commercial band, another to shortwave broadcasts. Caracas radio was confining

itself to repeating press statements out of New York. A
cease-fire agreement was still being hammered out in a
conference room in the Waldorf-Astoria, one statement
advised, but optimism prevailed among the partici-
pants, and it was considered likely that ratification
would come before the end of the day. Georgetown
radio, by contrast, mentioned nothing about a cease-fire
and instead broadcast reports that the early-morning
Venezuelan advance was being systematically repelled.
Zoccola decided that trying to distinguish truth from
fiction on Georgetown radio was as entertaining an
exercise as a game of poker with a bad hand.

Periodically Zoccola walked outside to find men
stretched out reading magazines in hammocks or else
swatting the intimidatingly large black flies that enjoyed
picking at human flesh.

At five that afternoon Lawson noticed Zoccola
wandering about on break and asked him if he'd heard
anything that might be worth his attention.

Zoccola shook his head.

"Thought so," Lawson said sourly.

The artillery fire could still be heard, but it was such a
commonplace sound by now that it went ignored.

"They're still expecting to sign a cease-fire agreement
in New York," Zoccola added.

"They can do whatever they damn well like. Ain't
going to change a fucking thing."

They eventually returned to the communications
room and checked out the decoded reports from the
battlefield. "Hot damn, we're not doing so bad after
all," Lawson said, obviously indentifying with the
Venezuelan successes.

He was still perusing the reports when a station out of
Ciudad Bolívar interrupted its music to announce that a
cease-fire agreement had finally been reached.

"Shit," Lawson said. "A little more time and we
could pull this one out."

"In New York City," the announcement began, "a
spokesman for the United Nations stated that a cease-
fire would go into effect between the armed forces of

Venezuela and the armed forces of Guyana and the armed forces of their respective allies at midnight Eastern Standard Time, at one A.M. Caracas time, and at one-fifteen A.M. Georgetown time. At that hour the disposition of forces on the ground will be frozen in place.''

According to the agreement, negotiations between Guyana, Venezuela, the United States, and the Soviet Union would begin in three days' time in order to lay the groundwork for a phased withdrawal and a rectification of the borders acceptable to all parties to the conflict.

''Still seven hours away,'' Lawson said. ''Any damn thing can happen in seven hours.''

Nonetheless, he proceeded to contact the military airfield at Ciudad Bolivar to arrange a pick-up by chopper at a prearranged rendezvous point some six and a half miles away from the village.

''We'll be airlifted out and be back home in good old Ciudad by oh-three hundred.''

''Where exactly is the rendezvous point?'' Zoccola asked.

''You want to know everything, don't you?''

''That's right.''

''Who are you to want to know everything?''

Zoccola maintained his composure. ''Told you, I'm just curious. I have friends who encourage my curiosity.''

''You have friends and I have friends, but I have this feeling about your type of friends. I knew some of your friends in Nam. They disappeared people. Suspected Vietcong, they just went puff in the night when they ended up in the hands of your friends. They poached on our territory.''

''I don't doubt that they saved your ass more than once.''

''Hey, I didn't say I didn't like your friends. I just don't fucking associate with them.''

With that, Lawson walked out of the communications room.

The airstrip turned out to be situated near a deeply

eroded sandstone ridge that extended for a mile above the forest. To reach it, the Special Forces were obliged to march through a savanna that was particularly wet at this time of year.

They had started out early, just past six, when the sun was still high in the west. Lawson was determined to get his men to the rendezvous point at least an hour in advance of the scheduled pick-up.

Throughout the afternoon and into the night, the Soviet column, composed of rear services logistical support troops under the command of Captain Valeri Bahkman, had been slowly making its way back toward the Guyanese frontier.

For reasons that had not been fully clarified to Bahkman's satisfaction, the order to withdraw had not come until 1:30 in the afternoon. What had caused the delay no one seemed to know. At any rate, until his force could be flown out, they would remain badly exposed in Venezuelan-held territory. Should any of them be captured, it would constitute a grave embarrassment for the Soviet Union, which continued to deny that any of its armed forces were operating in the war theater.

Bahkman's unit had been providing security and supply support to a larger Cuban force ever since hostilities were initiated. Like the Americans, the Soviets were to maintain a noncombat role.

But a Venezuelan counterattack three days previously had cut off the Cuban brigade from the Soviet rear services group, and it seemed, at least until this afternoon, that it had been all but forgotten by headquarters.

Bahkman had begun his career in the Carpathian Military District and had later been assigned as an adviser to the Sandinista army in Nicaragua prior to being sent into this part of South America. Those under his command, on the other hand, were detached from the Russian Northern Army Group and from East Germany, and had been transported by air to Georgetown. As a result, Bahkman had only a passing acquaintance with his men; they tended to grumble too much, in his opinion. More than bullets and bombs, they feared contracting some dread tropical disease, a fear not without some basis in fact, for five of them had already come down with hepatitis.

Encased in life jackets and with their Kalashnikovs tied to them, Bahkman's force crossed the Carrao River on inflated rafts at half-past nine at night. The crossing took the better part of an hour.

Once ashore, a reconnaissance patrol fanned out to insure that the area was secure. The others stayed behind until Bahkman received word on his field radio that they could proceed.

Half a mile beyond the river the reconnaissance patrol was alerted to the sound of men approaching. With the darkness, however, it would be some minutes before they'd come into sight.

Acting on the assumption that they faced a Venezuelan force, the patrol sought to obtain an estimate of the number of men in the approaching party. Quickly the patrol scrambled through the brush parallel to the advancing force.

Lawson didn't know what he heard, but he was damn sure he heard something off to the side. Without hesitating, he fired off a flare.

Two figures were immediately silhouetted in the blinding flash of light.

"Intercept them!" he ordered.

Twenty men drove through the brush in an attempt to cut them off.

At this point no one had any idea who the two men were.

The radio operator nodded. "I can't be a hundred percent certain, sir, but it sounds like they're speaking Russian. It seems like whoever's in charge of that patrol out there has some friends he's in contact with. Can't understand a word of what he's saying, but my guess is he's asking for help."

Lawson looked uneasily at Zoccola, who was close enough to overhear the operator's words. Nonetheless, the Lieutenant Colonel appeared to be unconcerned.

Lawson was determined to keep the patrol bottled up and either force its surrender or else eliminate it altogether.

"They've got the river behind them, we're right on top of them, so they're fucked," he told Zoccola.

"What the hell are we doing?" Zoccola said. "The war ends in a couple of hours, we can just go on our way. There couldn't be more than half a dozen men out there. It's not like they're any threat to us."

"You all think the same," Lawson said, but Zoccola had no way of knowing to whom he was referring.

At any rate, before they could move in on the patrol, the main Soviet force materialized nearby; it announced itself with a flurry of grenades and a savage burst of automatic fire.

"What the hell?" Lawson spun around to see what had happened.

"Shit!" somebody shouted out. "It's fucking Ivan."

Lawson exchanged a glance with Zoccola. The definite knowledge that it was the Russians, not the Cubans, they were pitted against changed the picture entirely.

One way or another, Lawson was not about to let his force be trapped or delayed in its goal of reaching the rendezvous point on time.

"We're going to fight our fucking way out of this," he said.

"Look," Zoccola said, "this is crazy. We don't want to go fighting Ivan."

Tracer bullets from Russian gunners stuttered into a tree four feet from where they were standing. Zoccola dropped down but Lawson stayed upright.

"You want to be a fucking hero?" Zoccola yelled up at him.

"That's the way I am, spook," said Lawson.

Seeing the flare, the Soviet recon patrol retreated back toward the banks of the Carrao, somewhat upriver from where they had made their crossing.

With their backs to the river, the patrol leader, a twenty-year-old corporal from the Ukraine, radioed for assistance. He was still under the impression that he was confronting Venezuelans.

Although he had no direct orders to open fire, he could see no other choice. It was imperative that he avoid capture; he'd heard stories of atrocities committed on Cubans who'd been taken by the Venezuelans, and he believed them.

The patrol's fire was meant only to arrest the enemy advance, which accounted for its random and sporadic nature.

The Special Forces returned the fire as they temporarily fell back.

So close to the rendezvous point, about the last thing that Lawson had been expecting was a pitched battle.

The radio operator by his side was bent low, trying to make out the radio traffic coming over his receiver.

"They're speaking Russian," he said. "I'm sure they're speaking Russian."

More tracer bullets whipped past them. For a moment a flare turned the forest into a weird sickly yellow; scrub plants and palms trembled in the violent light.

Machine guns up the river were brought into play. Two of Lawson's men were hit and collapsed in a heap. A third lay wounded and moaning.

"Hit back," Lawson screamed, calling to his men. "Molson, Hardwick, Tannenbaum, Smith, Orson, Manning, go around to the right. See if you can draw off some of that artillery!"

To another group, crouched amid the scrub plants, he shouted, "I want you to take out that machine gun coming from eleven-thirty."

Raising his Steiner binoculars, he strained to see which way the battle was going.

A Russian rocket detonated in the brush. To Zoccola it sounded like an awesomely large pneumatic hammer breaking up giant pavement. Black smoke cascaded above the palms.

A few moments later the Americans delivered their response. Two rockets, launched by hand, were fired downriver into Russian positions. One fell wide and detonated in the scrub, setting fire to the grass and brush in the immediate vicinity, but the second scored a direct hit, knocking out the machine gun and eliminating the crew manning it.

Recognizing that the patrol was unequal to the task of sustaining a protracted engagement, Bahkman decided to order it back. To him, it made little sense for the recon force to engage in an all-out struggle this close to the cease-fire.

On the other hand, he gave no thought to withdrawing the main force and allowing the enemy to inflict a humiliating defeat on his troops.

He ordered the 140mm M1965—a self-propelled launcher in common use among the Warsaw Pact countries—to be fired again. The launcher held sixteen tubes and could be reloaded in four minutes, but Bahkman decided that only six should be used now, discharged at the rate of one every three minutes.

His objective was to keep the Americans off-balance and held down upriver until the cease-fire at one A.M. He also hoped that the rocket barrage would help the battered patrol to make its escape if indeed any survivors were left in it—the patrol's radio had seemed dead for some time.

"Our best hope is to hang on until the cease-fire," he told his aide. "Let's just pray that the crazy Americans abide by it." Then he turned and gave his gunners the order to fire.

Lawson was growing frustrated; he'd lost twelve men and had little to show for it, but he was determined not to retreat in the face of the Soviet assault.

For his part, Zoccola could not believe what was happening. After forty-five years of uneasy peace, U.S. and Soviet forces were finally shooting at one another. This wasn't a matter of spy planes, manned or not, being shot out of the air; it was something much worse, possibly a prelude to combat on a far larger scale.

There were still sixteen minutes to go until the cease-fire. But as the battle raged time seemed to slow to a crawl.

The Russian rockets kept falling at regular intervals along the part of the river bank that the Americans controlled. But as their trajectories could be predicted, it was easy enough to avoid them. Zoccola surmised that the Russians wanted only to pin Lawson's forces down, presumably so that the remnants of their patrol could escape, rather than cause a great number of U.S. casualties.

But unknown to the Americans a machine gun emplacement had been moved forward and concealed in a bed of high grass directly across from U.S. positions. Once it started, its fire was particularly withering and, more than the rockets, forced the men under Lawson's command to lie low.

Lawson didn't like it. He was everywhere at once now, directing the fire and urging his men forward. One thing he obviously didn't lack for was courage.

He, like Bahkman and Zoccola, was very much aware of the time. But his intention was different from theirs; he was obsessed with the idea of punishing the Soviets before the cease-fire.

By eight minutes to the hour he had quietly led ten of his men in a circle generally in a downriver direction, taking them on a snaking path toward the Soviet positions. From time to time he'd fire his gun, a 7.62mm Bren, but mostly he exhorted his troops to quicken their pace.

Three Soviets behind a machine gun panicked and fled just when Lawson and his men were almost upon them.

A burst from Lawson's Bren brought two of them down. One of his men took out the third.

It was four minutes to the hour.

It could have been Nam, it could have been Cambodia—Lawson was in his element. He no longer gave a good goddamn about the time. With the Soviets in disarray and close to retreating, he had no intention of stopping.

A grenade went off behind him, but he ignored it. A second erupted at his feet, catapulting him high in the air. When he came down he was still alive, but both his legs had been blown off. There was a hole where his genitals had been, but he was so numb from the shock that he felt nothing.

He lay there, his eyes burning, until his life quietly flickered out.

At exactly one o'clock Caracas time, the American and Russian guns fell silent. The cease-fire was now in effect.

22

JUNE 18,
TRIAD HEADQUARTERS, VIRGINIA

It was four in the afternoon, and William Drexell had assembled the members of Triad in the headquarters conference room to consider the events of the past several days.

While James Lisker and Jerry Hahn appeared relatively relaxed, the same could not be said of John Zoccola. He'd arrived back in the United States by way of a specially chartered Lear jet from Caracas only three hours previously. The debilitating effects of the knife wound he had sustained in Fort-de-France combined with the exhaustion and sleeplessness of battle to give him a ghostlike appearance.

Drexell began the debriefing session by announcing that he'd just received word from the White House regarding the clash between U.S. and Soviet forces in the Venezuelan border region.

"After all-night consultations with members of his cabinet, the President has decided against making public any of the details of the fight," he said. "He and Kadiyev have apparently been in contact and they've reached an understanding of sorts. The Russians won't say anything if we won't. American losses will be attributed to a helicopter crash. As I'm sure you're aware, the Russians usually don't have to go to great lengths to cover up incidents that might prove embarrassing to them."

"Doesn't the President believe that the families of the dead have a right to know what happened?" Hahn asked.

"I can't speak for the President." Drexell said, an unusual note of apology tingeing his gravelly voice. He was uncertain of the wisdom of the President's decision, but he could understand its reasoning. An event of this significance could have devastating consequences once word leaked out that ground forces of the two superpowers had been engaged in combat. On the other hand, he didn't know how long such a thing could be kept secret, since there were any number of witnesses to the battle.

One way or another, Drexell felt sure, news of the clash and subsequent cover-up would leak out, and then there'd be hell to pay. It might even be sufficient to bring down the administration, with unforeseen consequences to Triad's future.

"What's most important, Jerry, is that we try to avoid something like this occurring again. I'd say the fact that Kadiyev and the President have consulted on this is a favorable sign."

"But you don't hold out much hope that it represents any real change in Soviet policy," Hahn prodded.

"You suspect right. I think everyone, the Soviets included, is in something of a state of shock. So long as both American and Russian soldiers were in the field the possibility of a combat situation always existed, but no one thought it would actually happen. But that's nothing new; people have more often blundered into war than gone ahead and planned it out carefully in advance."

Although he was older than anyone else in the room, Drexell had more energy and would have thought nothing of conducting a full-scale debriefing that went on for hours. But he recognized it would make more sense if the group members rested and had a chance to collect their thoughts.

After a short discussion of the situation that now existed on the ground in the disputed border region, he dismissed the meeting.

He stopped Zoccola at the door. "Have you seen a doctor, by the way?" he asked, a stern look on his face.

"I haven't managed to fit one into my schedule."

"Well, see one, for chrissakes. And if he puts you in bed, stay in it, goddammit." Ignoring the younger man's smile, he left the room for his office.

An hour later Lieutenant Colonel Cavanaugh brought Drexell a report that had just been transmitted from the Pentagon.

"It may be nothing, sir," he began by saying, "but satellite recon has just picked up some significant troop movements in the Urals and Volga. It seems that three divisions of the Central Military District are joining up with the eighteen divisions now in the Southern Military District."

"That's it?"

"That's it."

"Thank you, Colonel, that will be all."

As Cavanaugh had indicated, the information might be unimportant—just a transfer of troops in anticipation of unannounced war games. But it unsettled Drexell just the same. The eighteen divisions that composed most of the Southern Military District—the remaining six were deployed in Afghanistan—presented the main threat to Iran, which lay just south of the Soviet Union. But as many strategists had noted for years, no invasion of Iran would be possible without drawing down divisions from other districts.

Was it possible that Kadiyev was hoping to distract the United States by negotiating a settlement in the Guyana-Venezuela dispute so that it could prepare for an invasion that might take its troops all the way to the Persian Gulf?

There was no way of telling at this point. At the moment there was, if not peace in the world, at least a cessation of hostilities. For now, all Drexell could do was accept the lull at face value.

He put away his papers, shut off the computer console in his office, and thought about returning to his home on the outskirts of Washington. He hadn't been outside once today. Everyone had said it was a beautiful afternoon and he, for one, intended to enjoy what remained of it.

About the Author

W.X. Davies is the pseudonym of a well-known writer. He took on this new series both to entertain and to argue for a more sophisticated espionage capability for the U.S.

The Strategic Operations Group is an informal advisory council whose military, intelligence, and security experience provides much of the background for the series.

THE NEW YORK TIMES BESTSELLER
PULITZER-PRIZE WINNING AUTHOR OF
ADOLF HITLER AND <u>THE RISING SUN</u>

JOHN TOLAND

INFAMY

PEARL HARBOR AND ITS AFTERMATH

A Selection of The Literary Guild and
The Military Book Club With 16 pages of photos

0-425-05991-X · $3 95